Lemon Tango

It Takes Two

Jo Milanne

Lemon Tango ~ It Takes Two

Copyright © 2024 by Jo Milanne

Contents

The Office

I CAN KEEP A SECRET

G uilt impelled me to begin a list of my virtues.

   Number one: *I Can Keep a Secret.*

So far that's all I've got.

My lone virtue came about for not ratting on others. I think there is a sort of honour in that.

If further worthy traits come to mind, I will add them to the *Miss Dimity Minto Virtue List* - aiming for at least five.

I keep my cards close to my chest. So, apart from you, dear reader, I will never tell anyone else my own worst secret. The secrets kept for others are nothing to be proud of either.

My defence strategy is playing dumb. I have a natural talent for it. Some say I'm slow on the uptake.

My life of guarding secrets evolved around a man I adored.

Working at a city firm of property developers on the Australian East Coast, my heart throb handsome Italian boss, Fabio Ricci, had been my private passionate obsession for years.

Events came to a head after Fabio began humping his new secretary. No love triangle existed. When it came to office romance I was simply never in the picture.

No one, least of all Fabio himself, knew or even suspected that I kicked his lover down the stairwell.

Had Fabio ever found out, he might have expected me to share that little nugget. He came to share so much with me, in strictest confidence.

My desk dwelt amongst several others populating the busy open office floor.

Daily I languished merely ten steps from Fabio's office, aware of his every movement, however blurred behind frosted glass.

Only Fabio's secretary shared the hallowed ground of his private domain. Secretary Cynthia Nagy had been Fabio's keen partner in their torrid office affair.

It must be said: Cynthia was an awful bitch. Admittedly, I can hardly claim any moral high ground.

Fabio and Cynthia rose to stardom in a sizzling block-buster scandal. The office peanut gallery gave it five stars for thrilling entertainment.

The pair unknowingly provided an explicit peep show most days. Despite the frosted glass panels in front of Fabio's office, their silhouetted sexual exploits left little to the imagination.

If the gossip-mongering staff ever sniffed out the slightest inkling of my pathetic addiction to the boss, I would be ridiculed. None would pair my prim persona with fabulous Fabio. His handsome looks were likened to the iconic film star, Paul Newman.

I was so hooked on Fabio; I looked up the meaning of his name. Fabio means bean farmer. What's in a name? Eventually, I found a theme. But that's another secret.

Taming the electrifying tingle felt whenever Fabio was around required diligent effort. An inscrutable face constantly practised; my neutral portrayal held me in good stead after Cynthia's mishap came to light.

To start at the beginning: Gossip rioted throughout the workplace when Fabio hired Cynthia Nagy: Tall, blonde, beautiful, yet at barely twenty years old, far less qualified than other applicants who had applied.

Senior staff members were among hopefuls who vied for the plum secretarial position, only to be outbid in the glamour stakes.

Dapper senior clerk Sherman Knickerbacker also fostered romantic designs on Fabio and been the most peeved of applicants when Cynthia got the job.

I had not applied. Given my ridiculous crush, any hint of rejection would devastate. My suave superior only ever behaved properly friendly towards me, befitting our business acquaintance. Fabio addressed me as Miss Minto. I addressed him as Mr. Ricci.

In any case, the secretarial position was a permanent one. Barring death of course.

I was not best candidate, having every intention of leaving city life, dreaming of a place in the country. My goal, spurred by hopes of living in sight of Nero, my sturdy black horse, kept in expensive luxury at seaside stables.

The one reason I stayed so long in the city was to be near Fabio, my heart at odds with my head.

Now my escape to the country had to be fast tracked, all due to Cynthia and her caustic tongue.

Discretion

WOULD BE NICE

Discretion, the key to keeping secrets in our close-knit office environment, had been wasted on Cynthia, who never cared to be discrete.

Fabio had no idea Cynthia flaunted notoriety, or that the gymnastics of his affair became clearly highlighted on sunny days.

Fabio's office privacy, supposedly enabled by frosted glass panels, had a major flaw. He was blissfully oblivious that sunny days back-lit images inside his office, sharply outlining explicit physical activities between himself and Cynthia.

"Pornographic!"

Declared in scandalous glee by the peanut gallery. The spectacle that appalled and depressed me, titillated other bored sods chained to desks in everyday humdrum existences.

With the lurid displays as catalyst, respect waned for Mr. Fabio Ricci. I hated that I was still obsessed with that gorgeous man.

Cynthia never earned respect in the first place. The promiscuous young woman was deeply scorned. Most likely the majority of office staff were privately enamoured with Fabio. I couldn't blame them.

Rants against Cynthia became *commonplace. She's so up herself... What a tart... Uppity bimbo* and so on. The secretary was deemed poison. Always expensively dressed, well-groomed and never seen without perfectly applied full make-up, yet Cynthia's beauty and polish were only skin deep.

The secretary's speciality was zoning in on insecurities, and many, including myself, fell victim to her spiteful tongue.

Cynthia had the nous not to pick on Sherman Knickerbacker, aware his wit far outstripped her malice.

Sherman dubbed 'Cyn' as a corporate hooker and coined the name *Cyn Bin* for Fabio's office.

People in our office found Sherman's scathing critiques hilarious. I struggled to quell giggles at his best barbs too. Surrounded by several others, I resisted joining in snarky remarks. Careful not to 'protest too much' with my awkward secret fixation on Fabio to be forever guarded.

Spite really hit the fan when the payroll clerk discovered Cynthia was outrageously overpaid. The word got out. Fabio's young secretary was taking home much more money than anyone else. Sherman Knickerbacker had his low opinion of Cynthia confirmed.

"Corporate hooker. Big bix for turning tricks."

Cynthia basked in glory at Sherman's envy, unperturbed. One-upmanship had always been her favourite thing in the office. Opinions differed whether Mr. Ricci would be culpable of paying a hooker out of corporate funds. I abstained from comment in keeping with my prissy role but felt certain my idol Fabio would never stoop to the transgression.

Happy Hour

SPIDER

Fridays after work, five or six office friends habitually gathered at a nearby club.

"Are you coming this evening Dimity?" someone asked in passing.

I hadn't planned to go. I wanted to drive to the coast to visit my horse and had no intentions of wasting time drinking at the club.

"Sounds good...." I began.

Cynthia rudely cut me off mid-sentence with her own input, before I could add thanks but no thanks to the happy hour gathering.

"I won't be there," Cynthia chimed to the visible relief of all. "I've got bigger plans for this weekend."

Her brag included a jingled set of car keys bearing the distinctive company tag. The company keyrings were not difficult to come by, but as far as I knew, only Fabio, Sherman and I, from our office, had those tags. Clearly the keys must have been Fabio's.

"Assuming with the faaahbulous Fabio." Sherman Knickerbacker drawled wrinkling his nose like the idea stunk.

Cynthia smugged a smile while dropping the set of car keys possessively into her glossy red handbag. A flutter of her heavily made-up eyes emphasised raunchy intentions for her weekend. Sherman couldn't let her get away with it scot free.

"Eek a spider!" Sherman shammed jumping away from something scary on the floor.

Everyone jumped.

"False alarm. Relax everyone. It's only one of Cyn's false eyelashes." he said.

Cynthia dove back into her handbag for a compact mirror only to find her lashes intact and she the subject of much chuckling from all the onlookers.

Sherman swiftly minced off to the mens rest rooms before Cynthia could retaliate.

"I'm off to powder my nose." Sherman winked to all and sundry amid the laughter.

I really did not want to waste time at the club, preferring an early start to my weekend. When people began leaving towards the lifts or into the loos, I quickly tidied my desk and prepared for a speedy getaway.

Sadly, at the same time I slipped out via the back stairs to underground parking, Cynthia was hot on my tail and in a foul mood. She seethed from the trick Sherman played and took a spiteful dig at me.

"No drinkies with the crew then? Home to your knitting and cocoa?"

This rankled being rather too close to the bone. Plus, I so envied her sexy weekend jaunt with Fabio. Sarcasm may be the lowest form of wit, but I am not above resorting to it in a pinch.

"Do take care on the stairs in those absurd high heels dearie. It would be such a crying shame if you broke your neck." *Not.*

Tottering in tight skirt and on her towering stilettos, Cynthia bossily elbowed me aside. I rankled at the contact. How dare she touch me. Her next shots pushed me over the top:

"Can you go any slower? You'd think in those clodhoppers you wear you could move your fat arse, Miss Minto."

"How rude! You'd be well advised to dress more appropriately for the office."

"Huh. I wouldn't be seen dead in your ugly shoes. No wonder you're an old spinster."

Bitch!

Enough was enough. My sensibly clad foot connected forcibly with Cynthia's sashaying backside. I'm no gym fanatic but quite fit from frequent horse riding.

I should be ashamed to admit my deep satisfaction as Cynthia hurtled to the concrete landing below. The thrill of achievement will just have to remain part of my secret.

Cynthia landed face down, long legs askew despite her tight skirt. A glimpse of red panties flagged a stop to her weekend tryst with Fabio.

For shocking moments Cynthia lay inert, ungainly sprawled on the hard damp floor. I might be slow on the uptake, but immediately realised I could be in trouble for this.

Oh my God. Fark. What did I do?

With a rush of relief, I saw the despised young woman roll over and begin to sit up.

"Ow." Cynthia winced, moaning on the floor.

A thin trickle of blood ran from her once perfect snooty nose that now looked slightly squashed. *Oh dear. Tut tut.*

Irrelevantly I noticed the red trickle of blood matched her glossy lipstick and red handbag. One red shoe lingered halfway down the staircase. Cynthia liked her accessories to match. Betting her bra was red as well. If she even wore one.

Before Cynthia's expected screeching began, I judiciously retraced my steps back into the almost deserted office space. The door closed silently behind me on its hydraulic arm. No noise could be heard from the stairwell. Nobody still around on the large office floor took any notice.

Chatter and laughter came from the ladies' loos. I ducked in to blend with the bevy of women and girls fixing their hair and makeup. The opportunity to innocently join the party for Friday evening drinks, too good to ignore. So much for an early start to my weekend with Nero.

One white wine spritzer didn't go far in appeasing mild guilt, as much as I told myself Cynthia deserved that swift kick in the backside. I mean, how bloody dare she take for granted I'd be home to cocoa and knitting. Nothing wrong with knitting anyway. It's a noble craft.

I joined the cheerful chat hoping to nod or smile in all the right places but I wasn't listening. Cynthia's barbs still grated on my nerves. Home to my cocoa she assumed. So what? Cocoa is nourishing, it is chocolate after all.

I said nothing about it to anyone at that happy hour. They'd find out soon enough. I'd probably get sacked on Monday and that bitch Cynthia would have the last laugh on me. Inwardly I fumed: It would be justifiable homicide if she had broken her elegant neck.

Ugly shoes she said. Huh! My quality leather brogues might not be the latest fashion trend but certainly highly appropriate footwear for the office. And hadn't she mentioned my fat arse? What's the point of nice pants if you can't fill them out. Then the thing about being an old spinster. I don't want to go there.

"Relax Dimity" someone said perhaps noticing my tension. "Can I get you another wine?"

"No thanks. I'm driving. My shout anyway."

Faking a smile I made more innocuous comments to cover up. In their cups, the company at our table paid little attention to me. Gladly, more interest was shown in the shared platter of nachos as they chattered about their own weekend plans.

I longed to be with Nero at the seaside. Or almost anywhere else but where I currently sat.

"Looking forward to a nice weekend Dimity?"

"Yes" I shook myself "Yes, of course. Looking forward to more time with my horse."

Eye rolls from every one.

"The horse? Or the hunky horse guy? Duncan isn't it? Hunky Dunky. Is he your dark horse?"

All grinned at this teasing suggestion. Sure, I was considered classic horsey old maid material though barely 30-ish years old. I can stretch. I laughed along with them. *Bastards all.* Gladder than usual to soon be going home that Friday.

Ever since I'd mentioned the Irish farrier at the stables, mountains were made of mole hills. At least Duncan made a topic change from discussing the infamously obscene scenes provided by Cynthia and Fabio.

Nobody even knew Duncan O'Day, but he provided good value for the little amusements concocted by the office staff.

The horse guy, Duncan O'Day shod horses and generally seemed to do odd jobs about the boarding stables. He was a trusted help with my horse Nero. Apart from my stocky gelding, equine boarders were mainly racehorses whose jockeys used the hard sandy beaches for training gallops.

Monday to Friday limited my riding time to the indoor arena under lights at the stable complex at night. Weekends were bliss with canters along the shore, spritzed by sea spray, in all but dangerous stormy weather.

On the beach, my thoughts drifted towards the dream of someday moving further inland where Nero could run free on grassy pastures. A tree-change featured high on my wish list. Main stumbling block: I would be leaving Fabio.

Brought up by a grandparent, I sadly but gratefully inherited Grandpa's compact city home unit. The windfall allowed buying Nero and keeping the big Quarter Horse at the seaside racing stables.

It niggled that full time stabling seemed an unnatural existence for any horse, since their ancestors ran free and wild across vast tracts of land.

Dreams of rose covered cottage plummeted every Monday back to city grind and the reality of my unrequited yearning for the ever so sexy Mr. Fabio Ricci.

Gone

I SHOULD BE

The weekend after my sorry fit with Cynthia, I miserably anticipated the bollocking in store from both Cynthia and Fabio.

If I confessed to pushing Cynthia down the stairs, I would surely get the sack. God forbid, I might be forced to sell Nero. No way. Better to deny everything.

It would be her word against mine and I held status of senior clerk with unblemished record.

On the other hand, Cynthia was Fabio's lover which gave her the edge.

Clerks were a dime a dozen whereas beautiful sex partners who were up for anything in the office, may be a tad rarer. I couldn't find any statistics for that on Google. At an educated guess I surmised it high time to leave for pastures anew. I would just have to sell my city unit asap.

I was very late for work that Monday due to a flat battery. Stupidly in my angst, I had left my car headlights on all night. A long wait for a taxi and slow trip in peak hour traffic allowed even more time to worry. Not a great day to turn up late. I spent the taxi ride agonising over what to do when I arrived at the office. Should I confess or bluff it out? Slim chance the gorgeous bloody Cynthia might have amnesia.

The taxi dropped me in front of the building, and I took the elevator up from the foyer. The lift doors opened to reveal an uproar in the office.

Holy crap! I hoped this wasn't about me. What was happening?

Despite the hour, the place was agog with noisy chatter. Animated groups milled about all talking at once. Not the usual sober Monday morning heads bent quietly to their tasks.

Cynthia was apparently DEAD! As in not alive. No longer with us. Deceased.

But hadn't she sat up and even said ow? I am sure she did. What have I done? *Oh no.*

"You're late today, Dimity." someone observed.

"Sorry. Killed my battery."

As well as...?

Cleaners had found Cynthia dead very early that Monday morning.

After what seemed a routine police investigation, her body went by ambulance via the underground parking area. The staff were at least spared seeing the stretcher paraded through the office. Speculation was rife. General opinion was that Cynthia had come a cropper down the stairs.

"Those wicked shoes!" Office staff agreed. Not without a smidgen of glee I must add.

Few if any tears were shed. My numb state of shock went unnoticed in the hubbub. Initially police asked the staff the obvious - who had seen Cynthia last.

"We all said cheerio together last Friday." Sherman Knickerbacker offered.

"Cynthia wasn't joining us for drinks." someone else said.

"She had places to go." Sherman added.

"People to see." someone murmured.

"So the rest of you left together by the lifts at the front of the building?"

"The Friday night stampede. But no head count."

People shuffled feet and looked at the floor seeming to distance themselves from any knowledge that Cynthia's plans had included a rendezvous with their boss, Mr. Fabio Ricci. Yet they all knew. Cynthia made sure everyone knew of it herself in her usual manner of braggadocio.

"Was Cynthia generally well liked?"

An officer asked the pertinent question, sensing, as they say, an elephant in the room.

"Of course."

The lied reply was chorused in almost perfect multiple part harmony which made it infinitely less believable somehow.

"Liked more by some than others." Sherman said pursing his lips.

The interviewing police person took that comment as a generalisation. Everyone twigged Sherman meant Cynthia was more liked by Fabio. Sherman's sarcasm was fed by his jealousy of Cynthia, but we all knew Sherman would never actually dob the boss in.

Detectives commandeered Fabio's office for individual interviews since our boss had taken a few days leave. He was possibly the only person upset over Cynthia's untimely demise.

"Why are they giving us the third degree?" was asked.

"Surely it's just an accident?"

Having so much to lose, I fervently hoped Cynthia's fall would be seen as accidental.

Three cleaners who discovered the body, let it be known that it would certainly be deemed a mugging as Cynthia's handbag was missing - if she'd had one. That dramatic news evoked more garbled comments:

"She always has a flash handbag."

"Always matched her shoes. She must have had dozens of them"

Reminding all of her generous pay, Sherman added:

"She could well afford it on her wage."

Robbed as she lay helpless, dead or dying, was the new sensation. I could choke down causing death by accident but not being branded a thief. I remembered the glossy red handbag. Cynthia definitely had it last time I saw her. But I had reason to say nothing. Someone else had to be involved. Maybe another staff member.

Apart from Sherman who wore his heart on his sleeve, I had no idea who else might harbour enough resentment for Cynthia to rob her in such a callous fashion.

The three cleaners who found the body comprised one elderly man and two women. The trio had arrived at their usual time of 6am. Privy to the entry code, they gained access via the underground car park and came across the body.

The three hailed a security officer doing his rounds as he entered the car park. All four people had stayed with Cynthia's sprawled body after phoning police and ambulance.

"There she was bleeding on the cold wet floor. Blood trickling from her nose."

The cleaning man shook his head, reliving the shock discovery. A leaky pipe kept the floor wet. The leak should have been repaired but apparently nobody considered it their job or responsibility.

"Her nice coat was soaked through. She was an awful colour. Kind of grey." the younger cleaning lady shuddered.

Fingers crossed, any trace of my footprint on Cynthia's back might be lost in the soggy wetness of her coat.

"She was quite the hoity-toity young madam, but I didn't wish that on her. Not really."

On saying so, the older cleaning lady earned pointed looks to shut up from her two teammates. Dislike for Cynthia came through on that unguarded comment.

"Did you have some problem with Cynthia?" was asked.

"Just that she saw us leaving by the stairwell and told us janitors should use the back door."

"We said this IS the bloody back door. That sat her on her boney bum."

The three cleaners laughed heartily together before belatedly remembering sombre faces were in order.

"She put in a bad report about us but it got her nowhere. We were in the right."

Arms folded, united the three stood and would broach no argument. I knew that bad report would have gone across Sherman's desk. He'd have filed it in the wastepaper basket.

Who 'dunnit' was the general gist of office gossip:

"Robbed and murdered"

"Mugged"

"Mugging is murder if the victim dies."

"Isn't murder usually done by someone close to the victim?"

"We might have been last to see her alive."

"Who knows"

"Well, it's none of us. We were together in the loos before going for drinks."

Only Sherman was not in the ladies' loos. Unsaid.

No one could imagine Sherman capable of theft or violence in any form. Sherman reigned as master of catty comments but that was his limit. Also, Sherman obviously didn't see himself as being a probable contender if the event was deemed murder.

Sick realisation hit me that Fabio Ricci would be prime suspect. If he was accused, I would confess my part to save him. Otherwise, it would be my secret.

In due course, a check of security cameras in the parking area showed none used that external door until the cleaners arrived at 6am Monday. CCTV did not cover inside the stairwell or indeed inside the office space. *Phew.* I'd not even thought of security cameras.

The bag thief had to have come from inside the building. I had questions to consider: Could an unknown intruder enter the building unnoticed? Or was the thief a member of staff?

Security was fairly tight in reception. Staff wore ID tags. Any outside visitors had to sign in and out. Checks would no doubt be made.

I imagined it would only be a matter of time before the bag thief was found. I would have to sit it out and keep my cool.

Irish Charm

DUNCAN

During the following week, my big black horse Nero suffered a bout of colic.

Irishman Duncan O'Day phoned to say he'd walked Nero for hours to ease the painful condition and the vet had been, examined Nero and given the all-clear. Although Nero was OK, I made a special trip to the stables to see for myself.

"My darling boy Nero." I crooned, stroking his sleek black neck.

Nero snuffled obviously enjoying the attention.

"He wasn't too bad," Duncan's voice came from behind me, "thought you'd want the vet called. Maybe I should have checked with you first?"

"You did right Duncan. I am so grateful. What do you think caused the colic?"

"The chaff and feed pellets look clean. The others ate the same with no problems. Nero could be eating too fast."

"I guess feed time is a highlight of his day."

Once again, I wished Nero was on pasture.

"I'll add some big rocks to his manger to slow his eating. Maybe it will be better to keep him on plain hay for a while too."

"Thanks Duncan. I am giving serious thoughts to relocating to the countryside. Nero would be happier outdoors and I would be happier living beside him."

"You'll be leaving us?"

"If I can sell my unit and find something affordable. Quite a few ifs."

"Long commute to work though."

"I'll look for other work wherever I end up. If I'm frugal I'll scrape by."

Duncan looked downcast.

"Geez Dimi that's a big step." Duncan.

He shortened my name, annoyingly.

"My name is Dimity. It's just one more syllable. Dunk."

I corrected the big Irishman with a smile hoping not to sound too pedantic.

"You're so proper." he grinned.

If only he knew.

"Well, how would you like being called Dunk all the time?"

"Wouldn't bother me. I've been called worse."

Duncan laughed in his easy-going manner.

"Guess not much bothers you Duncan."

I envied him this. Suddenly earnest, Duncan's voice deepened.

"You bother me Dimi–ty."

With his coal black hair, emerald-green eyes and cheeky grin, the handsome Irishman would be a fun temptation in different circumstances. Though he was a bit of a scruff who obviously didn't shave every day or bother too much about appearances. I replied avoiding his meaning.

"Go on with you Duncan. I can't be that bothersome."

Duncan stepped closer, pulling me into a clumsy bear hug. If only he knew my darkest secrets he'd run a mile. It wouldn't be fair to lead him on, as much as I needed comfort.

"No. Please don't." I whispered turning away to bury my face in Nero's thick mane.

Duncan turned me around firmly but gently. My back was against Nero's warmth. Trapped emotionally more than physically it was too easy to yield when the big guy raised my face to his. His kiss was soft and full of promise. I had to stop it going further.

"NO. No. Duncan. Don't come at me with your Irish charm and twinkle in your eye. I can't deal with this."

I felt angry at myself for the mess I was making of my life and having to leave Fabio. Duncan released me but found something positive in my rejection.

"Huh. My Irish charm, is it?" he grinned.

"Go away. I mean it. I can't do this now."

"What now? Or never? Surely wouldn't be never with my Irish charm and twinkling eye."

"I don't know. Just leave me be. Please Duncan."

"You've got someone else?" he asked quietly, crestfallen.

"No. I've not got anyone." I truthfully replied. "I'm just trying to get over a thing. Long story. It's complicated."

Parting as friends despite the awkward encounter, Duncan said he sometimes worked in the countryside and would look out for any suitable smallholdings for sale. I thanked him politely for that, but did not expect anything to come of it.

Little did I know.

Frankly

MISS MINTO...

Cynthia Nagy's sudden exit created anew the secretarial vacancy with Fabio Ricci.

Hope was immediately rekindled among likely applicants with the natty fellow Sherman Knickerbacker leading the charge.

Certainly, Sherman would make a super-efficient secretary, though popular consensus had it: Sherman was barking up the wrong tree if he ever imagined himself sitting on Fabio's lap. Sly smirks and digs were shared among the office workers at Sherman's expense. No one was exempt from becoming a source of entertainment.

To my great surprise, Fabio called me to his office, ostensibly to help with a backlog of correspondence. Over the years, I'd hardly set foot in this space and then only briefly. With some trepidation, I tapped on the door obeying best office etiquette.

"Miss Minto." Fabio greeted as I entered his domain.

"Mr. Ricci."

"Call me Fabio. Please. And may I call you Dimity?" *gulp*

"Thank you of course Mr. er um Fabio."

"Can we talk frankly Dimity?"

"Of course Mr. um Fabio."

"Dimity I think you may be to blame."

What? Fark! How could he know? Almost collapsing in shock I struggled to squeak a reply.

"You do?"

Fabio kept me waiting in the time it took him to access his office mini bar. How the other half lived! Cynthia had bragged of having use of his private bathroom which I guessed must be behind a closed door I could see partly hidden beside his bookcase.

Without asking my preference, Fabio topped two heavy crystal tumblers with scotch and very short squirts of soda. Fabio knocked back most of his drink. To hell with it, I followed his example.

The good scotch went down smoothly. Obviously only the best would do in the dire circumstance. I thought of this as my inevitable downfall: *The condemned woman drank a hearty dram.*

Fatalistically I imagined Fabio shooting me dead where I sat. Glad I'd worn decent underwear this day.

I knew I'd rather be shot than suffer most alternatives that came to mind. Nero was my prime concern, maybe I'd give him to that nice Irishman Duncan, at the stables.

The peanut gallery outside would relish seeing this final chapter, if Fabio did pull a gun from his drawer and put a slug through my heart. Sunlight brightened the room. I knew it clearly silhouetted our outlines to the outside view.

I looked back to see who might be witnessing this from the greater office area. Of course, the frosted glass was quite opaque with sunshine smote hard on it. I had no view to outside Fabio's office.

I waited for the axe to fall, but Fabio confused me by going off on a what seemed to be a tangent:

"If only YOU had applied to be my secretary Dimity. Had you done so, I would never have met that young woman and never become so bewitched by her."

"Me?" *Moi? Huh?*

It took a while to fathom that Fabio blamed ME for his decision to take Cynthia on as his secretary. Better than the other thing by far. Relief surged through me. I almost peed my pants. Almost doesn't count. I struggled to make some sort of acceptable reply:

"Mr. um Fabio, surely I could not foresee..."

"No. You could not Dimity. Sorry. I don't know myself lately. Just kicking myself. I should have asked up front if you'd take the position without even advertising for a new secretary. It had crossed my mind but certainly, please be assured you are greatly appreciated and suited as head clerk. However, I do apologise if you feel to have been overlooked."

"Not at all. You see, I didn't apply because it would have only been temporary. I have plans to move on from this firm and relocate."

"Ah. You have been head hunted by the opposition? I wouldn't blame you if they've offered higher wages."

"Ha ha no. nothing like that."

I outlined the situation with my horse. The firm we both worked for dealt only in re-purposing urban acreage and demolitions pursuant to that, it would not list the humbler type of property I hoped for and I told Fabio I understood this.

"I will be sorry to see you go. I guess you will be after a smallholding."

"Yes that's right. I have a good idea of what I want."

Nervously talking too much, I detailed what I hoped for, a few acres with livable dwelling, in a small community or not too far from a town where I might find work. The quality of land was more important than the dwelling... blah blah blah. I went on and on ad nauseam until petering out seeing Fabio had a faraway look in his eye. He must have found my long-winded litany dead boring.

"I see," he said even if he didn't, "well I do wish you all the best".

Only then did Fabio get to the crux of this meeting:

"Something else I need to run by you," Fabio began uneasily, "it seems my, er, liaison with Cyndi did not go unnoticed. The police inspectors made out it was common knowledge."

"Cyndi? Oh you mean Cynthia of course." *Cyndi. How cute.*

"Wasn't she generally known by her nickname?"

Fabio looked askance having assumed Cynthia or his Cyndi would be unanimously well accepted as a friend by all.

Everyone's friend? Not bleeding likely. But I didn't say so. I couldn't let on how disliked Cynthia had been. His Cyndi had been called by several different names, none of them cute.

Fabio was very out of touch with the ordinary folk of the firm. Seemed he wanted my feedback on his dalliance with Cynthia.

"We were so discreet," he puzzled, "how could our...alliance... be common knowledge?"

To tell him Cynthia had been anything but discreet, how she'd constantly boasted of their relationship, would be to speak ill of the dead. I also did not want to burst his bubble. He seemed genuinely at a great loss.

Fabio topped up our drinks with generous measures. I didn't say no. Emboldened with Dutch courage aka best Scotch whisky, I dared asked a personal question that had been bugging me. I intoned it as sympathetically as possible.

"So Fabio, did you see a rosy future together with Cynthia?"

"I am not free to make that call." he answered distractedly.

Perhaps Fabio replied without thinking since he'd downed two strong drinks in quick succession. Now I was puzzled. Surely, he wasn't married. I wondered why he wasn't free to make the call. He noticed my raised brows. He hurriedly revised his answer into an excuse:

"Ah....Call it mid-life crisis. I just turned forty."

Forty made Fabio around eight years senior to my thirty something. He looked a lot younger. I thought he would have been nearer my age. I could definitely live with that slight difference. If anything, it would be perfect. *Dream on.*

But forty years old made Fabio a long twenty years older than Cynthia. I hoped my inscrutable face would not abandon me as my thoughts ran to *Baby Snatcher* and *Gold Digger*. I tried for a fair reply:

"Nonetheless, you're entitled to your privacy Fabio. Your own affair."

I cringed at my own comment. Oh no, why say *affair*. Silly me. Too much alcohol.

"How on earth did the secret get out? That's what troubles me." he agonised.

"I could tell you." I paused, fuggy as ever after two strong drinks.

"What - but then you'd have to kill me?"

Ouch

Deftly, I thought, shifting the focus from myself, I deigned to point out the weakness in his private domain. I told him how activity in his office could be seen when the frosted glass became backlit by sunlight.

"It's just a trick of light," I explained, "hardly noticeable. But you know what terrible gossips the staff can be." *Hic.*

The peanut gallery would disown me as a traitor for that treachery, if they found out.

"NO! Oh my God." Fabio sounded mortified as understanding dawned.

A myriad of stricken tics flitted across his reddening features, learning at last that his raunchy activities had been exposed to the amusement of the greater office population.

Chortle. I shouldn't laugh. Not out loud anyway. I almost felt sorry for him. Another example of 'almost doesn't count'.

"They all knew? All saw? What were they saying? Or do I really want to know that?"

"Sorry Fabio but they all called this office the Cyn Bin." *Hic.*

"The Sin Bin. I suppose that is deserved." he groaned.

Fabio covered his face with his hands and shook his head to dispel the awful knowledge I'd given him. First losing his Cyndi and then finding they'd been entertaining the entire office with their sexy shenanigans. It must have been quite a lot to overcome.

Suffice to say, we did not make inroads on the backlog of correspondence that day.

"I can't face this paperwork right now." Fabio moaned.

"Never mind. Leave it to me. I'll fix it. And may I please be excused for the rest of the day?"

I was in no fit shape to be efficient in my work. To put a finer point on it, I was quite tipsy.

"Of course Dimity. I appreciated your input and trust we are friends."

Fabio rose from his chair, shook my hand and opened the door for me to leave with the armful of paperwork. I plonked the whole lot into the IN tray on Sherman's desk on my way out. I earned that half day off.

Sleepless that night, I stuck on Fabio saying he wasn't free to make his future with Cynthia. He cited his age as excuse. A twenty year age gap of concern to him in the happy-ever-after scenario? He hadn't minded the happy-before-commitment scenario.

Of course his young secretary may have been just a sinful dalliance for him. A fatal attraction. Considering Fabio's Italian heritage, a more chaste woman would surely be preferable for any long term commitment.

To put it crudely: Fabio Ricci would have made a prize catch for Cynthia if she could have led him down the aisle by his willy to the strains of the wedding march.

Cynthia hinted at having a weekend tryst with Fabio, but could she have lied? It was so like her to invent a vain boast to promote her standing in the office. The car keys may not even have been Fabio's. The business logo key tags were easy enough to come by.

Ground floor security cameras proved everyone, apart from Cynthia, exited by the wide front doors of the office building on that fateful Friday.

Some went on to the club, shopping in the city or to public transport stations. The car park could be gained from the street at any hour and most preferred that entrance rather than the dank and gloomy stairwell.

With everyone's movements accounted for, whatever became of Cynthia's handbag remained a mystery. I put it to the back of my mind.

The coroner found Cynthia succumbed to a ruptured brain aneurysm caused by head injury resulting from a fall. She probably died during the merriment at the Friday evening Happy Hour, while I seethed over her nasty digs and found excuses for my vengeance.

A dark cloud hung over my work days. I dreaded entering our building and taking my place in the office as if nothing serious happened. My one regret when the time came to hand in my resignation would be separation from Fabio. I was obsessively addicted to that man.

In private, Fabio and I remained on first name basis after that boozy meeting. The trust he showed in me, balm to my foolish sentiments. Thrilled by his seductive Italian flavoured accent, I loved to hear his voice, and just be near him.

Shamelessly, I imagined baring more than my soul and bending over the desk for his pleasure. The entire office personnel witnessed the position as one he favoured with Cynthia. However, the peanut galley was definitely off-putting to that fantasy.

Fabio did not employ another secretary. Either Sherman Knickerbacker or I stood in at different times as secretarial assistants. My plans to relocate were known to Fabio so Sherman seemed best bet to gain the eventual permanent position. Good for Sherman.

Having inherited my home unit from my guardian grandparent, I had no experience in buying or selling real estate property. Fabio's advice was sought, since I knew no one else to ask and it was his specific area of expertise.

Fabio suggested I list the unit for sale with an agency dedicated to buying properties for the immense rental market.

"Stipulate a contract to rent back for a designated time." Fabio advised.

"How long should the rent back period be?"

"Three months should be enough time to find your next place."

I could hardly believe I might get my tree change within three months. Suddenly ninety days seemed scant time to organise everything. A cleaning blitz at the unit had me sort and send lots of unused articles to charity or trash. I packed up what I'd definitely have to take leaving only bare essentials out for everyday living.

The estate agency recommended offering the unit fully furnished. Since I had no nostalgia over any pieces apart from Grandpa's old gramophone, I liked the idea. Furniture was easy to acquire. I didn't need much. Something to store food in and something to sleep on, a refrigerator and a mattress as a minimum.

Desperate to move on and relegate the horrible Cynthia episode to the past, I would gladly live out of cartons and suitcases, if necessary, at least in the short term. I had no delusions of grandeur.

Preparing the unit for sale, temporarily limited my time for riding. I still visited Nero daily but hurried through chores and skipped sensible warming up steps before stepping into the saddle. Less activity and my scant attention to horse sense attributed to Nero's friskiness.

Caught slacking, a bout of energetic bucking landed me in an undignified heap on the soft surface of the indoor arena – witnessed by that leering Irishman, to my utter humiliation and angst.

"You should have lunged him down." Duncan advised mildly.

An amused smile flirted about his mouth.

"I do know that." I growled through gritted teeth.

Annoyed with myself for taking foolish short-cuts I took it out on the stable hand with a barbed retort:

"Thanks for stating the bleeding obvious Duncan."

"You're welcome." he answered politely.

Duncan's soft spoken Irish lilt did not disguise the fun he found in the exchange. I could forgive Nero. Duncan was another case. That grinning Irishman could get under my skin, and well he knew it. His amusement at my tumble irked every bit as much as Nero galloping joyful laps of the arena with reins trailing.

Duncan dusted me off paying greatest attention to my backside.

"Having a good feel are you Duncan?"

"Yes thanks. All good."

I chose to ignore Duncan's facetious needling. To retort only egged him on.

"I've been just so busy of late I've let Nero get above himself."

"If you like, I can lunge him down before you get here." Duncan offered.

"That's OK." I said ungraciously. "I'm about done now getting my place readied for sale."

"So it's all on the go. You're really leaving?"

"Yep. And I can't wait."

I'd been looking online at possible properties to buy but could do nothing until my unit sold.

Bridging finance was a risky option I could ill afford. My expected budget would already be tight compared to what I hoped to buy.

I thanked Duncan for offering to lunge Nero. Of course the man mostly meant well. We had a chat about the type of next home I wanted.

"I know of a possible place," he said, "the house is empty but as far as I know it isn't actually for sale."

"Where?"

"Closest town is Clemency."

Duncan named a sleepy town within half a days drive inland.

"But don't get your hopes up."

"No. It sounds like a long shot." I replied.

"Anyway, I'll be out there soon. I know the old people who have the farm next door to that place."

"Are they friends of yours?"

"Friends and clients. Giorgio and Sophia. I go out now and then to trim their old cart horses. I can ask them about it."

"Thanks again then Duncan. That might be a chance."

His help was appreciated but the property didn't sound too promising since it wasn't even for sale.

"I'll ask about it anyway." Duncan repeated.

Nero submitted to being caught eventually. I looked forward to a day my horse might enjoy freedom of open pastures and become lazily content.

I'd be happy to ride about in open countryside and never see the inside of another enclosed arena again.

Real Estate

GET REAL

Weekends, I cut into my adored beach rides to travel far and wide checking out advertised smallholdings. Properties invariably appeared far better in online photos than in reality.

Real estate ad photos showed places for sale in the best light and without down sides. Many fronted busy highways. Some were overlooked by close neighbours. Larger acreages often turned out to be on impoverished land. A waste of my time and fuel.

Often an acceptable house had bad land or reasonable land had decrepit hovels as homes. Rarely did I get to the stage of wanting to inspect house interiors. Agents would say I might as well look inside since I'd come so far. A thorough inspection might give them brownie points from the vendors.

Get real. My annoyance at being misled on the worth of a property would always make me decline. Pretense wasn't fair on hopeful sellers either. Perhaps agents imagined a prospective buyer might change their mind from a closer look.

One evening I sped out after work excited to suss an ideal sounding property. Sadly, it was adjacent to an enormous chook farming complex ablaze with lights and with a definite guano whiff. Apart from the smell, the lights would be on all night. Strike that one off the wish list.

Despondent with fading hope, I was buoyed by encouraging news from Duncan. The Irishman had found out about the Clemency place with the empty house. Downside, it definitely wasn't listed for sale and had never been offered as such. Despite the lead being tentative it represented a slim hope when there had been not much to choose from so far.

"Giorgio and Sophia say they keep an eye on the place for an absentee owner. He's related to them somehow, cousin or nephew, I forget what. Anyway, they graze their stock in the paddock sometimes to keep the grass down, so the fencing should be alright. The house hasn't been lived in for a long while. The old couple say it is livable if you don't expect much."

I was more interested in the paddock. A house could be fixed in time, but the land had to be viable.

"How much land?"

"Fifteen acres. Good loamy soil. Good grass. Some groundwater too."

Fifteen acres of good grazing would be a dream. So far, in my price range, only three to five acres seemed possible without heading to the back of beyond.

"Really? Do they think the owner would sell? If I could even afford it."

"The old folks think he might be talked into selling. They said that the place doesn't hold fond memories for the owner. Hinted at some awful drama there long ago. Domestic violence thing."

"How awful."

"Well that's all in the past. Giorgio says he'll be in touch if or when he finds out anything. Could be a wait until they get into town. They don't have any phone or car. Rely on a weekly bus run."

"What! No phone? Or car?"

"Out in the sticks you know. It's another world out there."

"But it's only a few hours away."

"These people are very elderly, very self-sufficient. You'd have to meet them to understand."

Italian immigrants had originally pioneered the district circa mid 1800s. The old couple, Giorgio and Sophia Gallo were probably descendants of those earlier settlers.

On further research of Clemency, I found the demographic was mainly ageing, Catholic and of Italian descent. Population hovered around 3000. The town fell within the temperate zone with an elevation of 477 metres or 1558 feet above sea level. I did my homework to be sure.

If I lived there, I would not be running to the seaside for a quick dip on an impulse, that's for sure. I would miss the coast, but 15 acres of good grazing had to be well worth the sacrifice.

A Mean Streak

NO DANCING

Meanwhile, the agents received a low offer for my home unit. I needed more money, but didn't want to lose a sale.

Anxious whether I should hold out for more, or not, I sat on the problem for another week.

No other offers came in. About to bite the bullet and accept the low bid, the prospective investors upped their offer nearer to my asking price. Once again, I went to Fabio for advice:

"You might not get a better offer, but it is entirely up to you of course Dimity." Fabio said.

I was keen to get the ball rolling and felt that Fabio leant towards the opinion that I should take it. I signed on the dotted line. The purchaser was a faceless business name of some company. I didn't care who bought it. The unit was to be a rental so no doubt would house scores of tenants as time went by. Fabio made sure to stipulate a clause that gave me three months rent-free before I must vacate the unit. Thank goodness for his help.

Mine had been a lonely existence there since Grandpa passed away. I was not sorry to be moving on.

Grandpa had always said, 'follow your instincts' so I had no qualms he'd disapprove of selling his legacy for the country dream. My instincts confirmed the move was right and best for Nero.

With only three months to find a place, I nagged Duncan to chase up the Clemency property. The idea of fifteen good rich acres made it my absolute favourite even if the house proved so derelict I'd have to pitch a tent inside the dwelling.

In the meantime, I kept seeking out other possibilities but as before, found nothing acceptable in my price range. Anxious to secure a place, I went to Duncan to nag him some more:

"My unit has sold. I have three months to move out. The purchasers might extend my tenancy at a cost, but the negative rent period ends soon."

"Well done," Duncan enthused, "good for you getting a sale and rent free for three months on top of it."

"But I need to know about Clemency. Pronto. If it's no go, I have to find somewhere else."

"Don't fret. If you end up homeless you can doss in with me."

"Thanks. You're all heart."

"Plus, Irish Charm don't forget." he twinkled.

"Wish I'd never said that. Get over yourself Duncan."

The incorrigible man made another unhelpful suggestion:

"How about we celebrate your sale. You get yourself into a frock and I'll take you out dancing. I'd like to see you kick up your heels Dimi-ty."

The fact I'd never been taken dancing in my life, was definitely not something I cared to admit to the Irishman.

What's more, I owned no garment that could be described as a frock. My wardrobe consisted of boots, jeans and shirts for riding or tailored suits for work. Not to mention sensible shoes appropriate for office wear.

"No dancing. I'll buy you a fish and chip dinner. How about that." I compromised.

"You're on." he high-fived almost knocking me over but caught me just in time. "Oops. Don't know my own strength."

"My god you're an asset sometimes Duncan."

"That could be a good thing."

"Hmmm."

Too bad if he expected a posh restaurant because dinner meant sitting by the shore eating fish and chips out of newspaper. Duncan supplied a six pack of stubbies.

The cold beer went perfectly well with the salty vinegary fish and chips. We sat in companionable silence watching sailboats glide by, way offshore in the misty distance.

"Just a thought," Duncan ventured, "don't bite my head off, but if you stay overnight here with me, we could get an early start and go out to Clemency tomorrow."

"That'd be great!"

"It would?"

Duncan grinned so delightedly I think he imagined I'd agreed to a roll in the hay. I had no idea what his digs would be like, but if I wasn't mistaken, he entertained a fantasy.

"Not staying overnight Duncan. I mean seeing the property tomorrow."

"You have a mean streak Dimity".

"That is so." I agreed.

He might as well know it.

Beyond the Sea

ANOTHER STREAK

The morning star twinkled brightly in the east and a full silver moon hung in the western sky as I headed out for the stables before dawn the next day. Thankfully Duncan had mucked out and was lunging Nero under lights when I arrived at the indoor arena. This saved so much time and I was super keen to view the fifteen acre property.

"That should do him for now." Duncan said. We cooled the horse out and put him back in a clean loose box with a full hay net. "One of the lads will check on him later" Duncan promised.

Day broke pinkly as we embarked on the road trip. Duncan was driving. He shoved some junk off the dusty passenger side seat of his ute and bid me get in beside him.

"This is us off to Clemency together." he winked and patted my knee.

I put up with that familiarity since he was doing me this great favour. The charm of the great handsome cheeky man wasn't lost on me. I'm absolutely sure he knew it too. Neither of us had eaten much of a breakfast that morning. I was feeling the pinch and in need of a loo break by the time we had travelled part way to the district of Clemency. At the halfway mark, we breakfasted at a petrol station roadhouse. I slipped into a window booth in the diner, while Duncan ordered.

"Hiya Irish! You're a gorgeous sight for sore eyes."

The sassy and voluptuous female shop assistant behind the counter obviously knew Duncan well.

"Mornin' Darlene my darling. Light of my eyes. You're looking lovely as ever."

Duncan flirted outrageously. My eyes may have rolled of their own accord.

"Want your usual Big Trucki Special?"

"For two." he said holding up two fingers in a V for victory sign.

His darling Darlene, light of his eyes, noticed my presence with far less enthusiasm. I am not sure if her top lip didn't curl in derision, or maybe she had something stuck between her teeth. Darlene hollered through a hatch in the wall, while never shifting her beady eyed gaze from me.

"TWO B.T.S."

Maybe the cook was hard of hearing. As Duncan took his seat, I clocked Darlene checking me over with a critical eye. In return I assessed her as quite attractive in a tarty-diner-waitress-obvious kind of way. I gave her a nice smile that wasn't returned. How rude.

"Ever the flirt aren't you Duncan." I said.

"Worth an extra sausage." he vowed. "I always get this. Best breakfast this side of nowhere."

Whatever that meant. Darlene served our double breakfast tray. Eggs, bacon, sausage, tomato, all topped with a mountain of hot chips, the obligatory norm in truck stops across this broad brown land. Steaming mugs of tea had the teabags left in of course.

Unused to going without sustenance for long, my tummy rumbled. The hot food looked and smelt scrumptious. Duncan did indeed get an extra banger. Darlene set Duncan's plate before him gently and lovingly. Mine was somewhat clattered down, just short of spilling chips on the table.

"Swap plates?" I asked in case Darlene had laced mine.

"Are you after my sausage?"

You wish.

"Nope. Just a precaution."

"Aha. You think Darlene spat on it." Duncan twigged. "Two beautiful woman after me and the day is yet young." he preened. "You can wrestle for me. Reckon you could maybe take her Dimi-ty."

"Dream on Duncan."

"No really. You're fairly athletic and I've seen you bounce well off the horse."

"Ha ha. Seriously. Are you game to swap plates?"

"Never fear. Darlene isn't the cook anyway. Her father is. And Cookie is fastidious. For a bikie."

"You know this how?" I asked.

Feeling starved, I began to hoe into the big breakfast, regardless.

"Old pals. They dote on me here you know."

"Pfft." I think I managed not to spray him with crumbs between mouthfuls.

"No really. See, a while back, Cookie sneezed in the kitchen and lost his best gold nose ring. Later on I found it in my stew. I recognised it right off. Of course."

"Of course you did."

"Anyhow, I cleaned this precious ring up with a wet teabag and a paper napkin. Cookie was that chuffed to get it back. Family heirloom see. Priceless to him. Shed tears of joy he did."

"Right. That explains your extra sausage."

"That's nothin'. Cookie said I could have the hand of his only daughter."

"That would be Darlene."

"The one and same."

"But you haven't taken up the generous offer."

"Not yet. Maybe later. I figure she needs both hands in her job."

"That is so lame. No wonder the Blarney Stone is supposedly smooth from all the Irish kissing it."

"You don't buy it? Was it the stew?"

"Yep. You always get the Big Truckie Special."

I cleared my plate, sat back full, and needed to loosen my belt a notch.

"I love a woman with a grand appetite." said Duncan.

"I love a man with no opinion." I countered.

Duncan laid a proprietary hand on my back as we exited the diner. I cast a foxy smile back at Darlene. That's just my competitive streak. *Eat your heart out Darlene.*

Refuelled, we continued our journey to Clemency. Duncan clicked a CD on. *Beyond the Sea* by Bobby Darin filled the cabin. My Grandpa used to play the same tune on his gramophone; the older version known as *La Mer*. It had always been my favourite. Bobby Darin's upbeat rendition, newer, yet a golden oldie.

"I love this song," I approved, "you share my taste in music Duncan."

"I do have a lovable sensitive side on top of my Irish Charm and twinkling eye."

"Modest to boot."

"I am. That is true. I'm so modest I could win competitions for it." he boasted.

Clemency

ENZO APPROVES

My mood lightened evermore as we headed westwards and the landscape opened to broader skies over undulating downlands.

I dared to wonder if distance could blank out the years squandered loving Fabio. A clean break might be the only way to get over him.

Cutting ties with my office past might prove helpful in fading out the shameful Cynthia thing as well. I could only hope.

Turning off the busy main highway, we travelled another ten minutes on a minor road before coming to an old timber bridge spanning a wide and picturesque river.

Delayed, parked on a grassy verge, while a herd of dairy cows sauntered across the bridge, I noticed a crooked signpost partly obscured behind a bush.

The sign read: *Danger Deep Water – Dangerous Currents - No Swimming - No Fishing Off The Bridge.*

I got out of the vehicle for a closer look. Swirling eddies and fast-moving flotsam denied first impressions of peaceful waterway. This river roiled and sped along its way. Perhaps recent rains from surrounding mountain ranges helped feed the racing spate.

Three people, blithely fishing from the bridge, gave us friendly waves. We waved back.

"They seem friendly."

"It's a friendly place." Duncan agreed.

"But the river looks fast and furious. I wouldn't want to swim here." I shuddered.

"Let's look for a safer place downstream. We'll go for a skinny dip, if you like."

"I didn't bring swimming togs."

"Geez Dimity. You must know skinny dipping means swimming in the raw."

"The raw what?"

"You're slow on the uptake sometimes Dim–ity."

Huh. Who is slow on the uptake? He is so easy to kid. Fun to yank his chain for once instead of the other way around. I let him think he had the upper hand to massage his ego. As I have said, playing dumb is my favourite strategy. It's a talent that has held me in good stead so far.

A young boy riding bareback on a fat pony followed the last of the dawdling cows as they cleared the bridge. He whistled a couple of kelpies to heel and politely tipped his hat to us as he rode by. I compared the farm boy to sneering youths idling in the city mall, evil yobs who flicked cigarette butts at people's heels.

"What a charming young man."

"Welcome to the country." Duncan smiled.

"That's a very encouraging start."

After the bridge, we came to a cross roads. Straight ahead went into the township, right fork led downriver. To the left, Duncan said was Gallo's farm next to the empty house on the fifteen acres.

"I'll take you around a quick tour of the town first."

Driving ahead on the main travelled road, we passed a service station, produce barn and showgrounds with an oval racetrack. A loop around town revealed three churches, a rural fire brigade, police station and general hospital with just one ambulance parked outside.

The pretty town was quiet. Few road signs cluttered the layout and there were no traffic lights at all.

We saw only one example of bustling industry, a building development under construction, signed as: *Clemency Retirement Village.*

"A lot of elderly in this place." Duncan remarked. "I could think of worse places to retire."

The townships one main street had three hotels and every variety of small shops including a hair salon. Roberto's Hair Salon advertised a special on streaks.

"See that? A special on streaks. You can add to your mean streak." Duncan quipped.

Mention of streaks evoked memory of one day back at the office. Cynthia turned up with hot pink streaks only to be studiously ignored by all. Flicking her long blond and pink hair to draw attention, the secretary aimed snarky unwanted advice in my direction:

"You should get streaks. Your drab brown hair could use a lift."

Sherman Knickerbacker, bless his heart, had leapt to my defence:

"You leave our little Miss Minto alone. We love her drab brown hair."

"Penny for your thoughts." Duncan said. "What do you think of the town?"

"Looks like everything is catered for."

I didn't want to bring up the office memory. One twinge of worry: What chance of employment could be found within this close-knit community. IF I even ended up in the area. I wouldn't mind doing work other than office administration. As long as it wasn't any type of meat works.

At length we reached our destination to meet the old couple. Their farm was nestled in wide open grazing country surrounded by forested hills. It dwelt off the beaten track but only thirty minutes drive into the centre of town.

Duncan pulled his ute into the farm driveway beside a roadside stall with a sign: *Gallos Fresh Veg & Eggs*. Shelves and open boxes displayed fruits and melons. No shopkeeper in sight, just an honesty box for payments.

"Giorgio and Sophia don't expect us today but don't worry, they always welcome visitors."

A young black and white border collie barked and ran to meet us. The dog's one brown and one blue eye offered a bright and merry greeting, while his whole body wagged in rapture.

"Hi Enzo. Who's a good boy. Who's a good woggy doggy." Duncan chuckled.

Elderly Giorgio waved from between rows of grapes in a vineyard. Sophia, picking beans in a vegetable patch greeted us with a broad smile. A variety of hens and ducks wandered about the gardens and orchards. It was rural paradise. I felt to have been transported into a time warp.

The Gallos, both grey haired and dark eyed, had short sturdy builds. Giorgio wore bib overalls over a plaid shirt and Sophia had on a plain calico pinafore over a floral dress.

The farm couple certainly appeared very 'olde worlde' in keeping with Duncan's description.

Welcomed for coffee on the front verandah of their rambling farmhouse, we chatted. I felt it was something of an interview, since I was applying hopefully to become their neighbour.

Enzo, the friendly dog, flopped at our feet. His odd-coloured eyes beheld our party of humans in good humour. I patted the dog's head, and he licked my hand.

"Enzo *approvare*" Sophia noted.

It seemed a test to see how the dog perceived me. Just as well he hadn't taken a chunk out of my pants. Enzo was indeed a lovely dog.

A narrow lane ran beside the big farmhouse. Appearing disused, the overgrown gravel driveway led to the smaller neighbouring property with the empty dwelling on fifteen acres.

I itched to inspect the little old house. It was partly visible behind some big trees and there looked to be a hay shed out back with green fields beyond. The house on slightly higher ground, fronted the narrow lane.

The land sloped gradually down to a watercourse, marked by a mixed vegetation of various native trees and bushes. Waiting to be invited to inspect the property tantalised.

I put my case to the old people, saying, should I buy the place, I would be a very quiet neighbour, keep to myself, but always be there for them if they needed help.

"It will be just me and my riding horse Nero, unless I get another horse in the future."

"But will you need paid work? There is no paid work to be had around here." Giorgio waved an arm to encompass the empty surrounding countryside.

"I will need a job but expect to drive into town to find work."

"You have a car? You drive?" Sophia and Giorgio seemed amazed.

Having assured them I did indeed have wheels, the old folk visibly brightened. At their age and so isolated, a neighbour with a vehicle could mean the difference between life and death.

"Dimity you will make a lovely neighbour" Giorgio decided. "Our nephew is owner, son of my dear sister Fiorella."

Giorgio and Sophia each made the Catholic sign of the cross, indicating Fiorella had passed away.

"Sophia, we must get onto the boy about selling."

"Now we have met and all is good. If you decide the place is for you, we will be blessed to know a nice lady lives next door." Sophia smiled kindly.

First hurdles achieved. So far so good. I passed the dog test and had the neighbours' approval.

"Go have a good look. The back door key is on a nail in the washroom under the house. You don't need us to do the tour with you, there are not many rooms in that place. You won't get lost."

"It will be a sorry state," Sophia apologised, "no one has been in that house for a long time. Come back for a bite with us when you are finished your inspections."

Albero di Limone

LEMON TREE

We drove up the overgrown lane for our first clear view of the abandoned home.

Ferny foliage of a grove of Pepperina trees veiled the smaller house from the Gallo's farmstead.

On first impressions, the little old weatherboard building, set on high stumps, could be likened to an old lady too tired to comb her hair or fix her face. Grey cobwebs festooned the eaves, her yellowing paintwork sadly faded and peeling.

We found the heavy door key hanging on its rusty nail in a laundry room under the house. An old pack of Persil washing powder and a well gnawed box of Silver Star Starch sat on a dusty shelf above double cement tubs.

A concrete floored storage cupboard held an electric hot water cistern and pressure pump. As expected, rain water tanks supplied the house. Two big corrugated iron tanks sat at ground level. Tapping the rungs to the sound of dull thuds established the tanks to be full. Hollow resonance would indicate emptiness.

"The tanks should be full since the house has been empty so long. But you won't get water upstairs if the power is off." Duncan said. "Probably be a dribble down here in the laundry but the pressure pump is needed for upstairs supply. It kicks in automatically when taps are turned on, but only if the electricity is on."

"Right. I'd have to make sure and keep bottled water and some emergency method of upstairs water storage, if I end up here."

"Or carry buckets up from the laundry." Duncan suggested.

We tried the laundry taps to be rewarded with a slow rusty brown trickle that turned clear in a minute or so. The pump didn't kick in so the power was off as expected.

A mummified rodent body in a rusted rat trap and a translucent scaly snakeskin graced the earthen laundry floor.

"Yew. There's a story." I said.

"The dead tell no tales." Duncan replied.

Hopefully. But I didn't want to think of her.

Climbing the stairs to the back verandah, a panoramic view earned our admiration. The green landscape took in the fifteen acres or so of paddocks. Beyond the property, a clear view of more grassland and surrounding hills showed no other houses. Across the sunny blue sky a few wispy clouds scudded along on a fresh breeze. I breathed deeply of clean smog-free air.

"I could live here." I said.

"You haven't seen inside yet."

"I'd be happy pitching a tent on this verandah."

"That's realistic. Lucky I'm here." Duncan laughed.

Duncan twisted the heavy old iron key stiffly in the back door lock. Obviously it had not been used for some time.

Entry via the back door revealed a wide boot hall. An ancient pair of cracked gumboots resided under a built-in bench seat. An old hat and mildewed raincoat took up two of a line of coat hooks on the wall.

Either side of the boot hall were a bathroom and kitchen, both with sloped ceilings.

The only stove, a wood burning range filled most of the space in a recessed hatch made of corrugated iron. An iron bucket and empty wood box sat beside. Below a window dressed by a tatty lace curtain, two brass taps serviced a rectangular porcelain sink.

A plain pine table, three mismatched chairs and an old kitchen dresser furnished the kitchen. Given my lack of furniture, all would be a bonus, if included with the house.

An ancient rust spotted refrigerator, door propped open, confirmed the electricity to be definitely turned off. Some mouldy remnant of something colourful stuck to the interior of the 'fridge.

"Yuk"

"You've given it a Yew and a Yuk so far. No Wows."

"I didn't expect any Wows to be honest Duncan."

In the bathroom, a commodious claw footed enamelled bathtub had a grubby mould spotted plastic shower curtain and a large round shower rose overhead.

The tub shared the space with an old-fashioned unplumbed washstand. Ever optimistic, I imagined a pretty violet patterned basin and matching jug on that washstand. Best china of course.

The old shower curtain would have to go. A plain white one would be my choice.

A timber mirrored door shaving cabinet was fixed to the wall over the washstand. A cistern plumbed toilet with wooden seat completed the bathroom furnishings. We had earlier noticed the septic tank out in the yard. I might lash out for a new seat too.

"All mod cons." Duncan observed. "Indoor dunny."

"Thank heaven for small favours."

"Yeah. Easier to see the red-backs under the toilet seat."

Two large square empty bedrooms opened straight off the main living area. The spacious living room, twice the size of the bedrooms combined, was punctuated by four sash windows and a solid front door that faced the lane.

That completed the extent of rooms in the house: Two bedrooms, one living room, kitchen, bathroom and the little boot hall. Floors throughout were bare timber boards. Tongue and groove timber walls and ceilings all could do with fresh paint.

"Not many rooms but at least all a good size." I said optimistically.

The heavy panelled front door opened stiffly on squeaky hinges, to disclose a collapsed flight of steps. The rickety staircase landed at a terra cotta paved pathway which vanished into nettles and long grass. I imagined the weedy yard might have once been laid to lawn. Jasmine and Honey Suckle flourished rampantly over a surrounding picket fence.

"Can see why they use the back door."

"You'd have your work cut out here Dimity."

I rubbed clean a tarnished brass nameplate on the front door, better to see its inscription: *Albero di Limone.* I pencilled the name into a blue pastel-paged jotter brought along to take notes.

More cobwebs hung from ceilings throughout the house and a massive tarantula spider adorned one bedroom wall. Window glass, filmed with grime, was barely transparent.

"Geez Dimity. I don't know if I can see you living here alone."

"I'll get a hound dog."

I knew a burst of joy that I could actually get myself a dog. This notion helped me keep upbeat despite the sorrowful little house.

Upside, the dwelling did offer adequate shelter. I wouldn't have to pitch a tent inside the house as no signs of roof leaks were evident.

Making the place livable required a hell of a lot of cleaning and I could afford a new shower curtain right away. The back stairs provided safe access, so fixing the derelict front stairs could wait.

"Everything looks doable. In time. Let's look out back. The paddocks look wonderful and must be safe since the neighbours graze stock here."

"Hmm. Maybe." Duncan seemed less convinced after viewing the house.

The high roofed, half-enclosed hay shed appeared solid. Grey doves cooed aloft in the rafters and fled on creaky sounding wings as we encroached the deserted barn space.

The earthen floor was mixed with wisps of straw from old bales. Heavy timber columns like telegraph poles supported the hay shed roof. Pole bases were blackened with oil or creosote to protect from white ants. Duncan searched for any telltale termite trails but found none.

"This is OK anyway." Duncan approved grudgingly.

A raised tank stand held a large round water tank, to store run-off from the extensive hay shed roof. Tank water gravity fed to a stock trough equipped with a control float to prevent overflow. The trough sat in shade beneath the high tank stand. I imagined Nero enjoying cool rainwater to drink instead of hard town water.

"Reckon you could also cart water from this trough if the power was off at the house."

Duncan seemed convinced of my water carting ability.

Walking the fence line, confirmed the mixed grassy pasture to be more than ample fodder for one horse. Maybe I could get a companion or two for Nero if I came to buy this place. A flutter of hope morphed into wishful thinking. I had to be realistic.

The better it all looked, the more my optimism waned into pessimism. At least with the state of the derelict house, the property seemed within my price range. The good shed, paddock and lush pasture made it seem unaffordable.

The property back fence ran behind a clear creek, its banks embroidered with red Grevillia Bottle Brush, small leaf Lilly-pillys and Maiden Hair ferns. A Willow wept over the widest waterhole where tiny flashing minnows darted amongst reeds and water plants. Colourful parrots flitted and chatted in the branches overhead.

The natural wonders enchanted. The decrepit state of the house became of little importance. Try as I might, emotion overtook me. I loved this place. Duncan saw my tears.

"I'm good for a loan if you don't have enough of the ready." he offered gently.

"Thanks man. I don't even know if the place is for sale yet." I sniffed.

I would struggle to repay a loan even if rash enough to accept money from Duncan. He was being a good friend, and I appreciated his care, but borrowing from him was not on.

We wandered back up the paddock to the frontage. Walking further up the lane that fronted the house, we found the way tapered to a narrower trail that led up a rise. From that vantage point, the township of Clemency could vaguely be made out in the hazy distance. No other houses could be seen in close proximity to Gallo's farm or this small holding.

The track ran unhindered alongside boundary fences of adjoining paddocks. Exploring the trails with Nero would be a wonderful pastime. If only wishes were granted.

While up on the rise, Duncan checked mobile phone coverage. Naively I hadn't thought of internet connection. The house had no landline phone and apparently no mobile signal down there either. I didn't jot that down in my notes as I wasn't likely to forget it. Hopefully that might bring the price down. Duncan announced the reality:

"There's signal up here but you'd have to hike up the rise for access every time, if you lived in that old house."

It was only a few minutes walk to top the rise. It wasn't perfect but I decided I could live with it. The exercise would do me good. I so wanted to have that place; I could justify almost any excuse.

Back at the big farm, Sophia had laid out a generous spread with fresh garden salads, home-made bread and a rich tasty quiche made with free-range eggs. My tear-stained face must have been obvious. The old couple looked apologetic thinking I had been very disappointed in the place.

"Sorry the house is unkempt, but the family will clean it up if you decide to want it. No worries."

"I see it needs work, but I would really love to make a home of it." I assured them.

The Gallo's seemed pleasantly surprised that I did still want it.

I took out my jotter of notes, asked the meaning of the house name *Albero di Limone* and was told the inscription was Italian for lemon tree.

I loved the romance of that name. It made me even more sure of disappointment if I couldn't acquire the property. I remarked:

"What a lovely name."

"My dear sister Fiorella named the property. It was her part of what our parents willed to us long ago." Giorgio replied with sadness.

"Fiorella tended a beautiful lemon tree in the front garden. Years ago," Sophia recalled, "before that pull-the-chain commode was put in the bathroom. Fiorella would empty the piss pots to feed her lemon tree every morning."

Almost too much information.

"Did the tree die? I saw no lemon tree there." I asked out of curiosity.

A sad glance passed between the old couple. Momentarily a pregnant pause stilled the conversation.

"Lupo, Fiorella's bad husband chopped it down." Giorgio divulged sadly. "Why? Maybe only because our Fiorella had loved it so much. Who knows?"

"*Bastardo*. Lupo was a very bad man. Crazy when he got drunk." Sophia explained.

This sad tale fed into the domestic violence rumour mentioned by Duncan. It was an awkward moment in the conversation and I dared not press them for more of that story.

"I am sorry to hear this. I hope if I come to live there I can plant another lemon tree."

"That would be a very good thing to do." Giorgio and Sophia both nodded in agreement.

I clearly printed my full name, address and contacts on a pale blue page torn from my jotter. Adding the utmost amount I could afford to offer for *Albero di Limone* - the lemon tree place.

The unsophisticated elderly couple gaped wide-eyed at the amount, but I remained painfully aware my best offer was scant compared to the current market. Perhaps I should have held some money in reserve to bargain with, but I didn't want my offer to be an insult.

"Please give this page of information to your nephew when you can. I am very keen on living here, but if he won't sell to me I must soon look elsewhere. You see, my town unit has sold."

The old couple were keen to oblige.

"We will write tonight and include this page of details." Giorgio promised.

"And will say it would be good to have a helpful young neighbour living so close in our old age. With a car too." Sophia added.

"This is true. It would be wonderful. We are not getting any younger."

"We have rarely been sick in our lives but it would be nice to have more safety. And such a lovely neighbour too of course."

Duncan and I bid our thanks and goodbyes and set out for the return trip as evening drew in.

Beginnings

GOOD MORNING MR. RICCI

Driving home, Duncan warned me not to expect anything to happen at lightning speed.

"Even if they finish their letter soon, it won't be posted before bus day when they go into town. Bus day is only once a week, and it follows some strange routine only known to locals. I can't tell you when their next trip into town might be."

Emotionally drained, exhausted, I reclined as far back as the car seat allowed, happy to let Duncan do the talking.

"How did you come to meet Giorgio and Sophia?" I asked to start him off.

"Well now, the big shindig on the Clemency calendar is the picnic races long weekend. Three days. Everyone goes. Are you listening?"

"Yes. Go on."

"One time, some gallopers from the stables were entered. I drove the horse transport, helped load, unload horses. Giorgio watched me tack on a cast shoe."

Duncan continued while I fell half asleep. He nudged me to see if I was awake.

"I'm listening." I stirred myself to concentrate.

"Giorgio and Sophia drove into town by cart, they had pumpkins and melons to sell there, but one of their heavy horses seemed sore. Giorgio asked me to take a look because he couldn't see any cause for it. Horse had a bit of seedy toe. It was easy to miss. I cleaned it out and doused it with iodine. No big deal."

"Ok. I'm with you." I stifled a yawn.

"Upshot was, I did Giorgio's horse as a freebie. He was chuffed. Gave directions to their farm. Asked if I'd visit on a regular basis to trim horses, cows, whatever. Now I make a weekend of it every so often and stay over. A few others heard of my visits on the grapevine. So I have a loose schedule of regulars. It's an interest. I like coming out here. It's a nice change of air and scenery."

Duncan paused his tale while shifting gears going up the steep range dividing cooler downs country on the west side and warmer humid coastal lands to the east.

"Where do you stay on your weekends out west?"

"I like one of the Clemency Pubs. Hot meal. Pool table. Game of darts."

"Raging in downtown Clemency hey?" I teased. "You're a devil."

"I can be." he confirmed, aiming a twinkling eye at me.

I'm sure he could be a devil. In another life I'd be chasing him. But for now, my preoccupation centred on my country escape. In my dreams, I envisaged *Albero di Limone* freshly painted light green with white trims. Maybe touches of clean lemony yellow. The front door sanded back and resealed. IF I was allowed to buy the place. The anxious wait, a seesaw of highs and lows, held me on tenterhooks in an agony of uncertainty. Within a long drawn-out fortnight, I had my answer.

As usual arriving home from the office just on dusk, I kicked off my sensible shoes and stripped off my torturous bra as soon as inside the unit. Donning floppy shorts and an over-sized soft t-shirt I padded barefoot to the 'fridge where a pre-cooked beef stroganoff waited to be reheated for my evening meal. Inconveniently, I heard a tapping on my door just after I put the casserole in the oven. I soundly cursed whoever it could be annoying me right on teatime, vowing if it happened to be bible thumpers again, they would meet a less than gracious response.

A quick peep through the spy hole delivered a huge shock to see who was standing outside. Oh My God! It was none other than my adored and handsome boss Fabio Ricci. Flustered, I invited the man of my dreams into my humble abode. Embarrassment at my loose attire was somewhat assuaged seeing Fabio wore running gear. I surmised he must have jogged over. I am quick on the uptake at times. Thank goodness the unit was beautifully shiny and tidy since my cleaning blitz for the real estate agents.

"We need to talk". Fabio declared.

Aware Fabio also seemed ill at ease, I feared his need to talk might prove ominous. My manners surfaced to stave off the problem whatever it might be. I invited Fabio to sit at my table. I quickly assessed the stroganoff would be enough for two if served with rice.

"Have you eaten?"

"No, but it smells delicious."

"It's only a simple meal but I would be pleased to have your company Fabio."

To my own ears I sounded overly formal, ridiculous when we saw each other all the time at work.

"Thank you so much. I would love to join you Dimity. I will nip down and pick up wine."

A bottle shop just across the road fulfilled a perk of city living. Fabio's swanky apartment, only a few streets away, probably made it his local alcohol outlet as well. Hastily I filled the rice cooker and set another place. Candles? No. Too over the top. I decided whatever Fabio had to say, we would eat first. I'd handle any upset better if not famished.

What on earth he needed to talk about I could not imagine. Then it hit me. Of course! Fabio's reason to visit suddenly seemed perfectly clear: He must be the buyer of this unit. The purchaser had been named as a business. I knew from sly sleuthing at work that Fabio had an extensive investment portfolio under various business names. In best voyeur style I had secretly spied on some of it.

Also, I had asked his advice about selling my unit. He was instrumental in achieving the terms of the sale. So I got that he called by casually to inspect his recent real estate acquisition. I supposed he'd been jogging by and decided on an impulse to drop in.

"Eat first talk later." I insisted on Fabio's return.

Confident I'd sussed the obvious reason for his impromptu visit, I relaxed. Fabio proceeded to open a very decent bottle of red.

"Apologies for the plain glassware. All the good stuff is already packed. I've only left out the bare necessities." I explained.

"No matter," Fabio smiled, "on my balcony I drink wine from a teacup to fool the snooping neighbours."

I believed he attempted to make me feel better that my cheap glassware came originally filled with Dijon mustard from a supermarket. Sweet man.

"So. You have packed up already." Fabio commented.

"Yes. I have what I want to take. As you know, I sold this place furnished including most of the larger electrical appliances."

"Oh yes I remember now." Fabio said.

"There is an itemised list in the contract." I reminded in case he needed to check it.

"Very good." he paused seeming to regroup. "But now I must confess there is a worrying reason I need to talk to you."

Fabio said it with a slight frown.

Uh oh.

"Is there an issue?"

Mentally on high alert, I felt afraid the sale of my home unit could still be made void.

"Forgive me. You must think me very remiss. I should have mentioned I am the owner before now."

Well, he might have said, but I didn't see it as a huge omission. Surely everyday real estate deals are done in company names.

"Not at all." I replied. "It is a business deal. Not personal."

"But Dimity. It is very personal to me!"

He almost choked on the words. Fabio stressed his dramatic exclamation with typically expressive Italian hand gestures.

"It is? Why is it so personal Fabio? I don't understand." I really didn't.

"It is where I was born and brought up. I still think of it as my dear mother's *Albero di Limone*. To me, it is very personal."

I was gobsmacked. Comprehension sunk in. Astonishment fed my question:

"You own the Clemency place? The lemon tree house?"

"You did not know?" Fabio was also amazed in turn.

"How could I?"

Fabio produced an envelope from his pocket and revealed a few pages he spread on the table. Reading upside down, the letter looked to be handwritten in Italian. I recognised the pale blue note page torn from my jotter that I'd given to Giorgio and Sophia with my details and wishful offer for *Albero di Limone*.

"This evening I found this letter from my family."

"You are the nephew? The owner?"

"Didn't I just say?"

We both struggled with confusion.

"I see that now. But I thought you meant you are the new owner of this unit here."

"No. I am not." Fabio said. "Why ever would you think I might invest here without saying?"

"Um. Never mind. But tell me why you are remiss?"

I ventured forth.

"Because, when you described the country place you were trying to find, to be honest, I knew that my empty house fitted perfectly." Fabio admitted. "But I said nothing. You see, I choose to keep my home life and work life strictly separate."

I chose not to say I already knew about his drunken father, Lupo, the man responsible for chopping down the lemon tree. Family violence and alcoholism would be a matter of great shame to anyone. Particularly for a proud Italian man.

"I'm sure you have good reason." I answered carefully.

"I have reasons. Yes." Fabio agreed.

We sat across from each other at the table. I marvelled at the turn of events.

"So you are the nephew owner. Your uncle and aunt didn't mention your name. You know they call you 'the boy'."

"I will always be the boy to them. They were never blessed with children, so I am like a son to them. Uncle Gio paid my way through business college. He gave me the best chance. I am forever indebted and of course I love my family."

While I busied myself making coffee, Fabio carried the dishes to the sink, ran hot water and suds, efficiently washed up and wiped the bench as if he'd done it all his life, which he possibly had. His domesticated side differed from the smooth businessman I'd always known at the office. We both seemed to need a break from the conversation. I didn't know where exactly this was heading. I only knew my wish for the lemon tree farmlet hung in the balance. Fabio took up the thread:

"There is a more serious issue Dimity."

"An issue? It's the money isn't it. You are insulted by my offer."

My heart sank.

"No Dimity, your offer is reasonable. The property is remote with few amenities. My uncle admits they have let the house fall into disrepair. I too have neglected it and have not bothered with that house for many years."

If not the money then what could it be?

"What then?"

"My family would be so disappointed, ashamed of me if they learnt of my – thing – fling with Cyndi."

Bloody Cynthia. Persisting as the thorn in my side even from the grave.

"Cynthia?"

"Uncle Gio and Aunt Sophia, they would push to know more about my city life once they learnt of our close connection, working together for so many years."

"But Fabio. I can keep a secret. I really can."

I bit my lip, as I felt my ambitious dream thwarted. *Albero di Limone* was slipping through my fingers. The disappointment was crushing. Karma for booting Cynthia down the stairs perhaps.

"Please understand Dimity. I need to protect my family from further pain. They know I am far from perfect but that wrong thing – fling – whatever it was with Cyndi would be too much. Trust me. I am ashamed of my sins."

We stood wordlessly for moments facing each other. I had to fight for a last chance at gaining that Clemency place. He even considered my offered price fair. If necessary I would stoop to beg. Hand on heart, I pledged sincerely:

"Fabio, I give my solemn promise that I will never, ever, mention anything to do with Cynthia Nagy to any living soul. And I will never let on that we ever worked together. I will pretend to not know you. It is not lying. Just not telling."

Fabio gazed at me for several heartbeats.

"Cross my heart and hope to die if I am lying to you Fabio."

I made the Catholic sign of the cross which I hadn't practised since my high school days. An opportune upside to being taught by nuns. There had to be at least one. In suspense, I watched different emotions flit across Fabio's handsome face. Finally, he capitulated:

"I trust you Dimity. The lemon tree place is yours if you really want it."

I hope I hadn't squealed like a silly girl – but I might have. Throwing myself bodily at Fabio, I embraced him and kissed his beautiful face in ecstasy. I'd always wanted to do that.

"Thank you! Oh! Thank you so much." I cried. "Fabio, I love y.....the lemon tree place. I promise to take best care and treat your childhood home with proper respect always. And I can keep a secret. Truly I can."

"As I said Dimity, I trust you."

Fabio repeated his statement in all seriousness but with a smile.

"I am over the moon happy Fabio."

"You've always seemed quite sad. I am glad to have brought joy to you."

We grinned at each other. All that elation had to go somewhere. Fabio looked at my lips. A fine sheen of sweat appeared above his own top lip. I thought about licking it off. He bit his bottom lip. Smiling shyly, I met his gaze that posed the alluring question.

Fabio tightened the hug, inviting a closer embrace. His immediate hardening nudged temptingly against my belly. His lips brushed mine. Even his aftershave smelt of fresh lemons. Holding back now seemed pointless.

"You could make me even happier." I breathed wantonly.

"I am hopeless. I never learn." Fabio groaned.

He shook his head at his own failure to learn from past mistakes, all the while running his warm hands under my loose t-shirt. Fabio murmured his desire as he gently squeezed my full breasts.

"Mama mia. Miss Minto's unattainable assets at last."

"Oh goodness me Mr. Ricci".

So, I had not been completely overlooked at the office. There was no way I was letting this sucker out of my flat without a full audit.

"I won't tell if you won't." I gasped. "I really can keep a secret Fabio."

Feverishly, in my lonely bedroom where I'd spent years longing for this man, Fabio made all my dreams come true. Then a while later, he made all my dreams come true again.

Fabio proved to be a masterful and considerate lover. The sweet, adorable man. It was the absolute best time of my life.

At last, sated, we lay naked side by side staring at the ceiling. A chink of light through venetian blinds palely illuminated my bedroom. Fabio and

I lived only a few streets apart, worked in the same building for years, yet always commuted separately and never socialised.

Reliving the random turn of events culminating so heatedly this night, a dreamy smile mellowed my thoughts. To my mind, the rosy outcome seemed spiritually ordained. Fondly imagining Fabio must be on the same page, I spoke softly, wanting to share my wonder:

"Fabio. Are you awake?"

"Mmmm."

"What are you thinking?"

A slight pause as he became fully awake preceded his sudden outburst:

"Oh my God! I forgot to feed my cat! How could I forget her. She will be starving."

His cat!? Leaping from my bed, Fabio searched for his clothes randomly scattered earlier. He let himself out. Plainly, no after sex cuddles or whispered sweet words afforded for this wicked woman.

The heartache of Fabio's swift departure would surely be analysed in the future. For now, I hugged the major trophy – *Albero di Limone* was really to become home to myself and Nero.

Just hours later I was back sitting at my office desk promptly at 9am. Fabio entered looking impeccable as always in smart Italian tailored business suit, crisp white shirt and dark tie.

"Good morning Miss Minto." he said nodding as he strode by towards his office.

"Good morning Mr. Ricci." I dead panned.

Piper

SMOKE

Neither Fabio nor I alluded to our energetic one night of passion. It was easier to pretend it had never happened.

To keep my end of the bargain, our occupational associations must always be kept secret from Giorgio and Sophia. My beloved Fabio trusted me and I would never betray his trust.

Duncan was a link between myself, Giorgio and Sophia, but I had never discussed office business with the Irishman. He was unlikely to even know the name of the firm I worked for. Certainly I would never have mentioned Fabio to Duncan or vice versa.

Superstitiously afraid of jinxing the deal, I resisted visiting *Albero di Limone* until absolutely certain the sale was watertight, done and dusted.

With a few weeks of negative rent remaining at the unit, some lazy days were free to spend riding Nero out on the sands. One morning, splashing through shallows on the seashore, Nero's flicking ears warned of approaching gallopers.

Soon the beat of many hooves sounded over the shooshing of waves, as several sleek racehorses thundered by. Inured to the spectacle, Nero paid little attention, although he'd been known to shy at a tiny bit of paper or a leaf blowing in the wind, when full of oats.

A rangey grey horse pulled up snorting alongside me and Nero. Duncan, astride the tall grey gelding, greeted me.

"Mornin' Dimity. Not long before your exodus."

"Morning Duncan. I know. It is looming. Are you still right to deliver Nero when the time comes?"

"I am," he replied, "and can I ask a favour?"

"Ask away."

"Any danger you could spell this fella for a while out at your new paddock?"

Duncan asked the question as he stroked the smooth neck of his horse. Piper, as the big grey was named, did duty as an escort for green youngsters on first outings. Being an ex-stewards mount at racetracks, this nice horse was stoic in nature. A light sweat darkened Piper's dappled flanks after his morning exertions.

"Of course. Piper deserves a break."

"Your black boy already knows him, so he'd be good company."

"I was just thinking the same thing. Piper will be a calming influence on Nero."

"It won't take him long to settle in the new paddock with Piper there." Duncan agreed.

I smiled at my friend and was glad we would stay in touch.

" I'm really glad you'll still be Nero's farrier too."

"So am I. We can get together whenever I'm up that way. I'll give you a game of darts at the pub."

"I'll have a go at it. But I've never played darts."

Duncan seemed pleased I agreed to the darts game. I could do with branching out a bit too. Another idea occurred to Duncan:

"They have dance nights at the Clemency Hall once a month. I could take you dancing."

"Well Duncan, I am forced to admit that I don't do dancing. Never have."

"Bull. Girls all do dancing."

Thankful for the 'girls' description anyway.

"Nope not me."

"So what do you do at night for entertainment?"

"Read mostly. Sometimes I knit."

"Knit? What do you knit?"

"Anything. Mostly squares to join into blankets. They don't need complicated patterns and are small and easy to knit in bed."

"I can think of better things to do in bed."

"Explains the smoke coming out of your ears Duncan."

He just laughed. I enjoyed swapping playful banter with Duncan. Our horses splashed along together through the salty shallows as we made our way back to the stables.

Frisky

SAUSAGES NEXT TIME

Fabio fast-tracked conveyancing on the lemon tree place. He invited me into his office to complete paperwork and share a celebratory Scotch. This time our drinks were in crystal rather than mustard jars.

Sherman Knickerbacker, installed as secretary, was sent outside to allow our privacy while the transaction took place. Poor Sherman was agog with curiosity, but I felt sure Fabio would cover all his tracks on this particular sale.

Everyone in the office knew I was leaving my job for a tree change. None knew I was buying a property from Fabio.

There was a bit of a going-away party for me at work. Cake, jokey gifts, well wishes. I don't like being the centre of attention but appreciated the thoughts. Leaving the building on my last day at the office, I felt liberated, light as a feather, walking on air.

At long last I drove out to *Albero di Limone* as its owner. Though my car was packed to capacity, a few trips would be required before I could properly move in. Glad to have whittled my belongings back to bare essentials, I realised what an onerous undertaking it might have been if everything in the home unit had been kept.

It was bus day so Giorgio and Sophia were not at home. This suited me well. I preferred a quiet time alone, on this my first day entering the lemon tree house as the new owner.

The back door key turned easily into an oiled keyhole. Power was on.

To my absolute delight, I found the house had been thoroughly cleaned inside and out. Windows gleamed. Cobwebs were gone. No tarantula in the bedroom.

A shiny new refrigerator hummed quietly in place of the decrepit old one which was nowhere to be seen. The wood burning range stove was spic and span, newly blacked. A full wood-box sat beside the stove.

The knotty pine kitchen dresser, table and eclectic mix of chairs remained, even those pieces looked to be scrubbed clean. What a boon that simple furniture was to me, since I had none.

I could hardly take in the changes. There was more:

The front door no longer creaked open, its hinges had been lubricated and its proud brass nameplate *Albero di Limone* shone, brightly polished.

The front garden had been cleared, showing the original paved pathway led to an ornate entry gate, a feature that had not been visible on first inspection. Jasmine and Honeysuckle creepers had been tidied.

It was all so lovely and unbelievable. I realised how worried I'd been about coping with all the work to make the house livable.

Overwhelmed, I wept silent tears of thanks while sitting on new sturdy front steps, remembering the fallen down old staircase that I thought would take years to fix. If ever.

Darling Fabio must have made all this happen. I reinforced my pledge to honour my end of our bargain and keep all prior work connections a closely guarded secret.

Duncan was not surprised when I described all the wonderful changes to the lemon tree house. He said he'd expected no less of the good Italian neighbours.

Privately, I credited Fabio, particularly for the wonderful modern brand-new refrigerator. It upgraded the old kitchen beautifully.

Fabio's name for the place as the lemon tree house also became how I thought of my new home. Hopelessly imbued with romantic longing for Fabio, I liked to share this notion.

I hung a new pristine white shower curtain; the $20 purchase hugely brightened the dim bathroom.

Before finally taking up residence, a bed must be bought. Duncan agreed to transport this essential item in his ute. To save time, he was pressed further to accompany me on a bed buying mission at city stores. I hoped to buy the bed and move into my house on the same day; however, the shopping expedition took far longer than anticipated.

Traipsing from one furniture warehouse to another, entailed driving and walking miles to find the exact bed I had in mind, at an affordable price. Luckily Duncan proved tolerant.

"That's alright. The bed is very important." he'd said stoically.

As a last resort, we went to a second-hand dealer. Duncan talked me into buying a big solid old-style wooden bed on long legs. I liked the idea of a high bed since it would be easier to roll out of on odd days when my back ached. Like when after Nero dumped me.

Having measured the bed for the correct sized mattress, we went to a mattress warehouse where we bounced on many, separately not together, before deciding. The salesman must have been glad to see the back of us, although I purchased an expensive innerspring.

Duncan offered to bring the bed and mattress up to Clemency right away, but that would make a late arrival time. Sidestepping any overnight sleeping issues with only one bed available, I opted for next day delivery. As soon as my new bed was in place I would spend my last night at the city unit and first night at the lemon tree house.

Duncan promised to bring the horses, Nero and Piper, within a few days time after delivering my bedroom furniture. What would I have done without Duncan's help, I don't know. The ever helpful, always cheeky, often annoying Irishman was indeed my best friend.

At long last I could turn my frisky horse out to pasture. Overly excited to be at liberty in the large paddock, Nero galloped about in wild euphoria, tail flagged high. My black beauty was in danger of getting hurt if he kept up the pace.

Fortunately, Duncan's steadier horse was only interested in cropping lush green grass, a delicacy to stabled horses. The grazing would be limited until their guts became accustomed, so I would yard the pair overnight.

At length, Nero settled and fell to grazing, following Piper's good example. I blessed the wisdom of bringing the steady grey horse. Once more, Duncan had bailed me out.

Duncan booked in to stay at his usual pub and invited me to a game of darts and a lunch there. Nero had settled well with Piper. We deemed it safe enough to go out for a couple of hours.

Duncan seemed popular at the pub and was welcomed by several people there. He introduced me as his lady friend.

I wanted to pay or at least go Dutch treat for the lunch meal but Duncan insisted on paying. Nevertheless, I ordered a grilled steak with tomatoes and mashed potatoes. Sausages would have been a cheaper choice, but I fancied a T-bone after the busy time of moving house. I'd just make the expense up to Duncan at some later date.

Our game of darts had people dodging as some of my throws went wildly astray, glancing off the edge and landing anywhere other than the target board. Still, it was lots of fun, and I needed a laugh. The pub had a bit of a dance floor, just a square of polished parquetry. Someone clicked music on the jukebox and a few couples got up.

"Time for our dance." Duncan announced.

"Oh no way. I don't dance as I have already explained."

Duncan grinned and ignored my refusal.

"Come on. I bought you a steak."

"Now you want payback? That's not very gentlemanly."

"Never claimed to be a gentleman."

True. Duncan had never made that claim. He dragged my unwilling feet to the dance floor. Fortunately, a slow number came on so I could get away with just shuffling around in Duncan's arms. He crooned soft words in my ear as his hands dropped lower down my back below my waistline and his Irish lilt became more pronounced.

"Babe. You feel so nice."

"Next time I'll order the sausages."

I pushed him gently away to distance the hold.

"Then there is a next time." Duncan twinkled.

The persistent cuss. I should have been flattered by so much attention from the handsome Irishman, and I was a bit, but he could be so pesky.

The man knew exactly how to push my buttons – to either annoy or flirt. His cheeky sexy suggestions often enticed me in a disturbing way. I am sure he knew it. That is exactly why he did it.

At the time, my obsession with Fabio stood between me and any other romance.

Frugal

A FRESH LOAF

I loved living in my lemon tree house and often looked out to see Nero and Piper grazing the paddock, just because I could.

Breathing in the clean country air was sheer bliss, always to be remembered as one of the happiest times in my life.

The back verandah became my favourite spot for meals. Two kitchen chairs served as temporary patio furniture, one to sit on and the other as a table.

A pity I had to find work. I'd have gladly lazed my days away in the beautiful place.

Seeking paid work took precedence over horse riding, home decorating and socialising during my initial weeks living in the lemon tree house.

Thrifty meal ingredients, vegetables and eggs, were bought from my old neighbours' roadside stall, although the township had a variety of shops offering anything and everything.

Having only a dwindling bank balance to live on, no garden plants or decorating items could yet be splurged on. However, my kitchen table soon became populated with paint colour charts, brochures, fabric swatches and a bevy of jotted wish lists.

Despite a need to be frugal, I could indulge in free window shopping, doubling browsing to spread word of my job seeking.

As expected, vacancies were few and owners of the small family-owned shops had their own kin to fill any gaps. In Clemency, anyone not at least born in the province would always be considered a newcomer, making it far more difficult to gain paid employment.

Snail mail delivered once a week on the bus, where, having no personal letterbox, I picked mine up at Gallo's roadside stall. All I ever got were bills and junk anyway. With no landline phone, walking up the lane to access mobile signal was the quickest method to check for job offers. One bonus, my physical fitness improved with regular walks up the rise to access the internet.

Frequent visits to that higher vantage point familiarised me to the lay of the land. I now easily recognised where the road branched off to the township and where it forked, veering to a tree-lined road heading for the river lands.

Glimpses of sun-sparkles glanced off distant water, marking where the river wended through the terrain. The track past my lemon tree house meandered down towards that river valley. I vowed to take Nero out exploring once we both became more settled, and my financial status improved. It could take a while.

Duncan texted most days to see how Piper was going and could be reassured his horse was well and content. I refused to accept Duncan's proffered agistment payment for keeping Piper no matter how long the quiet grey horse stayed at my place.

Having Piper paddocked in with Nero was an asset and I already owed an enormous debt of gratitude to Duncan. Apart from delivering my bed and horse, without Duncan's help I would never have found the lemon tree house.

Furthermore, I never would have experienced that unforgettable wonderful night of passion with Fabio, if not for Duncan finding the lemon tree house for me.

The two good men, Fabio and Duncan, were complete opposites, yet both unwittingly intertwined in shaping my destiny.

When Duncan turned up with a racehorse to be spelled for six weeks, the extra income was not to be sneezed at.

The agistment fee Duncan quoted seemed astronomical up front, but the elegant chestnut thoroughbred filly came with night rugs, day rugs and an attitude. She required careful management of time on grass and supplementary hard feeds twice daily.

Duncan had a long list of requirements for the filly's upkeep:

"...and if you could see your way clear to running a brush over her between rug changes..."

Duncan continued his speech of instructions as he unloaded horse rugs, feed bins, yard panels and all the paraphernalia that came with the chestnut princess.

"Not charity then Duncan."

"I don't do charity." he winked.

Resident geldings, Nero and Piper seemed enchanted as the elegant chestnut girl, Zoe, tip-toed into the paddock and coolly ignored their presence.

"Three is the magic number for this paddock," Duncan reckoned, "Piper will still have company when you take your black fella out riding."

"That's horse sense." I agreed. "I'll be sure to take advantage of that and ride Nero out exploring while Zoe is here. So far, I haven't ridden out, been too busy with everything else."

"There's a long waiting list for good spelling agistment. I'll bring a replacement when I come to collect Zoe. If that's ok with you." Duncan added.

An ongoing stream of agistment income was great news. I would be solvent, again thanks to the Irishman. He was making himself indispensable. I wasn't complaining, being in no position to do so. Despite the promised income from Duncan's thoroughbred boarders, I gratefully grabbed the only job offer received from all my forays into Clemency town: Sunday morning shop assistant at the town bakery. I had never done the type of work. It was mundane and luckily for me, not rocket science. I landed that bakery job as few locals were keen to work Sundays. The time frame clashed with sports events and morning devotions. Missing Mass posed no worries for me. I hadn't observed any church faith since waving a less than fond goodbye to the strict nuns at my high school.

For me, most days were now much the same including Sundays, so a higher weekend pay rate plus a free fresh loaf to take home sweetened the deal.

I had it all. Or so I thought.

Ghost

NIGHT INTRUDER

All was tickety-boo until the night I got the fright of my life.

It happened on a still and silent night when a new moon bathed my bedroom in a pale ethereal silvery glow.

The weather, yet balmy, would cool towards dawn. I chose to wear a pair of ski pyjamas, although I lay atop the bed covers.

Haunting hoo-hooting of an owl wafted in on a whisper of breeze, the bird call lulling and soothing.

I stretched luxuriously feeling perfectly comfortable, not too hot, not too cold – until some eerie sixth sense of being watched, prickled my scalp. At once stiff with foreboding, I slid my line of sight to the open bedroom doorway.

A scream froze in my throat. The doorway held a ghostly vision of a tall thin man. It so terrified me, for heart stopping seconds I was struck rigid, unable to move.

The apparition stood still at first, but then began to creep slowly into the room.

Survival instinct spurred me to action at last. In panic, I dove off the far side of the bed, hitting the wooden floor hard, but managed to scramble under the bed. It was my only option as a bolt hole.

Bellying about in the dark amid dust bunnies, I found nothing to use as a weapon. Apart from a useless pair of fluffy slippers all I had were my wits and bare hands.

Waiting, terrified, I watched the intruder's footsteps. The presence began a slow deliberate trudge around the bed. He would not find me on the floor there, so I knew he would look under the bed next.

Frantically I slid out from under the bed on the side nearest the doorway. I fled the bedroom and raced through the house.

The back door stood ajar. I must have forgotten to lock it. The key was in place, my pyjama top caught on it briefly as I ran by. I didn't pause to ponder but took the stairs two at a time.

Shit! Car keys! The keys were upstairs. There remained nothing for it but to race barefoot down the lane to the neighbours' farm.

Enzo barked at my midnight invasion. Lights went on in the farmhouse. Giorgio and Sophia came out in their dressing gowns.

"Dimity. What is wrong?"

Breathlessly I gasped: "In my house. A man. The door was open..."

Adding to my consternation, my garbled account made sense to the old couple. They didn't seem too fazed.

"It will just be Wolfgang again. Sorry. I better get him." Giorgio apologised.

Again? Holy crap!

Giorgio pulled on boots and stomped off in his dressing gown.

"Oh, poor Dimity, you got such a big fright."

Sophia sat me down at her kitchen table and patted my back.

"I will make tea. Lots of sugar."

"You know who that spooky man is?"

"Yes. He is just our nephew Fabio's brother. Half-brother I should say. Wolfgang."

"A brother?"

"Half-brother." Sophia repeated. "Wolfgang's mother is Agneta. Lupo's second wife."

I realised I knew little about Fabio's private life. The scary episode told me he had more to his family.

"What is this half-brother doing there? Why is he sneaking about in my house?"

"He used to live there. So, Wolfgang comes home sometimes. He has never gone inside before. He must be confused seeing someone lives there now. Don't worry Dimity. He is harmless."

I gulped.

"But I do worry, Sophia, he scared me almost to death."

"I know, I know this is bad for you. Wolfgang is like a child so don't worry."

Don't worry? This half-brother of Fabio's represented an unwelcome threat to my sense of security in my own home. My heart still raced.

"It was terrifying seeing him there watching me as I slept. He just stood staring at me. I hid under the bed. I could see by his feet he was walking around the room. As soon as I knew the doorway was clear I got away. Bumped my head too."

Sophia listened to my rave with suitable murmurs of sympathy.

"But all the time that man remained silent. He never uttered a word."

"Wolfgang doesn't speak." Sophia offered in a mater-of-fact explanation.

Presently, Giorgio entered the kitchen with the mute intruder Wolfgang, a younger, taller, paler version of Fabio.

I was politely and formally introduced as if perfectly normal to do so. Like a sleepwalker, the haunted man seemed to look right through me. What a spook.

Despite the hour, Sophia made a big pot of oatmeal porridge, dishing it up into four bowls, adding cream and honey. Saying I couldn't eat a thing, was ignored. The porridge was delicious.

We had almost cleared our porridge bowls when Enzo barked moments before a car was heard pulling up outside.

"That will be Fabio coming for his brother." Sophia said.

"Half-brother." Giorgio stressed the partial relationship.

I got that this half-brother would be no blood relation to Giorgio, since Lupo's second wife gave birth to Wolfgang.

Fiorella, Georgio's long-lost sister who named my house *Albero di Limone,* had only one child, my beloved Fabio.

"Fabio will take Wolfgang home. Our nephew is such a good boy."

Enter Fabio. I felt awkwardly conscious that I wore yellow polka dotted purple Pjs. No one else seemed concerned about that. Fabio said hello to the room in general.

"Dimity, have you met our nephew Fabio?"

"We have met." I could truthfully say.

"Of course. Sale of *Albero di Limone.*"

"The house contract was signed in my office." Fabio said.

Fabio's comment not a lie either. He rushed on to change that subject:

"Agneta phoned me in a panic. Wolfgang missing again. I sped out straight away. I will take him home now. Wolfy, you have upset your mother again."

Fabio chastised gently to no reply nor visible reaction from his strange half-brother.

"First you must drive Dimity back to her house." Sophia instructed.

"Oh, I can walk back it's not far." I insisted. Without meaning a word of it.

"Your feet are bare. There could be snakes, anything. No Fabio will drive you back. It will only be a few more minutes to do so."

In the car, Fabio apologised profusely. I began to better comprehend his wish to keep his work and home life separate. The retarded half-brother must be an extra embarrassment added to Lupo, the drunken father. Wolfgang's habit of wandering about at night scaring people would be another cross for Fabio to bear.

Fabio got out of the car and like a true gentleman, opened the passenger door for me.

"Dimity, thanks for your understanding. I will see it doesn't happen again."

"I did get a fright. I guess your brother lives not far away."

"No, not close at all. Wolfgang walks for miles when he goes bush. He usually comes back this way in the long run. It was our childhood home you know. Once again, I am very sorry."

"I need a hug." I said, shamelessly.

Fabio gave my back a brotherly pat, his arms stiff about me. I couldn't help but press myself more closely against his warmth. Fabio groaned a few words: *"Ahh...Tesoro mio bella."*

I don't know what he said but it sounded nice. Someday I should learn to speak Italian in words, rather than only in the language of love. Fabio's hands closed over my breasts while he sought my lips with his own.

In the dark before dawn, the cock crowed. Not the feathered variety.

I regretted that Fabio reluctantly pushed himself away and was back in his car, driving off within seconds.

Bummer. Alone, I climbed the stairs to my back verandah.

My shot in the dark was ill timed. Of course, Fabio must rush off since his family were all waiting. It wouldn't do to delay him at the lemon tree house, and heaven forbid, have the old relatives come looking for him. Not with what I had in mind, and he so hot blooded and quick to lust.

A hopeful idea came to me: Perhaps Fabio found a moment to send me a brief text message? I pulled on boots, grabbed my phone and gained the rise in record time. Nothing. No messages. Zilch.

From up on the higher ground, the headlights of Fabio's car could be seen cutting a path through the fading darkness. I expected him to take the town road – but the distant glow from his high beam illuminated the tree line along the river road. He headed out towards the river land.

Fabio's touch and hasty departure left me feeling so forlorn, for the next hour I sat at my kitchen table over an untouched cooling coffee.

My attempt at severing ties with my long-time obsession of Fabio had been to no avail. I was more than ever under his spell and had never wanted anything more than that man.

My mind turned over and over what I knew of Fabio Ricci: His secretary Cynthia must have been irresistible to his hot blood, especially as she surely chased him. No doubt Cynthia would have slept her way to the top with anyone, let alone with such an attractive man.

Fabio had been upset over Cynthia's death, but in hindsight, being found out seemed his greater concern.

He admitted to seeing no future with that beautiful young secretary, or at least he had said he was not free to do so. Cynthia might have been just a notch in Fabio's belt. As was I, surely. Being just another notch wouldn't make any difference to me. I yearned for Fabio. If he wanted me again, I would welcome him with open arms and legs. Pathetic.

Long ago at work in the office, I had surreptitiously viewed files to learn the address of Fabio's swank city apartment. Not that I would ever be so bold to visit but had walked by quite often. It wasn't too far from my unit, and everyone needs a constitutional to take the air. For all I knew, Fabio might have had a live-in girlfriend. I became obsessed with finding out all about him.

There were always other cars parked at his apartment block. He seemed the epitome of a confirmed bachelor but would surely have lots of women interested in him. My nosy sleuthing did not uncover anything of interest.

Fabio remained an intriguing mystery. At the time, little else occupied my innermost thoughts.

Sunday Bakery

TWO GERDAS

Another mystery - the Clemency Bus Day routine.

Bus days occurred on different days Monday to Friday. Maybe you'd have to be a born and bred local to figure out the eccentric schedule, changeable depending on market weeks for pig or calf sales, town hall meetings, nursing home excursions and whenever the lady bus driver had to babysit her grandchildren. Babysitting days depended on whenever her daughter had craft day or pilates. Craft and pilate lessons depended on when tutors were available.

Sunday was the one regular scheduled outing for my elderly neighbours, Giorgio and Sophia. Habit became to pick them up early on my way to work at the bakery.

The old couple always eagerly awaited, wearing their Sunday best. Giorgio in white open necked shirt and linen suit, his hair neatly combed with water. Sophia in smart navy dress teamed with hat and white gloves, her wrinkled face prettied with a touch of powder and peach lipstick.

They chose to sit together in the back seat of my car on those Sunday drives. I felt like a benevolent taxi driver giving them a treat.

The Gallos still doted on bus days but my Sunday morning job at the bakery doubled social life for them. Giorgio and Sophia could now travel in to attend Sunday Mass and go on to play canasta or lawn bowls with their friends.

Sunday afternoons, the old couple would have tea and cakes in the bakery cafe while they waited for my shift to end.

The inquisitive bakery staff soon learnt the Gallos were my neighbours. Customers and staff at the bakery were openly curious about me, a rare newcomer in their midst.

The other two women who shared my shift, oddly both named Gerda, made short work of extracting personal information.

Within my first morning working at the bakery, they learnt I was single, Catholic, owned a house and a car.

Anything I told them would certainly become common knowledge. Their attempts to winkle more information were blatantly transparent: A Gerda said she had two children and the spare Gerda said she had three, herself. I didn't take the hint to tell them how many children I had. So they asked outright:

"Do you have any children Dimity?"

"No I don't"

"Aw. IVF not work? Couldn't adopt?"

"Actually I've never been married so never tried to have children."

"Never married!"

I could see the cogs turning. They wondered if I batted for the other side. The two Gerdas mulled over how to phrase the lesbian issue. Let them stew. It became noticeable they avoided any hand contact in passing buns and strudels despite our rubber gloves.

"I have a very handsome cousin, still unattached." one Gerda began.

"Nando is a good-looking man." the other confirmed.

Cringe. What if the Gerdas had the eligible cousin come into the bakery to look me over? Yuck. Talk about market day. Deftly cornered into accepting or rejecting their matchmaking I was forced to divulge more of my personal life:

"I already have a man friend."

"Oh. That is good. What's his name?"

"Duncan." True. I counted Duncan as my good friend.

Now they were armed in finding out if I lived with him in sin.

"Does he live in town?"

"No. Duncan is from the coast."

That stumped them momentarily. They went off on another tack:

"So, Dimity, you live out near Gallo's vegetable stall? I didn't know any places were for sale out there."

"It wasn't listed for sale. I only heard of it through the grapevine, a friend of a friend."

"Really. Suppose that was lucky. Whose place was it?"

"I bought it from a man named Fabio Ricci."

Might as well tell them that much. They would find out anyway.

"Never heard of a Fabio but there was a Ricci at school, remember him Gerda?"

"Oh yes that weird boy. Wolfgang."

"Not the full quid. But I never called him Werewolf like some kids did."

"Kids can be cruel" I said. That fact was universal, city or country.

I had a reprieve from their inquisition on my personal life as the Gerdas paused for breath, lost in memories of their old school days.

"That Wolfgang boy didn't talk but he wasn't deaf. He always heard the school bell. He'd just leave straight away before being told. No one else would dare do that I can tell you."

"That's right he did. He was a strange one. Eerie. Another thing, he used to draw horror pictures all over his books. All death and doom. He liked to draw a clawed hand reaching up - like out of a grave."

"Remember the teachers said we had to be tolerant. He was unbalanced, they said."

"He just stopped coming to school. I wonder what happened to him?"

"Probably in some loonie asylum by now." spare Gerda mused without too much concern.

"Hopefully, poor thing. I never missed him though."

Gossip-mongering is also universal both in city office and country workplaces. I must never let on to the Gerdas that I had met Fabio's half-brother and been creeped out by him. They would have a field day with that little snippet.

Fabio

SUCH A GOOD BOY

Meeting Fabio's strange half-brother Wolfgang, and learning Fabio assumed responsibility for him, whetted my curiosity.

Before consenting to sell the lemon tree house to me, Fabio agonised I would be cajoled into divesting his private transgressions. He feared to expose his tawdry office affair. But there seemed to be a lot more to it.

I meant my solemn promise to Fabio that I would never speak of our past at the office, nor mention that C name to anyone. An easy oath to make, considering the wrong I did to that C.

Now the tables tilted. After the terrible fright his half-brother caused, I endeavoured to wheedle what I could about Fabio's country roots from his old folks. At the same time, I must be careful to guard the secret that I had known Fabio for many years before coming to Clemency.

An opportunity to pry soon presented itself. The Gallos invited me to a dinner at their place to make up for all the trouble and terror Wolfgang caused by invading my privacy.

Sophia went to a lot of trouble, serving a basil rich tomato soup, followed by a tasty lasagne. Side dishes of salads and figs filled the table along with fresh home baked bread rolls. A carafe of red wine graced the table, and our glasses were topped up generously.

"This is absolutely lovely, Sophia, thanks so much for inviting me."

"I will fix a bolt latch inside your back door so you can feel safer." Giorgio promised.

"Thank you. That is so kind. Sophia says Wolfgang is as harmless as a child, but I would feel safer if he can't get into the house."

"Wolfgang is family, he is worrisome, but we take care of our own. We all do. Especially Fabio. Even as a child himself, Fabio looked after his little brother. Fabio is such a good boy."

I didn't have to guess who was the favoured one, with *such a good boy'* repeatedly used to describe Fabio.

Perhaps I was a little paranoid to think the praise overstated. It almost sounded as if Fabio's behaviour needed to be defended. Angling to bring up some history to extract more information, I made a sympathetic comment:

"So Fabio must have been quite young when he lost his mother?"

"Only four years old when Fiorella drowned. The poor little fellow."

So Fabio's mother drowned. I could think of no delicate way to ask if she had drowned at my home, in the bathtub, water trough or even the creek down the back paddock. Perhaps Sophia had second sight. The old lady seemed to read my mind or my face as she said:

"Fiorella drowned in the river."

"We wanted our little Fabio to live with us, we pleaded and begged but his rotten father, Lupo, refused us." Giorgio added.

"Bastardo." Sophia muttered. I didn't need fluent Italian to recognise the curse word.

Giorgio poured more wine while Sophia served a delicious tarty lemon meringue dessert. I made a remark to keep them talking:

"How sad that time must have been for everyone."

"Not so sad for Lupo. He didn't grieve for long. The grass had not yet grown over Fiorella's grave plot before he remarried."

Giorgio shook his head sadly, reliving the heartbreak he felt for his sister.

"Lupo married a young strong girl who could do the brunt of work of course." Sophia added.

"Agneta came fruit-picking with other German backpackers but she wished to stay in this wonderful country, so to marry Lupo was a way." Giorgio said.

"Also Agneta was in love with Lupo, at first anyway. He was a very good-looking man. Like Paul Newman the movie star," Sophia added, "but he had a dark heart."

OK. Fabio definitely took after his father with the handsome Paul Newman looks. I had learnt a couple of things from this one dinner invitation. Fabio's mother had drowned in the river and his father looked like Paul Newman.

"Then there must be a strong family resemblance between Fabio and his father, also his half-brother has that same look."

"Yes. Fabio and Wolfgang share the comely face. Yet their mothers, so different. Our beautiful little Fiorella small and dark haired. Agneta a big boned German girl, tall and fair."

Giorgio brought out many old photos of his sister. Some had Fabio as a cute baby and a lovable toddler. Fiorella had been pretty, a petite raven-haired beauty. Her flourishing lemon tree, laden with fruit, featured as background in many photos taken at *Albero di Limone.*

If photos of Lupo, Agneta and their son Wolfgang existed, I was not shown any.

It was hard to imagine little four-year-old Fabio having to accept a stepmother so soon after losing his own, and then being withheld from living with his loving uncle and aunt. I wondered how it all worked out.

"So the stepmother was kind to Fabio even after her own baby was born?"

"Oh yes. Agneta was always kinder than his father. She did her best - does her best."

"Poor Agneta soon found out the real Lupo behind his good looks. His bad temper and cruelty did not remain hidden for long. She might have fled if not for her pregnancy."

"The German wife stayed because she was pregnant?"

"She was only a teenager with no money of her own. Also, I know she worried about our little Fabio."

"Sounds like Agneta did well for the family."

"Yes. We were sorry for what Agneta had to put up with. She would tell us things sometimes. She told us she named Wolfgang after her own father." Giorgio recalled.

"Lupo means wolf. So Lupo believed his younger son was named after himself. Agneta liked to have that secret against him."

Sophia smiled sadly.

"At least Agneta could defy Lupo secretly without getting a beating for it."

The old couple reminisced into the night. I learnt that the half-brothers Fabio and Wolfgang shared the second bedroom in the lemon tree house until Fabio went away to college.

They said young Wolfgang needed therapy, so Agneta moved into Clemency nearer the hospital. I gleaned that Lupo must have died sometime before Agneta and Wolfgang moved into town.

"Does Wolfgang still live in town with his mother?" I asked casually, curious as to why Fabio's headlights veered towards the river lands, not mentioning that I had watched this.

"No. They went to live up in the foothills on another family place. Originally my own father built the cottage out there as a retirement home. Stone by stone over the years." Giorgio said.

Sophia explained further. "Doctors said Wolfgang must attend public school, they said he should be socialised. But the boy was teased and bullied at school".

This much had been confirmed by the two gossiping Gerdas at the bakery.

"Agneta kept him home a lot. Soon she got sick and tired of being hounded by the welfare authorities and having Wolfgang treated badly. She was terrified they might take her son off her and put him into an asylum. He might get electric shock treatments. Maybe they do not do this anymore. But stories of what happened in the war were fresh in our memories."

"Agneta took Wolfgang out of school. She just stopped sending him and moved out of town. The authorities did not know where they had gone."

"The stone house is isolated. It is a safe place to hide." Giorgio said.

"It is a shame they had to hide." I said.

"Yes. A shame having to hide." Sophia agreed shortly.

"Agneta continued to home-school Wolfgang as she always did in the past with Fabio as well. Correspondence lessons used to come in the mail from the education department, but Agneta stopped getting them. She was too afraid their whereabouts would be discovered."

Agneta must have lived in constant fear, but maintained diligence in schooling the boys. Apart from fluency in English and Italian languages, Fabio gained German from his stepmother. Being multi-lingual boosted

Fabio's high profile career. I had long been aware his ability to deal with overseas phone conversations made him indispensable in our office. This fact I could not share with Giorgio and Sophia, of course.

"Lupo hated when Agneta or the boys spoke in German. He didn't understand the language and always thought they were saying things about him. Sometimes they did use it like that."

Sophia began to say more..but bit her tongue on that story after Giorgio shot her a warning glance that I pretended to miss.

Apparently Wolfgang wasn't born dumb if he could speak at one time. Another mystery. Ever besotted with Fabio, anything to do with him drew my interest, though I would be well advised to mind my own business.

Fortunately, I can keep a secret.

Ride to the River

THE WILLIES

Apart from Sundays, I was gloriously free to ride Nero after completing morning chores in the house and hay shed.

Cross country and bush trails were a nice change for rides. The indoor arena wasn't missed at all, but losing those bracing canters along the sandy seashore would always evoke some regret. Still, I counted my blessings in having a variety of picturesque countryside to ride through.

I began to take along a packed lunch, curious to explore further afield, confident in Nero's strength and surefooted agility. I would go out for several hours at a time. During those early trail rides I never met another soul and was content alone in the company of my good black horse.

On one such excursion I came upon an ideal picnic spot by the broad riverside. A grassy bank sloped steeply down to a narrow strip of gravelly beach. Nero could be led slipping and sliding down the incline to drink at waters edge.

The pebbly beach plunged abruptly into deep dark water where a swift current rapidly hurled away sticks I threw in to test the flow. It looked dangerous. No skinny dipping here or any other swimming for that matter.

One morning, not long after sunrise, Duncan arrived in his battered ute, towing a long horse trailer with another racehorse to be boarded as a swap for princess Zoe. The chestnut filly was to go back on the return trip. I spoke to Duncan from under the hay shed where I saddled Nero ready to ride.

"You're early."

"You just starting out? Mind if I join you? I've missed riding Piper."

"Sure why not."

Duncan had his riding gear in the trailer and swiftly had Piper saddled ready to go. We took the trail at the high end of the lane, past the mobile signal spot and onwards through bushland that bordered fenced paddocks.

"How far do you want to go Duncan?"

"I don't mind. It's a grand day."

"Well it's a bit of a trek but I found a nice spot along the river bank. I've packed some snacks we could eat there."

"Perfect."

We set off happily together astride the black and the grey.

The trail branched off a few different ways that all eventually rambled down towards the river. Since I was not alone, I decided to try a shadier path that went deep into patches of rain forest. Before, I had stuck to the more open tracks as a safer options.

We rode in companionable silence most of the leafy way, happy to listen to the sounds of bird calls and the muted thuds of hoofbeats on a carpet of leaf litter strewn over the moist ground.

Red and green King Parrots flitted high overhead through leafy treetops. Scarlet faced scrub turkeys foraged about the forest floor where huge fern fronds curled, amid moss covered tree trunks.

We bobbed our heads under overhanging branches where at one such place, an enormous bright green, yellow bellied tree snake writhed sinuously above us.

"Whoa! Is this the way you always come Dimity?"

"Nope. I thought I'd give you the more scenic experience."

"Thanks for that. I could do without the snake, although that thing is a splendid colour."

"I'd be more worried about the red-belly you're about to stand on Duncan."

"Holy mother of....geez!"

Although I did see red-belly snakes quite often, I made it up that time. It was fun teasing Duncan. He was so out of his natural element, and he needed a good nudge to watch the path ahead.

"At least there are no drop bears out here. None that I've noticed anyway." I mentioned.

"What the hell is a drop bear?"

Sucked in

"Don't tell me you've been in Australia all this time and never heard of a drop bear Duncan."

"No. I've heard of koala bears. I believe they are not actually bears but closer to possums and wombats."

"Drop bears are flesh eating bears. They look like koalas with fangs. They're very aggressive. They drop out of trees onto unsuspecting victims. That's how they got the name. Most Australians are safe because they eat Vegemite which is a known deterrent."

"Bull. Pull the other one. It jingles."

"Look it up on Australian Geographic when you get a chance. Foreigners are more at risk because they rarely relish Vegemite. There is some evidence Vegemite also works well if plastered over the skin particularly behind the ears."

"Well I find that hard to believe." Duncan said. The sceptic.

At times, snakes including deadly browns and red belly blacks were detected along the way, thankfully slithering away into the undergrowth. Truly, we are never far from a snake in Australia and not to be taken lightly. Snakes will usually avoid confrontation but not always.

Reaching the riverside picnic spot, we dismounted leading Piper and Nero down the steep grassy bank to the pebbly beach so they could drink at waters edge.

The two horses were firm friends. Nero had become steady through being free to roam and graze. I knew he wouldn't stray if Piper didn't. We were able to fix their reins up to their saddles and let them loose. They rested sleepily nearby just twitching their sensitive skins, flicking their ears and swishing an occasional fly with their tails.

Duncan and I sat on the warm grass where I shared buttered wholemeal Vegemite sandwiches, fruit and chocolate. If the Irishman had any distaste for Australia's favourite black savoury spread, he didn't say and ate his fair share. Pity he didn't smear any Vegemite behind his ears. That would have made my day.

White-faced grey herons perched on branches overhanging the river on the opposite bank. Now and then fish jumped above the river surface, only to drop back with a splash that interested the fish-eating birdlife.

"Be good fishing here." Duncan observed.

"Probably full of fish." I agreed sleepily.

Some sort of shed built at waters edge, could be seen further downstream.

"I wonder why that shed is so close to the water." I mused.

"It'll be a boat garage I think. Probably has a channel dug into the inside to float a craft."

"Some day I might take a closer look out of curiosity."

All was ideal while the sun shone brightly and bees buzzed in the clover. Clement weather changed suddenly, as a heavy cloud loomed up, darkening the day and abruptly gusting a chill breeze.

Unexpectedly, the horses snorted and started. Their pricked ears focused on something in the bush above where we sat. I sensed being watched. Maybe just a wallaby.

Glad of Duncan's company, as an ominous prickling sensation transported me back to the terror I'd felt the night Wolfgang intruded. Duncan must have felt something too.

"This place gives me the willies now." he said.

Nero and Piper had scooted off several paces downstream. We made slow haste to catch them, careful not to scare them further away.

We caught up with the horses near to the old waterside shed, its timbers silvered with age. The building jutted part way over the water. It did look like a boat garage. A small wooden jetty seemed likely for mooring a boat while the riverside doors were opened.

We calmed the horses and remounted. Circling closer to the shed, a faded hand painted sign could be read as *Gallos Boathouse – Private Property – No Trespassing*. A smaller padlocked door accessed the shed from the grassy bank. There were no windows, so we were denied a peek inside.

Seems we had inadvertently trespassed on private land owned by the Gallo family. Gallo was a fairly common surname in the district, but this could well be family property related to my neighbours and therefore to Fabio.

It occurred that Giorgio's father would have built his stone retirement cottage handy to this boathouse, if he owned it.

Fabio's headlights headed out this way when he drove his weird half-brother home. I felt certain the stone cottage must be further up the treed slope above the river and Agneta and Wolfgang probably still resided there.

Could it be Wolfgang who startled the horses, I wondered. Maybe he hid in bushland and watched us as we rested on the riverbank.

I didn't voice my concerns. Duncan didn't know about Wolfgang nor that I had worked for years with the Gallo's nephew. My instinct was not to mention it. Duncan might unwittingly let slip information Fabio wanted kept from his family.

Since I had been allowed the lemon tree house on the promise I kept Fabio's secrets, any speculation about Wolfgang and the stone house had to be left unsaid.

The forested foothills inclined gradually above the river flats, then soared to higher peaks of a mountain range. Duncan surveyed the lonely terrain and offered his advice:

"I don't think you should come out here alone. This place is too remote Dimity. It gives me the creeps to be honest. Why not wait until I'm around to ride with you."

"That sounds like a very good idea."

I agreed only to placate him. All the while I meant to investigate beyond Gallo's Boathouse on my own, someday soon.

Duncan's Confession

A NEW LEAF

Despite the weather turning sombre that first day Duncan rode with me to riverside, we rode back at a calm walking pace.

It wouldn't do to encourage the horses natural flight instinct to bolt after a scare. After initial high stepping intentions, Nero and Piper took their cue from us and travelled sensibly.

Return to the lemon tree house ended up being much later and in worse weather than anticipated.

I didn't like Duncan to be driving home tired, especially with a horse on board and in such squally weather. A strengthening wind whipped the Pepperina branches into a thrashing frenzy, and anything loose took off across the paddock. I would have to retrieve at least one plastic bucket if it could be found the next day.

Duncan didn't ask to stay. I offered.

"You'll have to stay the night."

I said it while wondering where to put him. I still only had one bed and no sofa. In fact, I'd not had time to think about furnishing the living room. Evenings, I ate in the kitchen or on the back verandah, had a shower and retired to read a book or do some knitting in bed. Duncan replied:

"I should stay till morning. Don't worry I won't jump on your bones."

The mind reader said: "There's a bunk up front in the horse trailer. I've slept in it many a time and keep a change of clothes under the mattress."

"Good-o".

Sleeping arrangements all sorted. We put the horses away, gave all four a feed, separated Zoe and the new boarder into portable panel yards and made our way upstairs to the kitchen.

"You have first shower Duncan. I'll rustle up something to eat. It'll probably only be baked beans and bacon on toast though."

"Yum," he said heading to the bathroom, "don't s'pose you have shaving gear?"

"There's a pink lady shaver on the washstand."

"Never mind."

Duncan had a cosy fire blazing in the wood burner when I returned from my shower.

Sitting in our clean track suits at the kitchen table, we ate our beans and bacon on toast, washed down with gallons of tea. Riding can be hungry and thirsty work.

"It'll only be porridge for breakfast." I warned.

"Done porridge before this. Can't think of anything better than breakfast at Dimity's."

Duncan grinned his hallmark grin, the one laced with innuendo. He also wagged his eyebrows suggestively. The cheeky sod. Wind and rain lashed against the kitchen window. Waiting for a lull so Duncan could hightail it to his trailer, eventually led to heavier discussions.

"Have to love Aussie weather. Beautiful one day, lethal the next." Duncan observed.

"There'd be worse places in the world to live."

"For sure. I can vouch for it."

"How long have you been in Australia Duncan? I can tell by your accent you weren't born here."

"Dead giveaway hey?"

"It is".

"Must be going on twenty years now".

"Why Australia?"

"Had my fare paid. I came over with a mate's Melbourne Cup team. Just as another strapper. A dogsbody shite-kicker."

Nevertheless I knew he must have been good to be included with a Melbourne Cup mob.

"And you loved the place so much you never left obviously."

"I didn't love the place at first to be honest."

Duncan paused gathering his thoughts. His face turned woeful. He took so long to say more I wasn't sure he would continue. I prompted a kick start from him:

"So why stay? Had you met some sheila like Darlene already?"

"Ha ha. No. I had every intention of going home to Donegal. But something really bad happened before I came over here. Put me off going back home to Ireland."

"Must have been something dire."

"It was indeed dire. I killed someone."

His green eyes darkened as he scanned my face for a reaction.

"Geez Duncan".

"You probably hate me now."

"What happened?"

"An accident. My fault. I don't expect you to understand."

"I might understand more than you'd credit me for."

"I got myself into a mad jealous rage. Drove like a maniac. My girlfriend died. Should have been me."

I felt his pain.

"Mistakes are easily made in the heat of the moment."

"This was a big one. I might have married Lexie eventually".

"What started it? If you can talk about it. Just say if you don't want to. I'm fine with that. Rest assured I would never repeat anything you tell me to anyone. I can keep a secret."

Duncan decided to talk about it.

"That's ok. It's been a long time now. We were at a race meet and a bloke I knew was hitting on Lexie. I thought she led him on, but in hindsight, that was just how Lexie was, always outgoing and a bit flirty. Like an idiot I grabbed her arm and made her get in the car. I didn't wait for her to fasten her seat belt properly. I floored the accelerator and sped down the road. Missed a corner. Rolled the car. Lexie was flung out."

I'd never seen Duncan so serious and my heart went out to him. I well knew how a moments rage could end badly. Poor Duncan.

"I understand why you would need to get away from any reminders."

"I copped a lot of flak over it. All deserved. I earned it. People saw me leave in a jealous rage. I'd been drinking. Only luck I hadn't been over the limit. I got off on a lesser charge. Did porridge as it is called. I was out in six months. Just in time to take up the standing offer of travel to Australia. I paid the debt to society, but it won't bring Lexie back. I've felt like a murderer ever since. So much for my Irish Charm hey."

So much for my hiding myself behind a prissy persona too, if it came to a contest. But I couldn't tell my secret to Duncan without implicating Fabio and the fact we'd worked together for years.

"Were you engaged to be married to Lexie?"

"No. I was still in my teens and had not long taken up a blacksmith apprenticeship. Lexie was a few years older. She hinted at wanting more but I wasn't ready or in a good financial position to settle down."

I realised a handsome fellow like Duncan would always attract women of all ages. I wondered how much older Lexie had been to him but didn't see it as polite to ask.

"I guess you've had other girlfriends during the past twenty years."

"No one significant. There's been no woman I could talk to. Until you."

"You don't owe me Duncan but I appreciate your trust. Thanks for confiding in me."

At least Duncan could tell me his worst. I could not reciprocate with mine. It was too complex with Fabio and his trust in me to keep his secrets.

"Better you know about me now rather than finding out later. I'd have told you before this but there never seemed the right moment. I haven't been trying to hide it from you Dimity. Admit I've been afraid you'd hate me".

"I could never hate you Duncan. I consider you to be my best friend. I'm very glad you decided to stay in Australia."

"You're a brick Dimity."

A brick. High praise. Could it be my drab brown hair? Maybe I should look into getting a few highlighting streaks to brighten my image above building materials.

Duncan went back to the seaside stables early next morning. He vowed that after the car accident that killed his girlfriend, he had turned over a new leaf and now strove to control his hot head. I had made a similar resolution. We had that in common. As well as both having caused a death.

Bean

THE STONE HOUSE

Before long, I did return to Gallo's Boathouse alone, riding Nero. Despite trespassing on private land, I could not resist riding further upland from the river to explore.

Cicadas buzzed as Nero picked his careful way amongst tall stands of blue gums and stringy bark eucalypts, making little sound apart from the snapping of dry twigs under hoof.

A speckled goanna ran up a nearby tree trunk on our approach. Nero had raised a sweat and couldn't be bothered to shy at the fast reptile.

We had left the cool morning behind and as noon approached, the sunny day grew hot and the atmosphere, humid.

Black flies were annoyingly sticky. I snapped off a leafy gum tree twig to fan the insects away from my face. I regretted my decision to make this long trek. Turning back now would not shorten the round trip, so I pressed Nero on up the hillside. I'd give him a good rub down when we got home.

A mob of kangaroos, not particularly worried about our presence, rested in dappled shade. A big male stood up and flexed his bulging muscles. That 'roo was taller than most men and could easily gut a person if pressed to attack.

Kangaroos prop on their powerful tails enabling sharp hind claws as formidable double weapons. I wasn't seriously afraid of the big man kangaroo, but I kept an eye on him and was glad to be safely astride a good strong horse. We could give him a run for his money if he fronted us aggressively. Thankfully, this time the buck's display was all for show as a warning.

Presently, I came across a disused forest track, wide enough to take a vehicle, yet rough. I could see the overgrown track wove down towards the river.

The area seemed completely uninhabited, until topping a ridge, a hidden valley came unexpectedly into view.

Nestled there dwelt a quaint stone cottage on a cleared patch of land. An advanced lemon tree, laden with fruit, graced the front yard. Vineyards and gardens spread down a long slope beyond and below the fairytale house.

Stone built dwellings are rare in Australia. Surely this place must be where Agneta and Wolfgang lived. I dreaded running into them, intruding on their privacy. Knowing I trespassed on private land, a small concern compared with coming face to face with Wolfgang. I also shrunk at having to explain my presence to the German woman, Agneta, whom I'd never met.

Nero's black coat felt warm and damp. The not unpleasant aroma of horse sweat filled my senses. I felt sorry for putting my good horse through this ordeal, owed to my own curiosity and obsession with Fabio's history.

I chanced sneaking quietly along a hedge row beside the stone house, to gain an access road seen further afield. The better travelled road would be an easier more direct route for home, rather than retracing any steps over the rougher bush trails.

Rounding close to the stone cottage, I was taken by complete surprise to glimpse Fabio's sleek company car parked nearby.

The unexpected sight gave me reason to stand in the stirrups and peer over the high hedge for a better view. Nero chose that moment to loudly snort some dust from his nostrils.

Fabio had been lazing in a deckchair. He jumped, clearly startled. My Italian lover panicked on seeing my curious face suddenly appear above the thick shrubbery. His mouth fell open in what could only be described as a horrified reaction.

"Dimity!"

"Hi Fabio. I'm...um...sorry to intrude. I became a bit lost while I looked for an easier way back home."

Wolfgang and a tall woman I took to be Agneta, could be seen busily working down in the vineyard. They were far enough away not to notice me astride my black horse, mostly hidden behind the hedge.

Fabio seemed gobsmacked but recovered quickly to point me in the direction of my home. I might be slow on the uptake but could tell he didn't want me hanging around. No cold drink offered on this hot day, either. The bum's rush was my sad lot. Clearly, I should not linger. Yet linger I did.

Nearby, on a smooth mown area of green lawn, a little girl played dress-up with several dolls and teddy bears. Oblivious to my presence, in a world of her own, she play-acted a tea party.

The little girl wore an oversized dress and big floppy hat. I fondly remembered playing dress up as a child so took a moment to admire her creative outfit. She had accessorised with beads, lots of bangles and carried a distinctive bright red handbag, just like the one stolen from Cynthia.

That red bag immediately explained Fabio's fearful alarm at my surprise appearance. Fabio noticed I ogled the red handbag. His guilty expression confirmed my guess. He knew I knew. I said:

"Oh dear. Fabio."

Fabio glanced down the long garden to ensure Wolfgang and Agneta were out of earshot.

"Dimity. Let me explain."

He spoke quickly, with a face heated almost as red as that damning handbag.

"Explain away Fabio. It's been a great mystery who took that bag."

"Cyndi was supposed to wait for me in the car. I waited for everyone to go from the office. Just killing time in my bathroom. Shaving."

Fabio said it all in a rush of nerves. He obviously had not rehearsed it, never expecting to be caught out.

"I could not believe it when I found her dead! Gone! She had fallen down the stairs. I had to get her phone to erase all the messages and photos. She liked to record everything. There would be lewd video of...ah...you know...things...plus I needed my car keys."

"You took the bag and left her there without reporting it."

I wasn't judging him, just trying to get it straight in my mind.

"Please believe me. She was already dead, Dimity. Past help. I was in a panic. I stuffed that red purse into my briefcase. I did not want to step over the body. Her staring eyes accused me. It gave me the horrors. So, I went back to the lifts and left by the front door."

I could see how it panned out. Fabio hid his attachment to Cynthia by taking her bag with the incriminating content and not reporting her death.

He left by the front door of the building which would be confirmed by CCTV. His tracks were covered. Until I sprung him with the red bag.

"Holy crap Fabio. The whole place knew about you and Cynthia anyway."

"I know that NOW. But I only found that out later after our talk, when you told me about the frosted glass silhouettes."

"Would everyone knowing about you and Cynthia have made a difference?"

"No. It definitely presented an added complication. At the time, I had to take the bag. If the press implicated me by name my whole family would hear of it."

As I suspected, Fabio's greatest concern had been his family finding out he had an affair with his secretary.

"I hope you do not think I killed her!?" he exclaimed.

"No. I don't think that for one moment Fabio."

Fortunately for Fabio and myself, the story had only made a few lines single column on an inside page – accidental death – possible bag snatch – no evidence – no persons of interest. I didn't want to go into it so segued into another topic.

"What's the little girl's name?"

"Bean."

"Bean? B-e-a-n? That's unusual."

"Agneta chose it. It is quite popular as a girls' name in Germany." he replied cautiously.

"Is she Agneta's daughter?"

"Yes." Fabio allowed me this brief and truthful answer.

While I fathomed possibilities, the small girl kept singing and talking to her dolls. At length, the child piped up with an explanation to her existence:

"Be good dolly or you can't go for a drive in Papa's big car."

Papa's car! Fabio appeared sheepish as if caught in an *Oops* moment. He shrugged in the Italian way with open handed gesture to emphasise his helplessness of the situation.

"With your stepmother Fabio? Your step-bloody-mother?"

He replied cooly:

"No blood relation."

Far be it for me to judge. Plainly, just as the little Bean did, I too had been playing a pretend game. A fistful of fantasies about Fabio were crushed.

Sophia's frequent declarations that Fabio was *'such a good boy'* I now recognised as excuse for the stigma attached to moral incest.

Little wonder Fabio didn't want the family to learn of his office affair with Cynthia when he had already made a baby with the woman who had raised him as her stepson.

Then there was me. I don't claim innocence.

Minutes ticked by as Fabio and I regarded each other wordlessly until I had to ask:

"Why didn't you just get rid of the red handbag Fabio?"

He had an answer for that:

"That Friday evening, I drove away in shock. When I got here, little Bean went through my briefcase looking for her treat. I always bring her something. For the first time I simply forgot. Lucky for me, Bean thought the pretty red bag was her gift. So I let her believe it. I emptied the bag and gave it to my little daughter as a play thing."

"Hiding in plain sight. Do you know how much that handbag is worth?"

"No idea." he admitted.

"Prepare for another shock."

Fabio's young daughter became sleepy. She rested her head on Fabio's knee. He stroked her head lovingly.

"Papa, will you stay with us tonight?" Bean whimpered.

"No, my pet, sorry. Not this time, I must go back to the city."

Reminded of her father's swift exit from my bed, I offered a sarcastic comment:

"Home to feed your goldfish Papa?"

"Cat." he replied.

Meow. I rode away before I choked on a hairball.

Lemon Tree

A SKINNY DOG

Once again, Duncan drove in to my place early one morning in his trusty ute. He was certainly notching up the miles but had refused any reimbursement for diesel.

This time, he arrived with a tree tied on the tray, its canopy protected with fine white mesh.

My lemon tree! I'd had it on back order but being distracted by recent events, completely forgot Duncan promised to pick it up.

"My lemon tree at last. How exciting. Thanks Duncan. You're a legend."

The good farrier replied with his usual bluster:

"I am that. Glad you know it."

The citrus tree was a real beauty with dark green leaves, white buds and fresh lemon scent. I could understand why Fiorella loved her own lemon tree years ago.

"Seems to have travelled ok. I gather you want it around in the front yard." Duncan said.

Fetching a wheelbarrow from the hay shed, we managed between us to manoeuvre the advanced tree undamaged in its heavy pot.

I hadn't owned a shovel but there was an old one in the laundry room. I'd discovered the heavy garden tool some time ago, concealed behind the hot water cistern where it must have fallen down.

Duncan wheeled the tree around to the front garden while I began scooping out the planting site in the exact spot where Fiorella's lemon tree had lived, as I'd seen in Giorgio's old photos.

Soon Duncan lost patience with my efforts and took the shovel from me. With much grunting, sweating and some cursing, the tree was released from its pot and planted in the rich loamy soil.

At long last *Albero di Limone* had a new namesake. I had made good my promise to Giorgio and Sophia, to plant another lemon tree in the front garden.

After all that hard yakka, I made tea and sandwiches that we had in the kitchen. During our morning tea break, Duncan said he'd take the wheelbarrow up the lane to get some big rocks to put around the new planting. We knew there to be rocks in the verge further up the lane.

"Oh, don't bother Duncan. Thanks for what you've already done. It's more than enough and I am truly thankful. I can always get a few rocks later on."

"Nope. Best finish the job properly Dimity. Or your dog might try digging the tree up."

"I don't have a dog."

"Yeah, you do. I got one for you."

I stared at him and could tell he wasn't joking.

"NO! You didn't! I don't want you getting me a dog Duncan. When the time comes, I want to choose my own dog."

Duncan wasn't fazed:

"Fair enough. Point taken. It's an ugly bloody thing anyway. Half-starved. I can probably fob him off on someone else."

What!? Fob it off? Half-starved?

"So where is this alleged damn dog?"

"Dropped him up the road on the way in, Enzo was giving it a hell of a beating. But no worries, the poor skinny thing seems used to being kicked about. Hardly a yelp out of him."

"How could you!" I cried. "Why not bring the poor old thing here right away."

"I thought I'd break the news gently and get your ninny-fit over with."

"I do not have ninny-fits" I threw a wet dishcloth at Duncan's head.

"I beg to differ" he said mildly, catching the soggy cloth and chucking it in the sink.

Duncan's ute had my car blocked in. Infuriated, I stomped down the lane to the neighbour's farm.

Whistling a ditty, Duncan strolled behind me.

For once, Enzo didn't bark at our approach. Laughter was heard coming from the farmhouse yard. Enzo the border collie was playfully zooming about with a sleek adorable puppy, both enjoying a great game together.

Giorgio and Sophia watched fondly, laughing at the dogs' antics. The sealskin coat of the gangly pup rippled over his muscles and shone with health.

I'd been had.

"Duncan you bloody bast...Irishman! You get a big kick out of tormenting me don't you."

"That I do. You're so easy." he admitted shamelessly.

I wasn't prepared to let go of my grouchiness but was forced to do so. I grumpily said:

"Trust you to get a racy one."

The leggy bright-eyed youngster had a whip tail, and his curvy bronze body, decorated by a hieroglyphic scribbling of black brindling. A crooked white flash lent a quirk to his face and his four white paws were as neat as bobby socks.

I knelt quietly on the lawn. Seeing me, the pup skidded to a halt. He looked all the world like a curious Meerkat as he regarded my presence intently. In seconds he bounded over in youthful exuberance and threw himself bodily into my arms.

Bundling him on his back like a baby, the puppy relaxed and fixed a loving gaze to meet my own. There was no way this confident pup had ever been ill-treated. The frame of his birdlike bones and hard muscles felt at once athletic and delicate. He stretched up to lick my chin.

"Is he a greyhound pup?" I asked.

"No! He's a whippet."

The reply in triplicate came from Duncan, Giorgio and Sophia. Eventually I acquired the t-shirt printed with *No It's A Whippet!* Perhaps only other whippet owners will understand.

While I fell deeply smitten with the 'poor skinny thing', Duncan in his faded jeans and work shirt, appeared nonchalant, casually leaning against a fence post.

I strongly suspected the purebred whippet pup cost a pretty penny, no doubt putting a big hole in Duncan's pocket. I knew to offer repayment would be an insult for the wonderful gift.

I felt teary and couldn't think what to say with the old folks also watching and waiting for my reaction. I only asked:

"What name does this whippet go by?"

"He hasn't said." Duncan replied.

Giorgio and Sophia got belly laughs out of that. My mind began whirring with all my favourite dog names, listed in my head.

Back at the lemon tree house, Duncan unloaded a carton filled with dog foods and puppy stuff. I let the little whippet loose in the front yard where he explored and squatted for a puppy piddle, before bringing him indoors.

"I am incredibly grateful Duncan; this little boy is exactly right for me."

"Knew he would be. What will you name him?"

"Shamus. I hope you're stoked that I chose an Irish name in your honour."

I punched Duncan in the arm and planted a big smooch on his cheek.

"Consider me stoked." he blushed.

It was a rare and surprising sight to see Duncan's face redden.

Shamus the whippet puppy was balm to my bruised heart, still hurting from shattered Fabio dreams.

<h1 style="text-align:center">Heart Attack</h1>

THE SHOVEL

On morning rides with Nero, Shamus the pup went for playtime with Enzo next door. Bus days when Giorgio and Sophia went out, Enzo came to my place.

One bus day, I walked up the rise to check the internet, leaving Enzo and Shamus happily romping together around the lemon tree in my front garden.

As I browsed messages and emails, an anxious phone call came in from Fabio. I answered it immediately. Fabio sounded frantic:

"Uncle Gio has suffered a heart attack on the bus. He has been taken by ambulance to hospital."

"My God. Oh No. How bad is it?"

"Not good. Can you give me an hour and call back please Dimity? I am almost to Clemency now. I will go straight to the hospital. Aunt Sophie is with him."

Sick with foreboding, I walked back up the rise again in an hours time, and called Fabio back. Giorgio's state of health was touch and go. Sophia and Fabio would be staying by his bedside.

"Aunt Sophie asks can you please lock the hens and ducks in for the night this evening and feed Enzo?"

"Of course I will. Tell her not to worry about that. Please give my love to Giorgio and Sophia. And my love to you too Fabio."

"Thank you, Dimity, my friend." he quietly replied.

Hastily I pulled dried washing from Sophia's clothesline, just before a soaking downpour. Rain made her poultry retire early to be secured against foxes and other nocturnal hunters. There would be no guard dog at the farm as I would keep Enzo at my place for the time being.

Enzo's sleeping basket would be brought back to go beside Shamus's in my kitchen.

Folding Sophia's washing, it occurred to parcel up several garments as changes of clothing to take to the hospital.

Next morning, clutching the bag of spare clothes, I crept into the hospital ward. Faces stricken, Fabio and Sophia sat at Giorgio's bedside. They had spent the long night there taking turns at napping on a hospital cot in the next bay. Giorgio requested a priest to hear his confession.

"I think it will be my last." The old man breathed weakly.

Knowing the end was nigh, Sophia almost collapsed. Convulsed with unshed tears, she didn't want Giorgio to witness her distress. I helped her to the spare bed they'd been allowed to use and poured a glass of water.

Pieces of conversation between Giorgio and Fabio were overheard as only lightweight curtains separated the hospital bays.

"For my sins. It is time..." from Giorgio.

"Then you must hear the truth Uncle. You did not kill him."

"...the shovel..."

Fabio's voice gasped in breathless sobs:

"He did not die. Not then. You are innocent of killing him Uncle Gio."

"Then...how?"

The priest arrived and spoke briefly with Sophia.

I left Sophia alone with the priest and stood out in the aisle nearer to Giorgio's bed, so I overheard Fabio's last sentence quite clearly.

"The priest is here. We will leave you in privacy now. I will explain soon Uncle Gio, after the priest leaves. But you do not have to confess to murder. You saved us all that day. I have prayed for you and for all of us. We owe you our deepest thanks. God will forgive you Uncle."

Fabio, Sophia and I sat on hard metal chairs in the hospital canteen while Giorgio made his peace with God and received the last rites. We were all too upset to speak. Later I returned home to take care of the animals.

Giorgio Gallo died peacefully in his sleep in the early hours of the next morning. He did not see another dawn.

Fabio Tells

ABOUT LUPO

Early in the day after Giorgio passed away, Fabio drove out to the lemon tree house to give me the sad news.

He said Agneta would be taking care of Sophia for a while, until after the funeral. I said to assure Sophia I would look after her place for as long as she wanted or needed.

"We are grateful for your help."

"I am so very sorry for your loss and glad to do what I can."

"Dimity, you must have heard what I said to Uncle Gio in the hospital."

"I didn't try to eavesdrop. Fabio please be sure I would never repeat anything and never make mention of it, ever, to anyone. I promise."

"I trust you Dimity." Fabio said not for the first time ever. "I want to explain and maybe you will understand why we, my family, have become like we are, and why I am, like I am."

"If it helps. I am here for you Fabio."

"My father Lupo Ricci was a savage man and quick to anger..." he began.

On the day of his death, Lupo Ricci had been drinking heavily, and a drunken state always fuelled his ingrained belligerence. The man had forever been paranoid that his family schemed against him. Lupo had

124

skulked in the boot hall slyly listening to conversations between his young wife and sons.

Agneta had sat with young Fabio and Wolfgang at the kitchen table, overseeing their school lessons. Agneta chose to speak German. She wished to have her son Wolfgang learn her native tongue. Fabio also gained the knowledge at the same time, which pleased his stepmother.

Furious that his sons replied in Agneta's language, Lupo burst in and knocked the chair out from under his young wife. Agneta fell to the floor unable to shield the boys from her husband's cruel onslaught.

Lupo took his belt to them all catching them with the metal buckle across their faces or wherever he was able to smite blows.

Agneta and the boys managed to get out of the house, but Lupo chased them downstairs and into the back yard. Agneta took the brunt while young teenaged Fabio tried unsuccessfully to intervene. Eleven-year-old Wolfgang raced next door to fetch their uncle Gio.

Giorgio arrived, breathless after running up the lane. Their uncle came upon the violent scene. Lupo still beat and kicked Agneta mercilessly in a prolonged attack. The hapless young wife lay whimpering and terrified, curled up on the ground.

Convinced Lupo would surely beat Agneta to death, Giorgio used what strength he could muster to grab a shovel and slam it hard down the side of Lupo's head.

Lupo fell to the ground apparently dead. The attack was over.

No pity had been spared for Lupo. Relief had been the upmost emotion felt by them all. Agneta was helped to her feet. She managed to stay on her feet only by leaning against young Wolfgang. Fortunately, the young German woman retained fortitude both in body and mind.

Fabio relived his part in it:

"I tried to stop my father kicking her," Fabio cried, "but he struck me away again and again."

"You were just a child."

"I was almost fifteen. Wolfy was only eleven."

"Wolfgang could speak at that time?"

"Yes. He only stopped talking after what I did."

The expression on Fabio's face could only be described as haunted. I took his hand in mine, while he continued trying to lay the ghosts of his past.

"Uncle Gio thought himself to blame, but I was responsible for killing my father. Uncle Gio's strength failed after the long run up the lane. He hadn't hit my father hard enough with that shovel. It only knocked him unconscious."

They all thought Lupo to be dead. I wondered if the shovel was the same one used to plant my lemon tree. Not that it mattered to me. It was still a good and useful garden tool. Fabio continued his story:

"Uncle Gio cried. He kept saying he would lose everything. He would go to prison. Who would take care of us all? What would become of us? By the time Aunt Sophie arrived Uncle Gio had to sit down on the ground. His face turned a sickly grey colour. We were all crying. Uncle Gio kept saying sorry, over and over."

Giorgio probably always had a dicky heart. Living remotely as they did and rarely having any obvious illnesses, routine medical check-ups would be considered unnecessary.

After the attack, Sophia helped them all upstairs to the kitchen. The aging farmwife treated their many wounds, made porridge and sweet tea and gave what small comforts she could.

Lupo had been left where he lay in the back yard while the family tried to gather their wits and recuperate. Eventually they had to confront Lupo where he lay.

"Black ants crawled over my father's face, there was some vomit on his mouth and blood on his ear that attracted them. He did not feel the biting ants of course. You understand, it added to our belief that he was dead, seeing all those ants all over him."

Sophia took charge as the only able-bodied adult.

"Aunt Sophie said Lupo must not win. He must never be allowed to ruin this family. His death was a godsend, she said. We must think of some way around this and come up with an idea."

The family schemed together against Lupo in the long run, as the man had always feared. So it came to pass that Lupo engineered his own fate.

"We made a plan to dump the body far away, so it did not look as if he had died at home. We decided the boathouse was the best place. No one ever went there. Gallo's Boathouse was known to be our private family property. Trespassers were warned off. Anyone fishing by boat on the river might see us, but that risk, we had to take."

Fabio took deep shuddering breathes as he struggled to revisit what happened:

"My father was not a really big man but his limp body was difficult and heavy for us to manage. Aunt Sophie tried to help me lift him up onto the truck tray. We couldn't do it."

Fabio's voice shook. I put a glass of water in front of him.

"Wolfgang tried to help but he has always been thin, and not very strong."

I could only listen in sympathy as Fabio continued.

"Without Agneta we would never have lifted my father onto the back of the truck. She dragged herself downstairs to help us, even with her bunged up eye and many other bleeding injuries. She told us later she felt so determined to get rid of Lupo, it lent her the power to do it."

Young Fabio had to drive the truck to the boathouse. Neither Agneta nor Sophia could drive, and Giorgio had been too sick. Agneta had exhausted her strength. On the point of total collapse, she couldn't accompany Fabio on that dreadful errand. That hapless young German girl surely regretted ever marrying Lupo in order to stay in Australia.

"We put a tarp over him and stacked a few hay bales around, so he would not roll off. Also to hide the body from view if anyone saw us. I knew how to drive, I had driven the truck about the farms since I was much younger."

Fabio sipped some water and continued:

"At first, Aunt Sophie and Agneta did not want Wolfgang to go. They said he is too young. I wanted my brother with me but I did not say. I did not want to sound scared of being alone because I was the eldest and almost fifteen. Then Wolfy asked how would I be able to drag our father off the truck by myself. This was also a concern of mine. Finally Agneta agreed Wolfy should go with me. She said best he sees the end of it so he can put it behind himself."

Fabio managed to drive the truck to the riverside boathouse. I knew the spot. No wonder the place had given Duncan the willies. He must have sensed some bad vibes. I now understood why the family didn't picnic there anymore.

"Going down the rough track from the stone house was the worst part. I had never driven down such a steep rocky place before. I rode the clutch and the brakes like I had always been told never to do. The truck was whining and clunking. We could smell burning rubber. I was afraid the brakes must be overheating and might let go. But there was no turning back. I probably could not have reversed up the hill anyway."

Those poor kids.

"We were supposed to slide his body off the back of the truck and run away. Just leave the truck like he had parked it there himself and put the keys in his pocket, or in his hand if possible. It was meant to look like he had suffered a fall and hit his head somewhere else but then tried to get back to the truck before collapsing and dying."

Fabio paused before getting to the worst part.

"But Dimity. You see, my father was still alive!"

"Oh my God Fabio."

Fabio looked into my eyes and begged for understanding. I nodded to reassure him. He went on with his tale of woe:

"He began to wake up when we pulled on his legs to drag him off the tray. We were terrified. He began punching at the tarp. Just lucky no fishing boats were out on the river, no one to see or hear what was happening."

Fabio's face told how the memory wrenched.

"My dear Fabio, it's all over now. In the past. You don't have to tell me everything. This is so upsetting for you."

"No I want it out of my system now I have come this far."

"If it helps I am here listening. Also breaking my heart for you and your brother."

"Thanks Dimity you are such a good friend."

Fabio's voice quietened. His calmness might mean he had confessed this sin to the priest at some point. It was not my place to ask.

"I could have let my father live. I chose not to."

Fabio explained how his decision had been deliberate.

"Instead of helping my father live, I ran back to the front of the truck and jumped into the cab. I released the handbrake and put the truck out of gear. Then I began trying to push the truck into the river, begging Wolfy to help. But Wolfy held back. He was stiff with fright. I kept yelling at him to help me push the truck, but Wolfy could not move. I know he feared retribution if our father survived. This fear also drove me on."

Fabio sipped more water:

"I busted my guts and at last the truck began to roll. Once it started moving down the steep slope, momentum took over. Our father got free of the tarp only when the truck was speeding faster and faster. He cursed us as he went to his death. When I am alone his curses echo in my head."

I remembered how the bank fell abruptly into deep water. The image conjured up by Fabio's description was clear.

"The truck sank. The river closed over it all. It was quickly out of sight. We waited to see if our father would come up. I could not believe he was really gone. I kept expecting him to surface like a demon. Already I thought of ways to push him back into the river. I took up a big branch to use."

"You suffered so much from that man. Even until the end. Even now."

"I felt justified that the river took that monster. I could never be sorry for making him drown there."

Dumping a dead body was a lot to expect from the youngsters. The fact Lupo had woken up was sheer horror. Circumstances dictated decisions made at the time. I could understand how it came about.

I couldn't feel pity for the evil Lupo, he deserved to know his own kin turned on him in retaliation.

$$\mathcal{Fiorella}$$

HER DROWNING

Fabio felt it represented poetic justice for Lupo's life to end in that particular place. In that river.

"He drowned my dear mother there in that same spot in front of the boathouse. It was justice to drown him in the same place. It was my revenge. I felt no remorse." Fabio confessed.

"Oh my God. You believe your father was responsible for your mother dying? Why do you think that?"

"I was only a small child at the time but over the years I pieced it together. The memories still stalk my nightmares, but I have learnt a way to forget even if only temporarily." Fabio said.

I had an idea of the way he used.

The Gallo families and friends used to picnic on the riverbank most weekends, in fine weather when the river was quiet. Fabio's grandfather kept a wooden rowboat in the boathouse. The men would row out and anchor midstream to fish. The womenfolk prepared food and minded the small children. Fabio continued the tale of losing his mother:

"One time there had been just me and my parents. Three of us in the boat, rowed out to the middle of the river to catch fish. I fell asleep after a while. My mother had a cushion in the boat for me to lay on. I barely remember hearing them argue and feeling the boat rock. It was not unusual to hear my father scolding. I would not open my eyes in case he started rousing on me. I have forever been unsure if I heard a splash or if I made it up in my mind later because it seemed logical."

"He drowned her? Can you be sure. I am not defending your father but you were very young at the time, Fabio."

"I know I was dunked in the water for no reason before we drove home without my mother. I found out much later he said my mother drowned trying to save me. That was a definite lie!"

I rubbed Fabio's hand. There was little else I could do.

"No one asked me what had happened at the time. I could not stop crying. I was four years old so I might have told them something useful. Who knows. Aunt Sophie and Uncle Gio wanted me to stay at their house, but my father would not allow it. Later on, I figured out he was afraid I could tell them the truth of what really happened."

I noticed Fabio never referred to his father as Papa or Dad, always only as my father or other name that distanced himself from any closer relationship. He was so ashamed of Lupo.

"Over the years the conviction grew that my father murdered my mother. I would wake in the night remembering parts of things he used to slur in his drunken state."

"So you became certain."

"I did. After Mama died he would get drunk and rave at her lemon tree as if it *was* her, as if her spirit was in the tree. He would rant things like 'it's your own fault – you made me mad – you answered back – who do you think you are?' All his usual rebukes when my Mama was alive."

Fabio explained about his mother's lemon tree:

"Just before my father brought his new wife, Agneta, home, he chopped the lemon tree down. I hated him all the more for that. My mother loved that lemon tree. It was all I had left to remember her and how well she cared for me and loved me."

What a sad history surrounded the lemon tree house. No wonder Fabio had stayed away and let it fall into disrepair. I vowed to tend my lemon tree well in memory of Fabio's young mother. If that tree died, I would plant another. Just as Sophia had decreed to her family, I would not let the evil Lupo ruin it for me.

"So your father must really have drowned Fiorella. How did he get away with it?"

"No evidence. Mama was found on a mud bank downriver the next day, but there was never any proof that he drowned her."

Fabio had known so much tragedy and hardship. I could never have guessed from his controlled demeanour in the office. That time seemed so long ago now, like another lifetime. Fabio tried to explain more:

"As a child, I feared he did it but was afraid to talk about it. I did not want to keep making Uncle Gio and Aunt Sophie cry and I was very afraid of my father. It seems cowardly now."

"Oh no Fabio you were only four years old. You were always very brave even as a small child. Also as a young teenager. Still now, you continue to cope however you best can. What has happened to you would destroy most people."

I thought of the tribulations that led to Fabio siring a child with his father's widow.

"Agneta couldn't have known what she was getting into." I said

Fabio nodded in agreement and spread his hands palms up.

Family

TRAUMA

Fabio strove to explain himself and his actions.

"Please understand Dimity. I know that having sexual relations with my stepmother must seem indecent to you. But, you see, I never considered Agneta to be my mother. No one could replace my real mother."

"I don't judge you Fabio."

Although I had judged him, at this point in time, I did not.

"I admired Agneta and appreciated all she did for me and Wolfy. I sort of love her. We shared hard times. She is family. We were all lonely and felt isolated from society. Agneta would only leave the stone house if it meant going back to Germany. I have led a double life. Keeping my two lives separate. I accept my fault for Wolfy being numbed speechless. Sometimes I wish Wolfy would scream or smash something. Anything would be better than his catatonic trance."

"Perhaps Wolfgang might benefit from advances in science now."

"Agneta agrees with your theory but is afraid of Australian authorities. She begs for me to send Wolfy and herself to Germany. The nagging has stressed me beyond endurance."

"I understand, you would not want to break the family up."

"Wolfy relates to me. I don't know how his mental capacity would cope with our separation. I could not leave my career and go traipsing off to Europe with them on a pipe dream. It all takes money. What would we live on?"

"So many problems, Fabio."

"It is my excuse for the office affair. I took the comfort Cyndy freely offered for a break and to forget for a while. My family would never understand it. They would be terribly disappointed in me."

Tears streamed unchecked down Fabio's face as he relived the tragedy of his messy life.

He shook himself and attempted further explanations on what happened the day he decided to finish his father. He needed to purge the memory. At least I could hear him out if it helped.

"Wolfy and I had to walk back home. That was always the plan because the truck had to be left at the boathouse. I do not know how long we sat by the river. It was long after the bubbles stopped coming up. A storm came over, so I took Wolfy up to the stone house to sit it out on the back porch."

I pictured the long steep walk up through the trees the boys would have taken.

"The house was empty. We could get inside but we sat outside watching the storm. I wanted to return home as soon as possible. I was hungry by then and I thought Wolfy must be. You might be appalled that I had any appetite for food. Truthfully, I felt pretty good. Free. The rain came down hard for a while and it felt cleansing. I told Wolfy the tyre tracks would get washed away. He said nothing. I did not know I would never hear his boyish voice again."

As soon as the storm passed over, the boys started the long hike back to *Albero di Limone.*

"It took hours to get home. The weather was not cold, but Wolfy shivered uncontrollably. I urged him to keep going. He sat down on the wet ground and refused to get up. I had to shake him and bully him to make him keep on walking."

"He must have been in shock." I supposed.

As Fabio continued with his tragic history, I made tea and toast for us both. We didn't want anything else to eat.

"We almost made it home when I found the truck keys were still in my pocket. That could have blown the alibi. Anyway, I ditched the keys in a big hollow tree. That tree is still standing but it has since died. You can see it from your front steps here. I could point it out to you if you like."

"No. That's ok. Not just now."

Someday I might identify that tree out of curiosity, but I considered it prudent not to take Fabio past my open bedroom door. He was so in need of comfort. I just wanted to hold him but knew where that might lead. When it came to Fabio, the stark reality was I simply didn't trust myself to act appropriately.

Fabio continued his sad tale:

"We got home, exhausted. Bedridden for days. Agneta was covered in welts and bruises. She had a split lip and swollen black eye. Uncle Gio was still poorly. Aunt Sophie had to look after all of us. I only ever told them I pushed the truck into the river with the body. I never said our father had woken. It was not for me to speak for my brother's side of it. Although I tried to force Wolfy to help push the truck, he is innocent. My actions turned his mind. It is my responsibility to care for him."

"Wolfgang's state of trauma can only be blamed on your father."

"Yes. But that is on my head as well. Sadly, even I ended up bullying poor Wolfy. I had to at the time. I wonder if he thinks of it now. Who knows what goes on in his head? Back then, we realised Wolfy had stopped talking. It seemed a logical result of what we'd all been through. We expected him to snap out of it once everything settled down."

The family waited weeks before reporting Lupo as a missing person. They didn't want to explain all their raw injuries. Authorities were told that Lupo had gone on a hunting trip, and they didn't know where.

The tale was accepted as Lupo had been known to go hunting leaving his family for long periods at a time.

At the time, they kept Wolfgang out of it. If the boy did snap out of his hypnotic state, he might inadvertently expose their lies. Only as time dragged on, did they realise Wolfgang's condition could be permanent.

Months later, human remains washed up on the riverbank many miles away. The decomposed body was identified forensically as Lupo Ricci. It was assumed the truck had gone into the river, but the vehicle was never recovered. I suppose those old truck keys are still in that dead hollow tree that can be seen from my front door.

Fabio explained that none of them wanted to mention the whole sorry saga again. Once again, I promised faithfully never to betray his trust. It was cold comfort to know other ordinary people hid skeletons in their closets.

Both men I held dear were guilty of killing another human being: Duncan did so by accident, paid his debt to society by serving out a prison sentence but forever rued his fault for Lexi's death. Fabio killed his father deliberately with no remorse. It was justifiable homicide committed out of terror, yet he avenged Fiorella.

Neither man would ever know I sent Cynthia on her way 'accidently on purpose'. Of course, I never imagined she might die, and my bad deed would become inextricably entangled with Fabio's secret and complex life.

Fabio revealed his main secret while sitting beside Giorgio's death bed:

"At the last I could tell Uncle Gio the truth. He did not condemn me for the murder. Some of his final words were to console me."

"Giorgio was a good man," I said in consolation, "I will miss him too."

Fabio seemed washed out with crying. He went to the bathroom. I heard the bath taps running knowing he would be splashing his tear-stained face with cold water. When he returned to the kitchen, he said:

"I am in great need of a hug now."

"Come here you poor darling."

I wrapped him in a caring embrace. Despite the sombre circumstance, Fabio sought comfort with sex.

"Dimity, my friend, I need to feel alive." he whispered.

"I know. You need an escape. I am here for you always Fabio."

"I so need you now at this moment Dimity. You are my lifeline."

I felt so tender towards him. He was so vulnerable. Leading Fabio to my bedroom was a natural way to lend comfort.

Fabio displayed no simpering need but seemed frantic in his wish for a swift relief. Despite the circumstance, I was a more than willing partner to his desire.

After his first quick release, Fabio took me more slowly, saying more of what he was feeling as he rocked a gentle rhythm that felt much too slow for my needy desperation.

"Ah my Dimity. The journey is as important as the destination." Fabio crooned.

Fabio was so experienced and adept in the art of lovemaking, he knew exactly where he had me on that trip. The build-up he created peaked in a shattering of fireworks for me. I felt to be his forever no matter what.

Vaguely it crossed my mind Fabio might still have it with Agneta. I wanted him regardless. I loved him. I love him still.

As night fell, I went to lock up Sophia's chickens and ducks and Fabio went back to join his family grieving together at the stone house.

Hair Salon

RETAIL THERAPY

During the week before the funeral, I endeavoured to make more of an effort to spruce up my appearance in honour of my old neighbour Giorgio.

A bell over the beauty parlour door tinkled, as on an impulse, I braved entry into Roberto's Hairdressing Salon. My drab brown shoulder length hair was pulled back in a scrunchy at the nape of my neck.

"I don't have an appointment." I began.

"Come in darling, take a seat. This is just so serendipitous! We've only just had a cancellation." Gushed the flamboyant stylist I took rightly to be Roberto himself.

Two ladies and a fat man, all three with heads full of tight rollers, sat in a row in front of a mirrored wall. A strong ammonia smell of perming solution proved my sinuses were clear.

"I don't want a perm."

"Heaven forbid." Roberto exclaimed in mock horror.

The three perm clients glanced up before resuming pretence at reading magazines.

"It's not for everyone." The hairstylist sung.

Roberto stripped my scrunchy away and dropped it with a flourish into a waste basket.

"Hey!"

"You'll thank me." Roberto said.

A second stylist entered from a back room.

"What do you think Toni?"

Roberto consulted with his female colleague. I wasn't asked what I wanted. Implied, was anyone with a scrunchy had no idea.

"I think short, layered, cut in here, more height here."

"Yes. Bouncy. And highlights of course."

"Maybe a pink streak?"

"No. Not pink." I quickly intervened, with sour memories of Cynthia's hot pink stripey locks.

"Right. I agree actually. I'm thinking gold. All-over foils."

"Perfect. Yes gold will accentuate her tiny gold earrings."

Tiny? I had never thought of my average sized gold sleepers that way.

"Are these your usual earrings sweetie?"

"Well, yes."

"The style I will create for you would be enhanced by much bigger hoops. We have a fabulous selection if you'd care to see?"

"Perhaps another time. You see I'm getting this done for a funeral."

"How sad. Hair styles should be just for yourself." said Roberto.

As expected, both hairdressers and their clients took great interest in my personal life and situation. Outdoing the two bakery Gerdas for speedy interrogation, they reaped that I was single, Catholic, straight, had my own home and owned a car even before the initial shampoo was rinsed off. The matchmaking followed:

"I have a brother, single, a very nice man…"
"Your brother? I hate to break the news Toni, but your brother is gay."
"He is not."
"He is." The fat perm-crowned man threw in the aside, without looking up from his magazine.
"Anyway, he is very clean in the house." Toni shrugged.
"What about Nando, Gerda's cousin?"
"That lazy thing?"
"Um. I already have a boyfriend."

I smiled to myself knowing I had two extremely handsome yet quite different man-friends, one suave, sensitive, polite and polished. And the Irishman.

"Oh. How fabulous. What's his name? Does he live in town?…"
And so on.
Nonetheless, I had to be pleased with the hairdo. I loved the chic look of the short layered bob. Subtle gold highlights lifted my dull brown hair to a crowning glory. I should have done this long ago.
I exited the salon not caring that the back of my shirt was damp from an enthusiastic rinse and a few loose cut hairs stuck to my neck. Roberto had been right. I didn't miss the scrunchy.

Buoyed, I succumbed to another whim and entered a fashion boutique to browse the racks for a new outfit. I was after something plain black or navy to be dressed up later with jackets or scarves for occasions other than funerals.

The shop assistant had other ideas, she talked me into trying on a flowing skirted frock in deepest green, pin spotted in silvery grey. The ruched bodice hugged my bosom and allowed a modest hint of cleavage.

"This is so you. Your hair colour is exactly right for this lovely dress"
"It does look nice."

It was a very feminine dress I would never have chosen for myself, but as I swirled the sheer layers of skirts before the full-length mirror, I had to have it. With my new hairstyle the frock was perfect. I sneaked a look at the hidden price tag. What the hell. I rarely buy new clothes and Giorgio's sending off was a special occasion.

I had a frock! Would wonders never cease.

On to the shoe store. Several styles were tried and rejected before choosing a classic matt grey pair with medium wedge heel. Higher heels might have been trendier, but I didn't want to fall flat on my face or turn an ankle.

Retail therapy: I am now a true believer.

Miracle

AWAKE AT THE WAKE

A full Requiem Mass was celebrated for Giorgio Gallo. The beautiful old church was packed with his family, relatives and friends. Giorgio had been well respected and loved by a great many people.

I sat towards the back and could see Duncan kneeling in prayer a few pews in front. I knew Sophia had asked Duncan to be a pall bearer, an honour he obviously took seriously. The Irishman joined the queue behind Fabio to receive holy communion. Duncan must have attended a confessional before driving up to Clemency.

I chose not to receive the Holy Eucharist on this occasion, since I had not confessed my numerous and various sins. The priest would need a fan, a cut lunch and a water bottle to hear me out.

I had been in school uniform the last time I'd been inside a confession booth. Then my worst sin had been writing *I Love Horses* in blue biro on my arm, to look like a tattoo. The nuns were outraged. They almost took my skin off scrubbing my arm with carbolic soap. If I'd said what I thought at the time, my mouth might have been scrubbed out as well.

In any case, at Giorgio's ceremony, I stayed in the background, bringing up the rear at the back of the funeral procession.

Giorgio was interred in a family plot in the Catholic church cemetery. Beside his prepared open grave site, a tombstone marked the resting place of his sister Fiorella, who I now firmly believed had been drowned by her husband Lupo. Her headstone read: *Fiorella Isabella Ricci nee Gallo. Beloved mother of Fabio Lorenzo Ricci.* She had been just 23 years old at the time of her death. So young. A tragic loss.

Weeping, Fabio was heard to say: "They are together now."

My heart bled for Fabio. Poor boy. Poor man.

Fabio had hired the grandest reception room in Clemencys best hotel for a wake following the emotional rituals. The venue was plushly carpeted in rich burgundy, chandeliers sparkled overhead. Several traditional sofas furnished the room, and there were tables set with starched white cloths for people who wished to sit and dine. Waiters hovered ready to serve at a generous smorgasbord.

I chose chilled white wine at the private bar while acknowledging the officiating priest, who ordered Cinzano for himself.

"Thank you, Father. You delivered a beautiful Mass and sermon."

"That is good of you to say so. Thank you. I hope to see you again." he smiled.

Maybe he might one day have that pleasure, if my coffin lid is left open. I beat a hasty retreat and wandered about the room.

Relaxing piped music played unobtrusively in the background. I recognised a few of my grandpa's old favourites: *Smoke Gets in Your* Eyes, Acker Bilk's *Stranger on The* Shore, Cole Porter's *Begin the Beguine,* among others.

I was accustomed to seeing Fabio looking sharp in a suit. On the other hand, Duncan was a complete surprise. The Irishman looked drop dead gorgeous in charcoal grey suit, white shirt and and navy blue tie. I had never seen him other than looking his usual scruffy self, in jeans, work shirts or track pants and t-shirts.

Duncan's green eyes twinkled, acknowledging my approval. He drifted over towards where I stood.

"You scrub up well." he said in a quiet aside.

"You're not so flea-bitten yourself today, Duncan."

"Go on with you Dimity. Is that the best you can say? I saw you droolin' over me." he said in an undertone.

"Get over yourself Duncan." I whispered in reply.

The background music segued into the *La Mer* tune of *Beyond the Sea*.

"They're playing our song." Duncan said.

"We have a song?"

"Of course we do."

"Well, whoever chose the tunes made excellent choices. Not too dreary, not too cheery."

"Please save us from being too cheery." Duncan quipped quietly.

"You know what I mean. You wouldn't want *Knees Up Mother Brown* or *Yakety Sax* played at a funeral wake, would you?"

"Hmm. Guessing you've never been to Ireland." he said.

Not sure if he kidded. I went to mingle. Before long, Duncan gained two doting matrons dressed in all black, who fussed over him. Possibly widows ripe to come out of mourning. I didn't think they were nuns with the way they primped over the big handsome Irishman. Duncan caught my eye from the other side of the room and wiggled his eyebrows in a self-satisfied gesture. The smug twit.

That day, at Giorgio's wake, was the first time Duncan and Fabio met. I formally introduced them. They shook hands, assessing each other.

It was also the first time I met Fabio's stepmother, Agneta, or seen her up close. With a jolt I realised Agneta was a dead-ringer for that tall blond secretary, Cynthia Nagy. Although an older version, the resemblance was uncanny. Make of that what you will. Perhaps Fabio had a 'type'.

Milling about, I overheard Agneta mention her daughter, Bean, to another guest, who remarked on the unusual name.

"I named her for her father." Agneta replied.

Of course she did. I'd looked up the meaning of Bean's father's name long ago: Fabio - The Bean Farmer. I had to work at quelling unkind thoughts. My failing. I am only human.

As soon as people drifted away from Sophia, I went over to offer my personal condolences. I hadn't seen or spoken to Sophia since before Giorgio had passed away at the hospital. Sophia was dressed in widows black. Her whole outfit, completely new. I guessed Fabio probably bought it all for her.

Sophia attempted to appear stoic but I could see the effort it cost her. The old lady hadn't been in her own home since Giorgio died. It must have been an awful strain on the old dear.

"Your birds and animals are all well Sophia. I am sure they miss you though."

"It will be different there without Giorgio. At least we finally said our marriage vows while the priest attended at the hospital." Sophia said.

I couldn't hide my surprise at Sophia's remark. She noticed my raised eyebrows.

"You are surprised? Yes it is true. I lived in sin with my Giorgio. If we were ever blessed with babies we might have bothered sooner instead of at the bedside with him fading. Of course it is not a legally registered marriage but saying the vows together meant a lot. We always think we have more time. Make hay while the sun shines Dimity."

I had been doing my best to do just that. But that was a secret between me and Fabio.

"You were blessed in many ways." I offered the old adage to Sophia.

It is difficult to know what to say but my well-meant sentiment struck a chord. Sophia began to weep. Her handful of tissues soon became wet through with her tears.

To the utter astonishment of those who knew him, Wolfgang stepped in and offered Sophia his own large handkerchief, and rasped out his first words in over twenty-five years:

"Don't cry." Wolfgang said in a hoarse stage whisper.

"Ach du meine Gute! Mein Gott! Wolfgang hat gesprochen!"

Agneta shrieked, reverting to her native language in the shock of the moment.

Wolfgang looked confused. He had begun to rouse after so long spent trapped in his mental fog. It had to be akin to finding himself waking up on another planet.

Fabio's tall pale half-brother swayed, unsteady on his feet. Agneta gently took her son by the hand and led him to sit on the nearest sofa. In danger of a swoon herself, Agneta collapsed on the couch beside Wolfgang. Fabio knelt before them. Tears flowed down his cheeks.

"It's a miracle." Sophia cried. Wide-eyed, my old friend placed trembling hands to her wet cheeks.

Many guests including Duncan knew nothing of Wolfgang's years of muteness, nor anything to do with the retarded state he subsisted in ever since witnessing Lupo's death.

People must have wondered at the surprised amazement shown amongst our small group who knew about Wolfgang. Emotions were expected to be high at Giorgio's wake, so no one approached to ask what was going on.

Fabio stood up and hugged his Aunt Sophie. I hugged Sophia and Fabio. Sophia's legs went shaky. She went to sit with Agneta and Wolfgang on the sofa. The women fawned over Wolfgang who seemed befuddled but happy at all the attention.

"Fabio. This is amazing. Surely this must be a new beginning for Wolfgang."
"I can't believe it. This changes everything."
Clearly astounded, Fabio spoke in wonder.

Fabio and I hugged again. He patted my back, and in an automatic reflex, my body reacted in memory of his touch. Unacceptable, given the company and the event. Perhaps Fabio was similarly effected in our shared emotion. We abruptly stepped apart, as if stung. Fabio took my hands in his, while we faced each other at arms length. Overcome with fervid endeavour, Fabio made new plans.

"Agneta has long wished to return to her homeland. She insisted there would be better therapy for Wolfy in Germany. I have been tied to my career and believed curing Wolfy to be only a daydream. I admit to having lost hope for him. But now this! It does change everything."

I dared to hope Fabio might stay in Australia.

"You'll go to Europe? All of you?"
"Yes. I will have to go too of course, to seek the best help for my brother. It will take some organisation before travelling. Passports etcetera. And much to do when we arrive in Germany."

Of course, Fabio would have to go. I must not make it about my selfish wishes and feelings.

"This day has been memorable Fabio."

"Dimity may I ask more of you? Aunt Sophie wants to return to her home this evening. She wants to sleep in her own bed. I worry about her being alone out there, but I must go back to the city."

Privately I though Sophia would be fed up by now living as a house guest. At her age, she might find the antics of a young child like Bean to be tiresome as well.

"Don't worry Fabio. I will take Sophia home with me and stay with her if she wants me to. Probably she'll want to be alone, if so, I will check on her every day. Make sure she is eating and coping. I think she will benefit from having her usual chores, her garden, hens and ducks to see to."

"What would I do without you Dimity. You are indeed a good friend. No. Much more than that. You are my best friend."

"Thank you Fabio. That means a great deal to me."

It did mean a lot and I felt slightly appeased. As always, I took whatever I could get of Fabio.

"I will be back in a week or so. Aunt Sophie wants my help in sorting Uncle Gio's belongings, to see if there are any small keepsakes I want for myself." Fabio said. "In the meantime I must research how best to go ahead with Wolfy. This miracle breakthrough today gives me hope that therapy might bring him completely back to us. Surely great advances have been made in the years since he opted out of reality."

Fabio and I chastely kissed cheeks. Duncan had been watching us for I don't know how long. He looked a bit put out. Serves him right. I couldn't resist a private sly wink to Duncan, hoping it said: I win. Eat your heart out Duncan. One Paul Newman beats your two old matrons in black.

Just my competitive streak coming to the fore again. My erstwhile prim Miss Minto persona wobbled under Duncan's influence and well and truly toppled under Fabio's.

I stayed on at the wake longer than planned, as I didn't want to hurry Sophia. Finally, I delivered Sophia home to her lonely farm, glad that she didn't want me to stay.

"You go home Dimity. I am so tired myself; sleep will come easily tonight."

By the time I returned to the lemon tree house, I felt ready to sleep for a week. Duncan had obviously been and gone. I hadn't asked for his help but gratefully saw the current racehorse boarder had been night-rugged and fed.

If Duncan had also fed the dogs, they got fed twice that night. I blessed Duncan's thoughtfulness. Good friends are hard to find.

Minding Sophia

VOLARE

Life would never be the same without Giorgio, but Sophia was practical enough not to continue wearing all black.

She had carefully wrapped her new widows' weeds for the town dry cleaners and wore her comfortable floral dresses and pinafores for her farm work. Animals and gardens still had to be looked after and the roadside stall kept up.

Gallo's roadside stall depended on the bus run for most of its customers. The stall, under a sheltering iron roof, was open at the front. Shelves usually held pumpkins and boxes of tomatoes, green beans and whatever farm produce was seasonal or available at the time. An old unpowered insulated icebox was used for storing eggs.

Once a week, according to its eccentric schedule, the bus stopped at the stall. Passengers got out, chose goods and returned empty egg cartons. The honour system had cash posted through the slot of a lockable metal letter box. With no way to dispense change, purchases had to be rounded out with extra produce. Somehow it all worked.

During the week following Giorgio's demise, minding the farm in Sophia's absence, I collected eggs to store in the icebox. Not knowing what else was properly ripe, I had not picked any vegetables or fruits, in case I ruined them.

Sophia's return to her farm was lonely without Giorgio but life must go on. I visited daily to keep an eye on how the new widow was coping. One morning, I helped take a barrow of pumpkins to replenish the roadside stall and Sophia remembered to check the honesty box.

The bus had been and gone, for once without Giorgio and Sophia as passengers.

"This can't be right. The cash tin is stuffed full of money. Lots of big notes." Sophia exclaimed.

Apparently, the honesty box usually held mostly coins and only a few low denomination notes. Sophia was puzzled.

"Where did all this money come from?"

"Sophia. I think the bus passengers have paid their respects to you and Giorgio by giving you these gifts."

"How can I thank them." her response hastened to their generosity.

"No need Sophia. They chose to give anonymously and to give is divine. The people will feel good in their hearts for having done something."

Sophia put hand to heart in a gesture of thanks.

"Speaking of divine," she said, "I will never forget every moment of when Wolfgang finally spoke. I relive it over and over in my mind. I wake at night and think of it. Better than mourning for my Giorgio. I feel blessed that Wolfgang's first words were to comfort me. Do you recall how it went Dimity?"

"Of course I do. I will never forget it either. Just seeing him realise you needed a handkerchief was amazing, even without hearing him say 'don't cry' in that hoarse voice."

"His voice is rusty of course. But do you remember the music? The melody of *Volare* was playing at the time. We used to call that song *Nel Blu Dipinto di Blu*. It was my Giorgio's favourite. He was always whistling that tune."

Sophia found great comfort in a belief that Giorgio had somehow intervened.

"He had to find a strong way to contact me," Sophia said in awed certainty, "to make me take notice to know he was with me. He knew I would relive that moment. And it would give me something different to think about instead of grieving."

"Miracles do happen."

The notion gave me goose bumps.

Sophia proffered payment for my farm work, but I would not accept her money. Perhaps that's a second virtue I can add to my original list, which remained short on credits.

Sophia said most of Giorgio's clothing would go to charity. I took some packing cartons saved from my move and Fabio arrived while I was there. I didn't want to intrude on their personal family clearance, but they both insisted I stay for lunch. Fabio had brought pizzas from the city, to be reheated in the oven. That tempting aroma of toasted cheese, capsicum, oregano and pepperoni, so delicious. I didn't need my arm twisted.

Although in the heart of Little Roma country at Clemency, I had not eaten pizza since my move from the city. Sophia said she must pick something fresh for a salad.

"Oh no don't go to that trouble." Fabio said. "Just this once let us be decadent."

Always happy to be decadent with Fabio remained my everlasting problem.

After we ate, I washed and dried the lunch things while Fabio and Sophia saw to their sad task of packing away Giorgio's clothes and belongings in a bedroom. The packing didn't take long. Sophia had already sorted things into separate piles.

Once it was done, Sophia excused herself, saying she needed her siesta. Fabio and I took our coffee outside to the verandah, so our voices wouldn't disturb her nap.

Fabio's Plans

GERMANY

Fabio couldn't help but be excited over the big lifestyle change and move to Europe.

"I have been busy at the office," he said, "planning the journey to Germany and researching what might be available to help Wolfy."

"You have much to do."

"Yes, and I have much to learn. It is very perplexing. There is behavioural therapy, depth psychology, systemic therapy. I think systemic therapy involves the whole family. This might be the best way to go."

"I guess it will take time. You could be over there for years. Or back and forth."

"I expect to be. Once Agneta gets back home she will never want to return to Australia. I would have to drag her screaming and kicking".

"I couldn't blame her for that."

I was reminded of how that warped man Lupo had damaged their lives.

"Of course I must come back from time to time," Fabio said, "there will be reasons I cannot ignore."

Silently we both realised Sophia's eventual passing would be one cause for Fabio to return. That would be a terribly sad reason to return. Nevertheless, perhaps Fabio would need comforting again when the time came. Our minds meshed on the unspoken. We blushed sharing a secret inappropriate sentiment at the expense of Sophia's demise.

"The move will end my career here, but I hope to find other employment before money runs short. At least Agneta has family to fall back on. Her ageing parents live in an apartment where we all might stay for a while. But their home is small."

"Will you sell your property here?"

"I will sell most. My city apartment must be sold to finance it all, but I hope to keep the stone house and land that runs down to the river. I do not wish to burn all my bridges in Australia."

"Does your property include the riverside boathouse?"

"It does. It is all on one deed but possibly could be subdivided."

"Do you mind if I still ride my horse out that way? I now know it is private property, but I hadn't realised before I chanced upon it."

"Of course I do not mind, Dimity. You are always welcome. And I do not grant permission lightly or to just anyone. Perhaps you will keep an eye on the place in our absence?"

"Glad to. Sometimes a friend, Duncan, rides with me. Remember you met him at the wake? Is that acceptable too?"

"Yes of course. I know Aunt Sophie thinks a lot of this Duncan, he must be a good man."

I noted Fabio's complete lack of jealousy. He was so different to Duncan. They really were complete opposites. We continued discussing Fabio's hopes to find employment in Germany:

"Have you spoken with the hierarchy at the firm? I had an idea they were thinking of expanding into Europe at one stage."

"They were tossing the idea about. It is a possibility. A long shot. But I have not told anyone at the firm about my plans. Sherman Knickerbacker realised something is afoot, but he does not know the whole story. I had Sherman do some of my research, so he put two and two together."

"Sherman was always very on the ball. I imagine he is an excellent secretary."

"He is very efficient. I intend to recommend him for my position. In fact I have handed some of my case files to Sherman already."

Geez. Go Sherman. Who'd have thought?

"One thing..." Fabio paused, "Sherman became most upset when he discovered I planned to leave the firm. He does not want me to leave. He even...ah...I am afraid you will be very shocked when I tell you this..."

Fabio's face reddened deeply.

"Tell me what exactly?"

"Sherman made a very odd confession. He said he is in love with me!"

"What? Oh my goodness. Imagine him saying that out loud."

"Indeed. Who would have thought Sherman was that way inclined? He must be a gay person." Fabio declared.

I had to laugh. I reverted to my Miss Minto office persona:

"Oh Mr. Ricci. Ha Ha. You have been so out of touch with the ordinary people at work."

"Do not tell me everyone knew about Sherman. As well as the other thing I thought to be a secret?"

"Yes Fabio. Sherman's persuasion was always known and accepted in the office. I am surprised you didn't notice."

"I more noticed the females." he admitted.

Dear Fabio was so worldly in many ways, yet so clueless in others.

"At least I could appease Sherman somewhat. I know the lease on his place ends soon because I originally facilitated it. So, I offered him first option to buy my city apartment. He is interested and jumps at the chance. I believe he has adequate means with the extra salary earned as my secretary."

"Sherman will be taking over your life Fabio."

"It works out for me in other ways. He agrees to keep my pretty little maid on there."

"Your little maid?"

Fabio had a maid?

"Esmerelda. She is so lovely. I am deeply sorry to leave her."

"Oh Fabio. No way. You have yet another woman on the go?"

Fabio afforded me an old-fashioned look.

"Esmerelda is my little pet cat."

"You actually have a cat?"

"Have I not mentioned my little kitty before this? You must have forgotten Dimity."

I'd certainly never forget his first mention of a cat the time he scarpered home with his pants inside out and his shirt on backwards.

"Would you like me to point out that hollow tree with the keys before I go?" Fabio smiled.

"Yes please. I would really love to. Love for you to...to point it out."

He knew exactly what I meant. We went back to the lemon tree house but got no further than my bedroom. His passionate kisses met with my helpless desire.

As my boss for so many years, Fabio had no problem supervising how he wanted this session to begin. My high bed was ideal for the position Fabio favoured to take the edge off his appetite. Enslaved by choice, keen to obey, I bent to his demands. The bed was far better than an office desk any day.

Fabio liked to go hard and fast at first. For his second time, he liked to be on top. He took my hands in his, and held me captive. I loved being at his mercy as he suckled my nipples, his instincts perfectly attuned to mine. When I thought it couldn't get any better, it did. Fabio tutored me as he re-entered for his encore. I trusted he would be right. He was.

"Wrap your legs around me. It will be better for you."

Cooling off, Fabio curled around me, nestling his face on my breast. I kissed his brow and stroked his shoulders. Fabio became that lonely boy again, the one who had too many burdens foisted on him at a young age. He continued burdened with his family responsibilities unto this day.

Parting was bittersweet. Fabio couldn't linger, he had to get back to the city.

"I sort of love you Dimity." he said with a final kiss.

"I sort of love you too Fabio." I replied in an understatement.

Life went on. Fabio moved his immediate family to Germany.

Spirits

ISSUED & DIVINE

My promises, love and lust for Fabio intermingled with a desire to protect him. I cherished our shared secrets.

I resolved to make the best of the lemon tree house to fulfill my own wishes. My promise to Fabio also made it a solemn duty.

Little by little, I undertook to furnish the empty rooms. A futon sofa and coffee table were on order from a city warehouse for the bare living room. Duncan delivered the items and in good spirits helped carry everything upstairs. To be accurate, he carried while I issued instructions.

Duncan frequently visited the Clemency district on his farrier rounds. He stayed at his favourite pub in town, always found time to see me, tend to the horses and look in on Sophia. He checked her retired cart horses and fixed whatever needed attention. Sophia told me he refused any payment.

"Silly man. His backside is almost out of those pants. He could use a new shirt too." she said.

I kindly offered the use of my new futon if Duncan wanted to save money by staying overnight at mine.

Ever graceless, he replied typically:
"Thanks anyway Dimity but if I'm ever lucky enough to stay overnight with you, it won't be on any fecking back breaking hard bugger of a futon."
"Don't beat about the bush Duncan. Say what you mean."

I suppose I could always sleep on the futon since Duncan helped choose the big bed and mattress, delivered it, carried it all upstairs and reassembled it. I can be generous. Could that be another virtue? I think so.
When Duncan came up for whole weekends, we usually took Nero and Piper out trail riding together. I never spoke of the long-ago drownings that happened at the boathouse, although at times we followed river trails that landed up there.

Other times, I rode out to the boathouse alone, taking a sprig from the lemon tree to throw into the turbulent river waters as a tribute to Fiorella.
I had never known Fabio's mother, but how could I not feel connected to that lost young woman. I loved and missed Fabio, her only child, and I lived in the little house she fondly named *Albero di Limone*. Our lemon tree house.
On occasion when birdsong suspended, cicadas ceased chirruping and silence prevailed apart from the rivers sigh, I imagined Fiorella's spirit visited me. I promised I would always be there for her son.

I understood Fabio the boy and the man. His frequent need for exciting sexual activity manifested as an escape from reality.

I expected nothing from Fabio except to share his passion when he needed me. Our connection transcended divine orders of our church that would condemn us as occasional lovers.

We did no harm to anyone and did not forsake others. I felt no guilt. Assuredly, neither did Fabio.

Village

SENSE

G iorgio's widow had visibly aged since losing him. Sophia struggled living alone in her rambling farmhouse.

Sundays, Sophia continued coming into town with me and would bring flowers from her garden for Giorgio's grave.

Afterwards, having tea and cakes at the bakery, Sophia's friends chatted about the newly built retirement village. Some had already secured places there. Overhearing conversations, I knew her friends encouraged Sophia to buy into it.

"I will be selling this farm." Sophia announced at last. "It is for the best. I am not getting any younger."

I didn't try to talk her out of it. I deemed it high time she moved into town.

"Where will you go?" As if I didn't have a clue.

"A friend wants me to look at the new retirement village where she now lives. She says I will love it there. I am not so sure. But I will consider it."

"Why don't I drive you in and we'll make a day of it. We can inspect it together. I am good at picking homes as you know."

"Ha ha. Not many people would have taken on *Albero di Limone* Dimity."

"But I could see the potential at least."

In due course, I took Sophia to see the new retirement village. The ageing population in Clemency meant places at the new village were at a premium. Although few could afford the new facility, I felt sure the sale of Gallo's farm should meet the high asking prices.

On arrival, we picked up brochures at a reception booth situated outside the main entrance of the gated community centre. A friendly sentry opened the gates electronically and encouraged us to take as long as we liked for a good look around. Approach into the centre led us along a wide gravelled avenue lined with Maples.

"It is beautiful. But it feels a bit like a prison to me. Being locked in." Sophia said.

"The gate is guarded for security. The residents don't have the worry of unwanted salespeople knocking on their doors. Or other intrusions."

"I suppose that is a good thing."

"This brochure mentions a one-way side gate. Residents are always free to go out. And look, there is a daily mini bus service just for the village. People can even request to be taken to the hospital or anywhere in town. The bus isn't limited to any set routes."

"Every day? That is good."

The compact detached houses were grouped in separate hamlets set around cul-de-sacs off the main driveway. Each of five hamlets had an open display home and separate identities: The Garden Closes 1 and 2, Mountain Vista, Green Fields and Lake View.

Well-kept community gardens had footpaths designed for safe progress of mobility scooters and wheelchairs. Pathways encircled a wide lake and branched to meander through pockets of forest. Garden benches set beside trails provided choices of shaded or sunny places to sit.

According to the brochure the lake was regularly stocked with fish. Fishing could be done from three jetties placed at regular intervals around the lakes edge. There were no boats, guessing in case someone fell into deep water, where it would be difficult to save them, or retrieve a body.

Wild brown speckled ducks swam amongst reeds on the shoreline, and the brochure claimed ducklings were already being bred and raised there. A few residents sat on lake side benches and threw special food to the ducks and wild birds. A sign forbade throwing bread. Going through the display homes, Sophia brightened. The modern interiors were impressive.

"This would be so easy to clean." she enthused.

"The brochure mentions house cleaning services if needed. Pets are conditionally allowed too."

Elderly people leading little dogs had already been noticed walking around the lake and through the parks and garden pathways.

"Looks like pets are not limited to budgerigars and goldfish anyway."

"It wouldn't suit Enzo here." Sophia observed in her practical way.

I knew she was right. The active border collie had never been limited to inside living and would miss running loose about the broad paddocks at home. He might never have known a leash either making him difficult for Sophia to manage on walks. I was sure Enzo and Shamus would miss each other too, as they had bonded as friends.

"Enzo always has a home with me Sophia".
"You are a good girl Dimity."

And why not? If Fabio could be a good boy, so could I be a good girl. Sort of a good girl. Sort of loved.

A choice of home styles at the retirement village offered one, two or three bedrooms. Interiors were tastefully decorated in neutral colours and owners could always change the décor.

"Which model would you choose if you bought here Sophia?"
"They are all lovely. Two bedrooms would be good so I still can have a sewing room. If I couldn't afford two bedrooms, I could set up my sewing machine in a one-bedroom place. The rooms are big, and I don't have any cats to swing."

I knew my old friend was warming to the idea. Sophia recognised and greeted people who were walking about in the sunshine, enjoying the outdoors. I was introduced to her friends who encouraged Sophia's possible move to the village.

"Sophia! Say you will be coming to live here amongst us."

"I am thinking about it." Sophia replied.

Driving home, Sophia was quiet. I noticed she referred to the brochures often.

"It's a beautiful village." I prompted.

"It is much nicer than I expected. And you know, another reason to go there would be to get all the old goats off my back."

"What old goats?"

"Ever since my Giorgio has gone to heaven, I am chased by all the old goats every time I am in town now. I know they are only after the farm of course."

"No! How rude."

"Yes, they are rude. Even Gerda's lazy good for nothing cousin Nando has put his oar in. Huh. Does he think I was born yesterday? I am old enough to be his....great aunt."

"This Nando must be a real catch, the Gerdas also suggested that cousin for me when I first started work at the bakery."

Sophia laughed then made a serious prediction. The old lady believed in her sixth sense. Though I'm not sure if she had the story straight. It was complicated.

"There is someone special for you Dimity. You will see."

"How exciting." I smiled, indulging her fantasy.

"Soon it will be. Mark my words."

Old Sophia waved a chiding finger as if she knew I only humoured her fortune telling. Maybe Sophia's gift of the second sight was a bit off beam. My love for Fabio had already come to fruition and played out. There was no way our trysts could be known. We were discreet with our prior and current connections and were both adept at keeping secrets.

The Farm

FOR SALE

By the time I dropped Sophia back home to her farmhouse, she had made the decision. She would sell the farm and move to the retirement village.

Sophia heaved a sigh looking around at her beloved gardens, vineyards and green paddocks beyond. With new owners, I'd have to contend with a possible stressful change as well.

There followed a bunch of back and forth emailing to Fabio to tell him of his Aunt Sophie's decision and catch up on his own news.

Arriving in Germany, Agneta enjoyed an overdue reunion with her ageing parents. It was very cramped with all of them temporarily accommodated in the small apartment. Despite the old folks' hospitality, Fabio was keen to find separate housing for himself and Wolfgang, and not wear out the welcome.

I didn't want to trouble Fabio overly, so offered to facilitate Sophia's sale of the farm. However, before Wolfgang's miracle breakthrough, Fabio had already looked into investing in the new retirement village complex at Clemency. With a view to the future, Fabio envisaged his elderly relatives might be well placed there eventually. He was always thinking ahead in their best interests but hadn't gone so far as to buy anything there. He said:

"My intention to invest in the retirement village changed at the last minute. I needed all my available funds to bring the family here."

All Fabio could do immediately, was secure a place in the village for Sophia, by a provisional contract made subject to the sale of the farm. She had only to choose which home to put on hold.

Fabio would use his expertise to liaise with real estate agents and make sure his aunt was treated fairly.

Homes were selling like hot cakes at the retirement village. It would be disastrous if Sophia signed over the farm only to miss out on a retirement village place. The provisional contract had a time limit. Hopefully a buyer for the farm would be found in good time.

The same agency that handled the retirement village, travelled out to the Gallo farm to assess its value and add the listing to their books. They had double incentive to sell the place as Sophia would then purchase her next home from them.

Another day was spent in Clemency town while Sophia chose her favourite little home at the village. It could only be hers if the farm sold in time and at the asking price.

Eventually Sophia chose a two-bedroom dwelling for its larger than average courtyard. Ever the gardener, Sophia planned to grow potted herbs and tomatoes in the sunny sheltered spot.

Plans progressed beautifully until negotiations hit a snag: The first potential buyers for the farm were rejected by Sophia.

"They don't deserve this place," she said, "horrible people."

"Oh dear. I am sorry that didn't work out Sophia."

"You know what they said? The bedroom wallpaper was ghastly. Ghastly! Giorgio and I imported that paper from Italy and we loved it. That is why we papered our whole bedroom with it. I know who is ghastly. Those people are the ghastly ones."

Yet to see her bedroom wallpaper, I sympathised but privately reserved judgement. The second potential buyers for the farm were also rejected by Sophia.

"They were going to raze the gardens for tennis courts! Giorgio and I spent our lives building up those orchards and vineyards."

"Oh that would have been a terrible shame. Some people! I can't blame you Sophia. But you know there is a time limit on how long your new village home can be on hold."

The third potential buyers also failed to impress Sophia. The real estate agents had been remarkably tolerant but were becoming edgy.

I continued emailing Fabio to keep him in the loop. He said his aunt's fussiness came out of difficulty for her to let the farm go. If it came to a crunch he might be able to come up with bridging finance. I felt this was an iffy solution given Fabio's expensive commitments to his family in Germany, but it was not my place to speculate.

Fabio's time in Germany had visa limitations so he might be jumping borders from time to time with Wolfgang, adding to expenses. At least therapy for Wolfgang had been sourced near the current location at Schwerin.

A pity Sophia's stubbornness added stress to Fabio's family commitments. His aunt might have to stay on at the farm longer if the initial retirement village deal fell through.

My admiration for Fabio grew knowing the increasing burden of responsibility he accepted for his family, particularly for Wolfgang.

I faced reality: I would always be available for Fabio if he needed me, but he could be away for a very long time, possibly for many years.

I had no intentions of living like a nun while waiting for Fabio to come back and he wouldn't expect me to do so.

Sold

SLEEPING WELL

In the long run, the real estate agents missed out on a double sales commission. Sophia found her own buyer for Gallo's Farm and Fabio facilitated the conveyancing.

"It will be sad to leave here after so many happy years, but it will be in good hands. I know who I will sell it to."
"At last! That's good. I hope I'll like them. Someone nice I hope."
"Duncan!" Sophia announced in triumph.

A wide smile lit her face. Oh no! I dearly hoped Duncan hadn't said anything idiotic just to be charming and given Sophia the wrong impression. The bloody big Irish sod.

The broad acres and solid farmhouse were worth a great deal and had been highly valued by the experts. The farm was assessed even without taking into account the little business concern of the roadside stall. The old Gallos had never kept records and would not know a profit and loss statement if it bit them. I tried to tactfully water down Sophia's expectations:

"Ha ha. Oh no Sophia. That would be a nice gesture to offer it to Duncan, but I don't think he would have the means."
"But Duncan says he would find a way if he could buy this farm, and I know he would take care of the gardens and our old cart horses."

Sophia seemed supremely confident she'd worked it all out. I could throttle Duncan. The flaming idiot.

"Enzo loves Duncan and of course he loves you."
"And I have grown very fond of Enzo."
"Duncan loves you, is what I am saying." Sophia explained.
"No Sophia," I had to laugh again, "Duncan is like that with everyone. He is just a big flirt."
"You will see." was Sophia's enigmatic reply.

I firmly believed a sale to Duncan could never happen. To my amazement, the Irishman did purchase Gallo's Farm. Duncan was to be my new neighbour. Could be worse.

"I had to sell the stables." Duncan said.

"What? You OWNED the stables?" I was astounded. "I always thought you were just - *chief shit kicker* - um head roustabout."

"So, you haven't been after my money? You've just been chasing me for my beautiful body. As I've suspected all along." Duncan grinned.

"Oh please. For goodness sake. Do get over yourself Duncan."

My heart lifted knowing that Duncan would be my neighbour instead of some other imperfect being.

Not all the furniture in the rambling five-bedroom farmhouse would fit into Sophia's modern two-bedroom home. She narrowed it down to taking her cherished lead-lighted china cabinet, formal dining and lounge suites, Singer treadle sewing machine, her double bed and another single for the sewing room.

I got to see her bedroom wallpaper on moving day. Oh! That glorious wallpaper: A pink and blue all-over heavenly depiction of chubby cheeked cherubs blowing trumpets amongst fluffy clouds. I sought to tease Duncan by saying he couldn't change it:

"Duncan, you know you have to keep the garish bedroom wallpaper. Sophia would be devastated if she found out you scrapped it."

Hands on hips, he surveyed the large bedroom.

"What's wrong with it? I don't mind the musical cupids."
"Cherubs."
"What's the difference?"
"It's subtle Duncan. I don't expect you to get it."

Actually cherubs/cupids are probably the same thing. This was just one of numerous verbal duels I got into with Duncan. Some minor, others major.

Sophia still had an off cut of leftover wallpaper and hoped to incorporate it into her new modern home. Eventually we had it framed as a picture that could be hung on a wall in Sophia's new bedroom. She was happy with that idea, and said it was like a window into her memories.

The grand farmhouse bedroom also featured an open fireplace, surrounded in highly decorative scrolls, in keeping with the wallpaper. Duncan installed a king-sized bed, and I helped make it up with fresh linen. Bushed from our efforts, we flopped on the bed and admired the ornate ceiling roses.

"Be nice in here on a cold night hey Dimity?"

"Very cosy." I replied, ignoring his nuance of suggestion.

Changes were happening for all of us. I could hardly believe Duncan sold his lucrative seaside boarding stables for an old mixed farm at outer Clemency. It seemed like a bad swap, but from my point of view, he would be an ideal neighbour.

Overlooking his annoying tendencies, I enjoyed Duncan's company and fun banter. I knew him to be a competent and helpful man as well.

Duncan's strong and trustworthy presence just along the lane, next door to my lemon tree house, added another level of security.

After Wolfgang's ghostly intrusion, deep sleep very often eluded me. Logically I knew that particular fright would not recur, yet even the soft hooting of an owl might prove enough to startle me from slumber.

Several times, in a half-awake state my imagination conjured up a transparent apparition hovering in the bedroom doorway.

I knew the dogs, bedded in the kitchen, would never allow an intrusion so I did not fear the dreamlike image. If anything, the wraith seemed gentle and angelic. Perhaps my subconscious mind conjured up the angel intervention to deal with my fears.

After each visitation of the kindly spirit, I fell easily into a deep untroubled sleep.

The Likely Lads

SID AND NOBBY

Although living in our separate houses, I spent time with Duncan most days. Enzo the collie and Shamus the whippet hung out together at either of our homes.

Duncan had a grand plan for his farm. He intended turning it over to racehorse spelling.

Apart from his grey riding horse Piper, he still wanted a racehorse boarder kept at my place, so I did not lose that vital agistment income. It certainly wasn't charity either.

Boarding a valuable racing thoroughbred to Duncan's high standards entailed a lot of extra work.

Gallo's roadside fresh produce stall looked likely to shut down through the new owner's disinterest and lack of time.

Duncan wouldn't foolishly get rid of the established productive gardens, but he had no green thumb to keep it doing well.

"Don't suppose you want to manage the chooks and garden Dimity? Keep that roadside stall going?"

"Nope. That's your baby now Duncan. Good luck with it."

I was busy enough painting rooms and doing minor renovations on my house and had no experience with growing the many and various fruits and vegetables.

"Fair enough. I'll see if one of the lads want to do it."

"What lads would that be?"

"I'm keeping on a couple of lads from the seaside stables to help work this place. Sid and Nobby. There's plenty of room in the farmhouse. Sid claims to be a good cook too."

"Guessing Nobby is a nickname."

"Short for Nobbler. Don't ask."

"As I said Duncan, good luck with it."

I imagined the lads would be spotty teenagers, skinny would-be young jockeys. However, the lads proved to be bowlegged wizened old retired jockeys. Sid and Nobby were still quite fit and agile. The ageing men, having few options once too old and heavy to competitively ride gallopers, were overjoyed at being taken on, with accommodation thrown in at the picturesque country farm. Sid could even bake bread.

Duncan may have been rather kindhearted but taking on the old guys turned out to be a wise move. They were loyal and very capable hands and revelled in taking over the gardens and poultry.

Duncan said they could split the honesty box takings between themselves, as incentive.

The name painted on the sign - *Gallos Fresh Veg and Eggs* – remained. No one saw any reason to change it.

The bus continued to stop at the roadside stall, providing a steady stream of customers.

Sid and Nobby had no vehicles, so they hopped on the bus as their day off outing, soon falling in with the eccentric bus timetable.

Duncan and the lads built a line of timber stables, loose boxes and a feed storage room down beyond the vineyard. Solar panels were fitted to the rooftops. A paved wash bay was set up with warm solar heated water sourced from a good windmill bore.

The bore water fed stock troughs in the paddocks for the cart horses. Duncan and the lads installed extra plumbing for the wash bay and to supply automatic water fonts to stables. Nothing was too good for the imperial equine guests at Duncan O'Day's Spelling Stables.

Another access road and marshalling courtyard came about by hiring a grader. The upgrades incorporated parking for horse transports. Duncan had kept his long trailer and one double horse float.

Soon an entourage of sleek racehorses arrived on agistment, some for a few weeks or up to a few months. Duncan had been correct in identifying a niche market for a state-of-the-art spelling farm, not too far from a city and reasonably near to a main highway for quick access. O'Day's Spelling Stables amassed an enviable waiting list.

The lads were kept busy. At times I helped out if necessary. I didn't mind as long it wasn't laundry or house cleaning. They could fend for themselves as well as I could.

Duncan bought a barbeque cooker and had the open verandah fly screened. Meals could be eaten out on the verandah without the company of flies. Sitting outside on warm nights unbothered by moths and other insects became the norm.

I had an open invitation to any meal. I tried not to take too much advantage. Tried and failed. Though I often contributed a sweet or dessert.

We had some hilarious dinners there. Sid and Nobby were full of funny anecdotes. They were cheerful company. Sid baked really good bread too. I paid him a compliment for it:

"Sid, I swear your bread is better than the town baker's. Where did you learn to cook so well?"

"Ah... I learnt in an enormous kitchen, one of Her Majesty's finest." he replied humbly.

"Gosh! That is a royal feather in your cap Sid. I'd like to travel to the UK someday myself. Take in the sights, London, Piccadilly and all that."

The three men smiled indulgently at me. I guess they hoped I might get a nice trip to England someday too.

No Date

WITH DUNCAN

Whenever Sid and Nobby went into town I liked to hang out with Duncan, just the two of us as best friends. One such time, Duncan sought my help in the absence of the lads. After completing the chore together at his stables, we lazed in the sun.

"Clemency picnic races are coming up soon Dimity. Want to go with me?"

"Love to. I've never been to a picnic race meet before."

"Call it a date then."

A date with Duncan. Hmm. Didn't think an actual date was a good idea. He looked a bit serious waiting for my reaction. I decided to keep the moment lighthearted, punching him amiably in the arm.

"You're a good friend Duncan. Always thinking of me."

"I am always thinking of you Dimity that's for sure."

I resisted Duncan's anticipated next move. Still freshly pining for Fabio, I did not want to complicate the easy platonic relationship I enjoyed with Duncan. Ducking away I called the dogs to me and began a game on the lawn with them.

Duncan strode into the feed shed and slammed the door. The big dumb cluck. It was going to get pretty boring locked in with bins and bags of feed. I only had to wait a few minutes before Duncan emerged, hands on hips, and he wasn't doing chicken imitations.

"Tell me something Dimity."

"You can't roller skate in a buffalo herd."

Duncan's lips didn't even twitch in a smile. The big killjoy.

"Seriously. Is there a personal thing between you and that Italian bloke?"

"What? Who?"

"The guy you introduced me to at Giorgio's wake."

"Don't know who or what you're on about." I fibbed.

"I'm talking about that smarmy Italian guy, the one who looks like Kevin Costner."

"Paul Newman." *Oops.*

"I knew it!" Duncan declared.

It felt like an accusation, and I rankled.

"How dare you question me! My personal life is none of your business. I don't know why you imagine it should be. But OK Duncan, if you must know, I once lured that handsome Italian guy into my bed for a naughty one-night-stand and we fucked our brains out all night. Is that personal enough for you? Happy now?"

"Bull. You did not."

Apparently, I can look like I'm lying even when I'm not lying. It's a talent.

Let him ponder. And I'd only told him the half of it. He'd never know the rest. I put my nose in the air and flounced off. To this day, I think of that as one of my better exits.

More and more these dummy spitting episodes arose from the Irishman. Did he really want to ruin our platonic friendship? I was having a great time as neighbours, able to socialise with him and the old lads at the farm with no hidden agendas or tensions.

That green-eyed Irishman could be so aggravating. I was even madder at myself for using that one-night-stand story to irk Duncan. It was supposed to be secret! I didn't want to lose number one off my measly short virtue list, and I promised Fabio faithfully I would never tell.

At least Duncan hadn't believed it. There was that. Therefore, I'd keep number one on the list but add an asterisk as a compromise.

I decided to ride Nero out alone early the next morning without inviting Duncan along. Serves him right. He can turn up at my house and I won't be there. It will be like *Miss Minto Has Left the Building*. I fumed.

Even if he turns up bearing gifts and apologies, it will be too little too late. The big interfering jealous sook. I hated that he baited that secret out of me. Keeping secrets had been my number one virtue.

Before sunrise, Nero and I hit the trail. With no clear plan on where to go and angry thoughts full of bloody Duncan and his hissy fits, somehow,

I ended up back at the river boathouse area. I don't recall making any conscious decision to go there. Maybe Nero chose that way habitually.

That morning, I'd worn a pair of stiff leather riding boots that hadn't yet been worn in. They pinched and started a blister. Sitting by the river on the grassy bank, I pulled boots and socks off, rolled up my jeans and went to cool my feet at the river edge.

Careful not to paddle any deeper in than a hands breadth into the water, yet I could feel the river gravel shifting and squirming beneath my bare feet. The river felt alive.

Nero dozed nearby. He was so used to this routine by now, I trusted him not to stray. Earlier, he snorted at something seen in the bush, I surmised probably kangaroos. I'd seen fresh scat on the grass and 'roo tracks in the gritty beach sand where the animals hopped down to drink.

Dawdling along the pebbly shoreline brought me near to the boathouse. I climbed the steep bank about to return to Nero when an oddity caught my eye. The padlock on the boathouse door was undone!

Fabio and his family were overseas, and as far as I was aware, only I had express permission to be there on their private property. Fabio had even asked me to keep an eye on the place.

I had never seen inside the boathouse and Fabio had not offered me a key to the padlock. Yet someone must have access and a right to be there. I'd message Fabio later and ask about it.

Canola

BALDWIN

Perplexed over who could have unlocked the boathouse door, I took a closer look. The padlock appeared much newer than the old tarnished one I remembered. I felt sure it had been renewed after Fabio left for Germany.

Gingerly I went to investigate. The door opened outwards. I had never seen inside this shed before. Stepping inside, it took a while for my eyesight to adjust to the dark interior. The timber floor seemed to be a used as a storage area. A stack of at least forty plastic wrapped parcels piled high against the back wall. Each parcel appeared to measure over thirty centimetres square.

The front of the timber deck edged up against an indoor pool of water. As Duncan once supposed, it was a boat garage. A boat floating there, not an old wooden rowboat as I might expect, but a more modern aluminium tinny with outboard motor. Closer inspection showed the parcels to contain bottles of canola oil. How strange. I had a trivial thought that being Italian, Fabio would prefer olive oil.

Suddenly the shed door slammed behind me. I heard the padlock click shut. I was locked in. If this was someone's idea of a joke, *we are not amused.*

"Hey!" I yelled angrily. "Let me out!"

No reply. No voices were heard so I assumed there might only be one person outside. A narrow view could be spied through a crack between the wall boards. I could see Nero beginning to mill about on the green grass several metres away, but my jailer stayed out of the picture.

"I'm calling the police." I lied.

My phone was in my backpack, beside my boots and socks. I didn't even know if mobile signal could be had here. Bet my jailer would know. Why store canola oil here? Then an alarming memory came to me. I had read of a drug bust where methamphetamine had been stored in canola oil. Crikey. The boathouse was being used by drug smugglers! I imagined a big haul of illegal drugs must be worth a great deal of money.

With a sinking heart I understood my peril. I might end up drowned, washed up on a mud bank further downstream, just as I knew others had. I identified with Fiorella more than with Lupo. No one would miss me for hours or even a few days. Nero might wander home eventually, but he would go to the lemon tree house. I didn't even know if Duncan would come looking for me. He might still be in a snit. Bet he was too. The big bloody goose.

I tried to kick the door open with my bare feet. It hurt like hell, and I couldn't budge it. Realising the doors to the river might be unlocked, I stepped into the aluminium boat. It rocked unsteadily as I tried the riverside doors. No luck. All tightly shut. I was trapped.

I searched overhead for any loose sheet of roofing iron that might be lifted. It all looked tight and secure. It would have been too high for me to reach anyway. The packs of canola oil would most likely collapse under my weight if I tried standing on them. I sat thinking on it.

Inspiration came once I'd gotten over my initial panic. There must be a gap underwater beneath the riverside doors. If I was to drown, it would be my own idea. I wouldn't allow the unseen enemy to dictate my fate.

Slipping into dark water that came up to my chest, I took a deep breath and submerged myself as quietly as possible in case someone were listening. There was a gap! I had to come up for another lungful of air before braving the escape route. The becalmed water inside the boathouse gave no clue to the strength of the living river raging freely outside.

I slid out underwater where the strong current took shocking control. Not much of a swimmer, my lungs burnt painfully before I came to the surface. Gasping, I looked back to see I had already been carried many metres downstream, but near to the riverbank. I attempted to grab overhanging Weeping Willow branches, to no avail. I felt my bare feet and ankles scraped by unknown fears underwater.

The river was too far inland for sharks and too far south for crocodiles, but I remembered reports of huge eels when police rescue divers had searched for missing bodies in near locations. Opinions had it they would never find any bodies due to the massive size of those carnivorous eels. The thought brought no solace.

Trying time and again to grasp anything was using up my energy. I knew once I became exhausted the roiling river had me. The terrifying knowledge helped spur greater efforts. I fought for my life.

In a stroke of luck, the current washed me up against a log jam. Struggles to get up onto the raft of logs only succeeded in breaking one loose. In despair, I kept a firm hold although splinters abraded my arms.

My log lifesaver sped downstream while I clung on in desperation. I didn't know where I might end up or if the bad guys were out looking for me.

Hopefully once my escape was discovered, the criminals might think I had already drowned to save them the trouble.

During that awful trip in the river, I thought of Nero, Shamus, Fabio, Duncan and my humble lemon tree house where I'd been so happy.

My dire predicament evoked all that randomly led to this circumstance: My crime at the office. Cynthia dying. The rush to leave for a country escape. Duncan suggesting Clemency. Finding out Fabio was the owner. My entanglement with Fabio.

All these recent life events passed before my eyes, so I feared this to be my final hour.

Sounds of dogs yapping cut into my muddled brain. I almost lost my grip as the log I clung to jarred and shuddered, snagged against some underwater obstruction. I looked up to see two kelpies barking at me from the riverbank. I recognised that I was almost under the bridge where I had first crossed into the Clemency district with Duncan.

Cows mooed as the dairy herd strolled over the bridge. The young boy on the fat pony came to my aid.

Thinking quickly, the boy pulled the bridle from his pony and tossed it to me as a lifeline. Befuddled, I missed the first time. The boy skidded further down the bank and tried again. This time I was able to grasp the metal bit while he wrapped the ends of the split rope reins around his wrists.

With our combined efforts at last I was pulled clear of the deep water, to lay like a beached whale, stranded and panting for breath on the riverbank.

"You're not supposed to swim here." The boy said in mild rebuke.

"I know. I...um...fell in. Thanks for your help."
"You're welcome."

The boy replied politely as he re-bridled the patient little pony and looked about to leave.

"Wait. Please. My name is Dimity. What's yours?"
"Baldwin."
Poor bugger. Hope he keeps his thick hair in later years.
"Baldwin, I need help. Are your parents at home?"
"Yes. They should be just finishing second breakfast by now."
"How far is your house?"
"Way up the road. I can get them if you want."
"That would be marvellous. Thank you, Baldwin."

Baldwin instructed the kelpies to stay with me before kicking his pony into a rolling canter. I flopped backwards to gaze at the sky.

My sodden clothes steamed as I collapsed in the hot sun, grateful to be alive.

"Good dogs." I said, as one licked my face.

Police

NANDO

Baldwin's parents arrived in a farm truck. They were full of questions. Apparently, it was an unusual event to have someone pulled from the river. Alive that is. I was recognised.

"Your son is a hero. He saved my life."
"Hey! Aren't you the new girl at the bakery?"
"You live out near the Gallo farm and have the boyfriend who is from the coast? That is you, right?"

They were abreast of the gossip.

"Yes, I'm Dimity Minto. But this is an emergency. I need to contact the police. May I please use your phone?"

Young barefoot Baldwin cantered the fat pony back to us. He was chewing on a piece of toast, quite unconcerned. He whistled his kelpies and calmly continued his task of herding the dairy cows to pasture, giving a parting salute to me. Baldwin's parents introduced themselves as The

Russos, Maria and Otto. They showed me to their landline phone in the farmhouse but blatantly hung about to listen.

"Emergency. Yes. Please connect me to the police. Hello, my name is Dimity Minto. I want to report a suspected stash of illegal substances in an old shed. No I don't own the shed. Look I have to hurry. My horse is loose. You can find me out near Gallo's roadside stall near Clemency. Everyone knows me." *Apparently.*

I rung off. The Russos were agog. They kindly drove me back to Duncan's place and stuck around to hear more. I had made their day if not their year, or even their lives. They could dine out on this story forever.

"Where are your boots?" Duncan asked on seeing me.

Not why was I being brought home by strangers. Or why were my clothes wet and muddy. Or why was my lovely new hairstyle so bedraggled. At least my favourite small gold earrings were intact.

"I left my boots at the boathouse. I've been in the river. Listen Duncan, Nero is loose out there near the boathouse. I have to get him."

"Don't tell me you went for a swim in that river! That was really silly Dimity."

"Aaargh. No. Listen. I have to go back and get Nero. I'll explain later."

"OK. Calm down. What happened?"

"A drug bust." The Russos volunteered. "Our boy saved her life. Baldwin is a hero."

"What?"

"The police have been called. I reported it but I think the call went to regional headquarters, not to the local Clemency station."

By now Sid and Nobby were interested spectators as well.

"Alright. We'll drive out there. I can ride your horse back. You need a hot shower by the looks. And, it must be said: You don't smell too sweet either."

Duncan pulled a piece of something slimy out of my hair.

"No. No. Wait. The bad guys are out there. They could be really dangerous. I was imprisoned. But I got away and nearly drowned. I am worried about Nero but we better wait for the police."

"No worries. We can handle them." Nobby said jutting his whiskery chin out.

"Yep. I say let's go and mix it with them."

Sid backed up the idea. Duncan was torn.

"Geez Dimity. I wish you wouldn't go traipsing all over the countryside alone."

"Well. You were having one of your childish ninny-fits Duncan."

"I beg your pardon? I was having no such thing."

"Were so."

"Was not."

The Russos intervened reluctantly just as the drama was getting more entertaining for them.

"Here comes Gerda's cousin. The lazy big lump of a thing."
"Surprised he's out of bed already."
"Who?"
"Gerda's cousin. Nando. The local policeman."

A big 4x4 police vehicle drove in, blue lights unnecessarily flashing. I had to stare. The middle-aged police officer who exited that vehicle was a veritable Adonis to behold. At least six feet five inches tall with a magnificent physique. His thick curly hair was neatly trimmed and his perfect superhero-chiselled face sported a golden tan. He earned a mental wow from me.

I couldn't at first understand how on earth Gerda's cousin Nando was apparently still footloose and fancy free. Or why everyone kept trying to palm him off. On second glimpse I got a hint.

"Why the blue lights Nando?" Otto Russo asked.
"Aw. Were they on? Must've forgot to turn it off since last time."
"Surprised you didn't have the siren going as well."
"Yeah. Ha ha. I still have to fix that."

Sid and Nobby were impatient with the policeman. Clearly, they did not welcome his arrival.

"Come on boss. Let's go get that black horse for young Dimity."

I nudged Duncan to comply. Nando bent to his duty:

"What's the story? I just got a call from headquarters saying to get out to Gallo's fruit stall a.s.a.p. I might pick up a dozen eggs while I'm here. Those melons look pretty good too. And the figs. I haven't tasted a fig for ages."

"Stay focused Nando." Otto Russo advised.

"A big drug bust." Maria Russo prompted. "Our boy Baldwin is a hero."

"Your Baldwin did a drug bust?"

"No. This new lady at the bakery fell in the river. But Baldwin saved her life."

Nando eventually found his notebook and looked about for his pencil.

"It's in your pocket."

"Oh yeah. It's always in the last place I look." Nando laughed.

He licked the indelible pencil. It made his tongue go purple. He was apparently preparing to take notes.

"Run that by me again? How do you spell Baldwin?"

"Bugger this let's go."

Nobby and Sid jumped into the back of Duncan's ute. Still barefoot, I got in the front beside Duncan. He pulled a face.

"Shut up Duncan. Just hold your nose."

"I didn't say anything."

"I read your mind."

We roared out of there leaving the Russo's (bless them) to misinform the local plod. I directed Duncan past the stone house. Soon we were bumping and slipping down the rocky overgrown track to the river.

My boots and old knapsack remained on the grass where I'd left them, but I couldn't see Nero. I looked around and whistled the two familiar notes used to call him up from the paddock at home. No response. Maybe he was making his own way home. That seemed the most likely explanation.

I sat to pull my socks on and spied a grubby note scrawled on the inside of a ripped cigarette packet. The alarming note was poked into one of my boots:

IF U WONT YUR HORS ALIVE U BETTA WAIT HEAR OR ELS.

I deciphered that horrible message and screamed:

"Duncan!"

Assuming only one criminal to be involved, he must have hedged his bets by leaving that note. He probably didn't expect me to turn up with a crowd, if at all.

Duncan came running, figured out the meaning of the note, and put his arms around me.

"Don't worry we're on it." he said.

Sounds of my mobile ring tone had me rummaging through my backpack to find it. At least that was still there. It was the police calling. Not Gerda's cousin thank goodness. My name and number had been recorded when I phoned from the Russo place. I answered the police question:

"I'm at the boathouse with some friends. It's on the Clemency side upriver from the bridge."

Sid had picked the boathouse lock in no time.

"There's lots of stuff still in here." he shouted back to us.
I relayed the message to the police:
"The stuff is still in the shed. It's canola oil. Heaps of it."

The police said to wait there. They were coming as fast as possible and were not far away. Nobby was scrutinising the ground for horseshoe tracks.

"OK. We'll be nearby but still looking for my horse."
"Leads uphill." Nobby called.

I pulled my boots on. We all followed Nobby. While hiking up through the bushland we heard the distinct whirring of an approaching helicopter.
Through the trees we saw a police chopper expertly touch down on the grassy picnic area beside the river. Several black clad officers jumped out. We waved to show them we were not the criminals.

"We're tracking the horse." Duncan yelled out to the police.

One of the policemen gave a thumbs up. Some of them proceeded to the boat shed while others stood guard. It looked like they were armed and ready. Good to see it taken seriously.

Nero's tracks went to the stone house. Thankfully, we could see him there, far down the hillside in the vineyard. He was still saddled. I cried out with relief.

Duncan and I went down to retrieve Nero. My poor horse was sweating and upset. He had crashed through some nylon bird netting and had it wrapped around his legs. Duncan took out his pocketknife and carefully freed Nero's legs. The leather reins had snapped but were usable.

Sid and Nobby went to look around. Shouts and sounds of a scuffle came from the direction of the stone house. Duncan ran to help.

Sid and Nobby had already ably downed a man who had been trying to scarper. Guess that man was my jailer who must have spooked on hearing the chopper.

Later it was confirmed he was a member of a gang of drug pedlars. He'd broken into the stone house and been squatting there, posted as a lookout for the boathouse stash.

I soothed and checked my darling Nero, mounted and rode down to the helicopter. The rotors had stopped turning. Nero was wary of the strange craft but behaved sensibly. He seemed relieved to be reunited with me and I appreciated his trust.

"I believe you found the goods in the boat shed Miss?"

"Yes, I did. I'm Dimity Minto. This is my horse that was loose. When I got back here with my friends, he was missing, and I found this awful message left with my things."

I showed them the cigarette packet. They put it into an evidence bag and kept it.

"We tracked the hoof prints up the hill. Thank goodness my horse seems to be settling down. He obviously suffered a bad ordeal."

"What were you doing out here? Were you alone?"

"It's private property. The owner is overseas. He gave me permission to ride on his land and I agreed to keep an eye on the place whenever I came here. This morning, I noticed the lock was undone so I went to check inside the boatshed. I'd never been in there before and yes, I was alone."

I suddenly felt faint and sat on the grass, holding Nero's reins. My horse snuffled my hair and snorted his disapproval at the smell of river mud and whatever else dwelt in there.

"Take deep breathes Miss Minto. So, you thought the contents were suspect?"

"Yes. I remembered some news story about drugs in canola oil. Before I could get out, someone locked me in. My horse was loose but I didn't expect him to go far. He is used to coming here."

"How did you get out of the boathouse?"

"I swam underwater. There's a gap under the river doors. I almost drowned as well. Fortunately, I had taken my boots off earlier to paddle."

Taking those new boots off turned out to be a stroke of luck. Had I gone in boots and all, the weight of water in them would have dragged me under.

"This is a major haul if it proves to be what it looks like."

"Is it thought to be drugs?"

"That is our guess. The people we believe responsible are considered extremely dangerous."

"I thought as much. That's why I braved the river. I'm not much of a swimmer. It's been really terrifying."

"It must have been. You were extremely lucky. We will take a full statement soon. You'll be informed where and when. This is an ongoing investigation. Do NOT discuss this with anyone."

"Of course not. I would rather forget the whole experience."

I saluted the police officer, then remembered to add:

"Oh. By the way, my friends have apprehended a suspect. Go up that track, you'll come to a stone house over the ridge. That's where they'll be."

After initial surprise at my afterthought, several officers hurried up the slope.

Police would enter Fabio's stone house and very likely record how the intruder made use of the place as a hideout.

A frisson of dismay struck. Investigators could come across Cynthia's red handbag bearing the extremely valuable label. Its history as presumed stolen from Cynthia's body would prompt deeper inspections.

Fabio's sudden overseas move would seem a damning factor in Cynthia's death.

Little Bean had kept the glossy red bag amongst her dress-up playthings, but even a rudimentary search would find it.

My next conversation with Fabio would be interesting.

My brave trio of men friends duly handed their somewhat battered prisoner over to police. Officers said his capture was a major breakthrough in an ongoing investigation. Strict instructions were repeated - we were NOT to discuss these events with anyone.

A pity Gerda's cousin Nando, the local plod, had not been reminded of protocol, as it later turned out.

Duncan insisted on riding Nero back home although I might just have achieved it myself. Sid drove the ute, I sat in the middle between Sid and Nobby on the trip back. Neither of them mentioned my odoriferous state.

"That bloke you caught looked like he took a beating."
"Yeah. The police mentioned that as well. Told them he ran into some star pickets trying to escape."
"Well, serves him right for being so nasty and for leaving that horrible note about Nero. I suppose he was in a panic and not looking where he was going."

Sid paused the ute at the crossroads.

"Why are we stopping?"

"The boss wants us to take you into the hospital to get checked over."

"No way! Duncan isn't my boss I'll have you know. And I've already been taken prisoner once too often this day."

"Thought as much. Told you she'd say that." Nobby laughed.

"I just want to get home. Come on guys. You can tell I badly need a shower."

I talked them into it. They dropped me back at the lemon tree house well before Duncan arrived riding Nero.

"You get into a hot bath and your jammies, lass. We'll handle Duncan." Nobby said.

"I've got a lovely pumpkin soup on the back burner. I'll send Duncan up with some for you later." Sid promised.

"I am being spoilt. I feel just like your old boss now Sid."

"Who?"

"Her Majesty the Queen of course."

They had a laugh. I guess they enjoyed spoiling me.

Sooking

SHOWER SHAMPOO & SOUP

Home at last. Never had a hot soapy shower and thorough shampoo felt so good nor so necessary.

I was covered in bruises and scratches from trying to grab branches and from hitting underwater snags as I hurtled down the churning river.

My arms, hands, legs, feet even my belly all stung from many dabs of iodine. At least the pain reminded me I was lucky to be alive.

The day was yet warm. I donned lightweight pyjama pants, and a singlet top. Despite it being too early for bedtime, I lay down for a five-minute catnap.

Three or four hours later I awoke. Duncan was sitting beside me on a kitchen chair I'd been using as a bedside table.

In surprise I saw my window darkened by an evening sky. Light streamed in faintly from the kitchen.

"Are you ready for some soup sleepy head?" he asked gently.

"Ah...Nero...the dogs."

"All safe and sound. All fed." Duncan soothed.

Thank goodness Duncan had handled my evening chores. He'd been home and changed into a white t-shirt and navy track pants. A pleasant scent of some spicy aftershave emanated from him.

"You're a legend Duncan. Thanks."
"That I am. Just relax. I'll fix some soup."

Duncan clattered about in my kitchen heating soup and setting a tray. I lay back and let myself be waited on. Duncan placed the tray beside me and plumped up more pillows behind my back.

Earlier while I slept, he had covered me with a hand knitted throw rug that had been draped over the futon. Now Duncan wrapped the rug about my bare shoulders.

Sid's pumpkin soup was delicious and there were hot crusty rolls as well.

"Do you want me to stay the night?" Duncan asked.
"Thanks, but no. You go home and get a good night's sleep yourself. It's been a hard day for all of us. I'm fine. Still a bit tired, is all." I yawned. "I'll just go to the bathroom and clean my teeth. Then I'm going to crash again."

When I came out of the bathroom Duncan had just finished washing up the tea tray things.

"Sure you're alright Dimity? Would you like a cup of tea now?"

That added kindness and sympathy chinked my resolve to tough it out. My voice wobbled tearfully as the events of the day caught me up.

"Oh Duncan it was so horrible. I thought I was trapped just waiting to be murdered. Going down the river. I couldn't get out. Certain I'd be drowned and end up dead on a mud bank. Then Nero going missing and that awful threat."

"There, there. You cry it all out. You'll feel a lot better afterwards."

Duncan hugged his strong arms about me. Sobbing I lay my head gratefully on his broad chest while he rubbed my back with his big warm hands.

"Thanks," I said with a final hiccup, "sorry for the histrionics. I'm good now."

"Come on. I'll tuck you in."

Duncan tucked me under the covers and kissed the top of my head.

"Sweet dreams. See you tomorrow." he said.

I might have replied, instead I fell into a deep sleep the moment my head touched the pillow.

From habit I woke before dawn. A faint snoring heard coming from the other room didn't sound like either Shamus or Enzo.

Not the dogs. Duncan's prone form occupied the futon sofa. He'd spent an uncomfortable night there, instead of going home to his own cosy bed. I'd told him I was ok. The silly sod. I woke him with tea and buttered toast.

"You lied Duncan."

"How's that?"

"You swore you'd never spend a night on the fecking back breaking futon."

"Yeah well. Would have jumped in with you but you snore so."
"Huh. I do not."
"Do so."

He groaned while stiffly stretching cricks from his neck and aching muscles. I think he was overdoing that groaning and moaning. I haven't had to spend a night on the futon, but it can't be all that bad. It was difficult not to talk about events of the previous day.

"What about the good old boys hey Duncan? Sid and Nobby were fantastic from the start. Overriding whatsisface the local cop while he dithered uselessly."

"Surprised you noticed with your eyes out on stalks ogling that big beefcake." Duncan remarked, green eyed.

"What? Gerda's cousin. You must be joking." I laughed.

"Gerda's cousin? You know him?"

"Everyone knows Nando. He's a local celebrity. Good looking. Gainfully employed. Single. The most eligible bachelor in Clemency. He's talked about everywhere I go. Truly he is."

I couldn't resist needling. It hit home. Duncan frowned but made no retort. He might have pouted a teeny bit. Ha ha. Got him.

"You're not the only hunky guy around these parts I'll have you know Duncan."

Aargh. I'd been doing well until I let that slip.

"Hunky hey? What with my Irish Charm and twinkling eyes I'd better watch myself around you Miss Minto."

"Don't forget to add your extreme modesty, Duncan."

"Ah yes. I'm full of it."

"No argument there." I smiled.

News

FROM NEAR & FAR

A shame Gerda's cousin Nando was not instructed to keep his big kisser shut about the drug incident.

The local newspaper screamed a bold front-page headline:
LOCALS FOIL DANGEROUS DRUG SMUGGLERS

A full-page blurb followed. According to a reliable source, the Clemency Police Force (Gerda's cousin Nando) cracked open a notorious gang of drug smugglers that had eluded the country's finest. A tip off from young local lad Baldwin Russo led to the bust.

One small photo of Baldwin looking courageous astride his fat little pony illustrated the mention.

Larger photos depicting Nando's handsome macho countenance filled out the content. A main image had a stern-faced Nando displaying a bag of white powder. Probably flour.

Seemed police headquarters had not shared the canola oil aspect with Nando. None who knew the true story could correct the misinformation since we obeyed strict instructions not to disclose details of the event.

A smaller mention on an inside page was made of a woman rescued from the river. It said she had been lucky the log she clung to had snagged on an old truck body jammed against the bridge footings under the water. Old truck body. Hmm. Betting no ignition key would be found in that rusty wreck.

The news story went on to state: 'The rescued woman who is employed by Clemency Bakery is known to be new to the area, so is possibly ignorant of the dangers. End note: A timely warning is issued: Never swim in the river. Strong currents and dangerous deep water present risks to perpetrators and rescuers alike.'

Now I was a perpetrator. Can't win for losing. Despite that, the event proved to be a flash in the pan.

I continued working at the bakery Sunday mornings. Sophia came in often to catch up. I would bring vegetables and eggs from the farm for her. Ripe figs from the Brown Turkey trees were prized and what Sophia said she most missed.

A landline phone had been installed in Sophia's new abode in the retirement village. The old dear was amazed that she could hear Fabio perfectly clearly on that phone, even all the way from Germany.

I could also hear Fabio quite well on my mobile, and without giving too much away, filled him in on the dramas at his property involving the boat house and stone house. He acknowledged my advice not to speak of events to anyone in light of police instructions.

Police had confiscated the aluminium boat found in the boathouse. Fabio said it definitely wasn't owned by any of his family. There used to be an old wooden rowboat in there, but he didn't know what had become of it. No one had used it for years.

"Don't worry Fabio, the stone house and boat shed are fully secured now."

Duncan and I had driven over there and nailed boards across all the doors and windows. The police had finished investigating and okayed us to do it.

"Thank you so much Dimity. I am very fortunate to have your help. Tell me, is it true you fell into the river? You must be careful. It is very dangerous."

"No I did not fall in. That is a long and exaggerated story. Take no notice of it. But something else worried me greatly. As you know the police had to enter your house and I am aware of a very valuable red handbag somewhere there."

The Cynthia secrets kept coming up to haunt me.

"Bean's favourite toy. Don't worry Dimity. She insisted on bringing it to Germany."
Phew.

Fabio went on to say they were all benefiting from family therapy sessions. Wolfgang had already improved immensely and was attracting romantic interest from a pretty receptionist at the clinic.

"Wolfy is like a shy teenager, but he is lapping up the female attention. I have kitted him out with some more up-to-date clothes and I notice he inspects his image in the mirror quite a lot now. I cannot remember him ever doing that before."

"That's amazing. I am happy all is going so well."

Agneta had been right about Germany being a good idea. I felt glad for them all. Yet I missed Fabio.

Picnic Races

THE IRISH

Clemency Picnic Races – a three-day event held over a long weekend – was celebrated throughout the town.

Every shop window had displays of hay bales, saddles, jockey silks and other paraphernalia associated with the horse races. Not to miss out, local businesses offered Picnic Race Specials.

Roberto's Hair Salon offered discounts, so I returned to select new and bigger gold hoop earrings. I made use of discounts at The Fashion Boutique as well. I asked advice about suitable outfits for the races. The helpful assistant said anything goes but personally she would opt for comfortable walking shoes, neat jeans or slacks and a cool top.

"Love your earrings," she said, "there's a pretty gypsy blouse that would perfectly complete that look."

Outfit easily sorted. I already had good jeans and several pairs of sensible walking shoes.

Duncan hadn't forgotten my casual acceptance to go to the races with him. He had been more affable since my near-death experience in the river, and I looked forward to going with him.

Sid and Nobby were driving the ute in together, and I was driving my own car with Duncan. Nobby had grown a bushy beard in honour of the day. Sid mentioned it was a good cover up. Not sure why. Perhaps he was prone to sunburn.

Clemency showgrounds blazed with colour and blared with noise. Side shows and whirley-girdies were in full swing and a ferris wheel dominated the skyline. Stalls with fairy floss and toffee apples did a busy trade, as well as those offering Dagwood dogs and hot chips. Sample bags and Cupie dolls could be had as well. It was all very festive even without the horse races.

The racetrack was in fine shape. Loudspeakers enabled race calls to be heard over the jumble of music from sideshow alley. Duncan bought tickets to the best grandstand where we sat viewing the grassed main arena that was surrounded by the sandy racetrack.

Between horse races, sheep dog trials went on in the centre arena. The dogs, mixes of border collies and kelpies competed herding small mobs of sheep around obstacles and finally into portable panel yards. Dog owners shut the gate at the end.

I couldn't remember enjoying a day more. Perhaps almost dying in the river now made everything more vivid and enjoyable.

Duncan took my hand in his at one stage during a race. I jumped up breaking the hand contact while clapping and cheering on my favourite horse, that I only picked for being a black.

As soon as I sat down, Duncan firmly reclaimed my hand. I didn't mind at all. Smiling happily, I snuggled up against him. He felt so good and solid.

A pavilion marquee set up as a dining tent advertised roast lamb with mint sauce luncheons and a sumptuous choice of desserts to follow. Hand in hand, Duncan and I wandered the grounds slowly making our way towards the lunch tent.

Buoyed at being partnered by the handsome Irishman, I clocked envious glances from other women. It was an opportune time to practice my smug Mona Lisa smile. Duncan in his well fitted jeans looked desirable both coming and going. He'd also shaved that morning and even wore an ironed shirt. I knew he'd gone to some trouble for this day.

We sat down in the lunch tent amongst a crowd of other diners. The roast dinners smelt delicious and there was plenty of it.

"Wow. This is OK." Duncan said.

"Very OK." I agreed.

Tables were nicely set and self-service from a warm foot bar had been easy to negotiate.

During our roast lamb meal in the marquee, an announcement came over the loudspeakers, asking if there were a farrier on the grounds.

"Oh. No. I'll pass on that." Duncan said. "I don't want to spoil our date and get dirty and sweaty. Let someone else do it."

So, Duncan did consider this a date after all, I hadn't been certain after our little tiff back at the stables. Minutes later the announcement was repeated at a more personal level.

"Duncan O'Day please go to the stables."
"Come on Duncan we know you're here." a second announcer added cheerfully.
Duncan still ignored the call. "There'll be other guys who can tack a shoe on."
Someone in the crowd was heard to shout: "He's in the dining tent."

What a dobber. But Duncan would not be moved since we were at the sweets stage of lunch. I couldn't blame him, tempted to indulge of trolleys laden with trifles, cream pies and pavlovas. The dessert trolleys wheeled around all the tables in turn, so diners could self-serve their choice of sweets.

Just as the yummy desserts reached our table, a burly man with a broad Irish accent and a cigarette hanging off his lip, accosted Duncan:

"If it isn't yourself O'Day. Bet you never thought I'd find you Down Under, hiding out all these years like a gutless mongrel. Ashamed to show your face at home after you killed my Lexie."

Duncan's expression registered surprise before darkening ominously.

"Your Lexie? I don't think so." Duncan replied quietly. "I did my time. Let it go Murphy. Or I'll be doing more time and you're sure not worth hanging for boyo."

The other guy threw the first punch. People screamed. Tables and chairs fell over. My beautiful new gypsy blouse got splattered with pudding and I felt something go splat in my nice hairdo. *That's it!*

Taking a big ladle full of trifle, I flung it at the mad boyo's face. Momentarily blinded, he crashed against a supporting corner strut. The marquee began to tilt.

Before he could recover, I upended a big bowl of jelly over his head. He tripped and sat down heavily on the ground. The soggy cigarette somehow remained in his mouth but bent down against his chin.

The yobbo swore some unspeakable curses. A woman took instant offence at the bad language and threw a bread-and-butter pudding in a heavy metal pan. It got him square on the forehead. That had to hurt.

Someone threw a cream caramel tart. It missed and hit someone else. Soon it was a free for all. The marquee partially collapsed. Last sight was of the boyo fending off an assortment of irate male and female locals.

"Let's get out of here."

Duncan took my arm, and we ducked under the slack pavilion wall. Once outside we attempted to appear innocent by casually strolling away.

"What the hell is going on?" Gerda's cousin Nando marched by.
"Not sure. Looks like the dining tent is wonky. Probably should be evacuated." Duncan said helpfully.

The local newshound was hot on Nando's trail ready for his next exclusive scoop. Neither the policeman nor the newspaper reporter looked at us, so they missed our incriminating state. Duncan took something off my hair and licked his finger. The feral.

We went by the stables on the way out. Duncan asked who had been asking for a farrier. A strapper said it was a big Irish fellow, but he didn't know him. It had to be the Irish yob called Murphy.
We found Sid and Nobby out the back happily engaged in an illegal game of two-up with a group of like-minded veterans. The simple coin tossing game is prohibited gambling in Australia except on Anzac Day and then only allowed if proceeds go to charity.

"Did you catch up with your mate from the old country Duncan?"
"He seemed dead keen on finding you."
"Murphy is no mate lads. He's out to lynch me. Dead set he is."

Sid and Nobby looked up from their game and saw Duncan's beaten-up face.

"Bloody hell. Your sins catch up with you?"
"Yeah. Something like that." Duncan admitted.

"Looks like we missed out on the fun." Nobby grieved.

"Best you all behave yourselves." I advised.

I bid the likely lads goodbye and dragged Duncan away, with a rueful parting comment to Sid and Nobby:

"I'm taking this fun date home. Catch you later."

When I next caught up with the old ex-jockeys it was rather later than expected.

Bail

HAVE A NICE DAY

I drove Duncan home. He nursed a swollen cheek, a sore jaw, a black eye and an even blacker mood.

"I take it you know that bloke from when you lived in Ireland."
"Yeah. I know Murphy. He was the one playing up to my girlfriend that got me so angry that day. Not that anyone else is to blame for my stupidity. Murphy and I go way back. We went to school together. Always been bad blood between us."

So, their feud had festered for a long time, worsened with their shared jealousy over Lexie.

"It's been twenty or so years. Wonder how he found you way out here at Clemency. It's hardly mainstream."
"Don't know. But I guess everyone at home must think the same, that I'm a gutless coward hiding out down here in Oz. I'll be going back to show my face as soon as I can." Duncan announced.

That statement troubled me.

"Back to Ireland? You probably couldn't go until the police take your statement for the drug bust."

"I'll have to sort it with them. They can't make me stay in Australia if I want to leave. I haven't committed any crime here."

Bruising bloomed to colour Duncan's face and the blackened shiner wept tears from his closed eye. He refused any help; just said he was hitting the hay. I left him to stew and went home to the lemon tree house alone. It was a bit of a let-down after the good day at the races. Good until Murphy showed up anyway.

Sid and Nobby didn't return that night, yet Duncan fully expected them home before dark. There was work to do and they had his ute. Early next morning, Duncan walked up the lane to ask if I'd drive him back to town.

First stop was the racetrack. We saw that Duncan's ute remained parked there.

Duncan questioned some of the racing fraternity still on the grounds. We learnt that Murphy had escaped the melee in the dining tent. He'd easily found out the utility was Duncan's vehicle due to a sign advertising his spelling stables in the rear window. Murphy broke in and slouched down in the cab expecting Duncan to return to his vehicle eventually.

Sid and Nobby, wise to the fact Murphy wanted to lynch Duncan, weren't best pleased to find the enemy lurking. They hauled Murphy out of the ute and advised him of their displeasure.

Sid, Nobby and Murphy had all been taken into custody for brawling.

"Why doesn't this surprise me." I sighed.

"I'm hoping that big idiot Nando is as dumb as he seems."

"Why?"

"Just saying." Duncan replied without saying more.

I never did find out about that enigmatic comment but had an idea it had been something to do with Nobby.

We drove to the police station. Nando was only too happy to release two of his house guests. As their employer, Duncan vouched for Sid and Nobby. They got off with a stern warning. The three all looked immensely relieved.

Nando didn't even ask about Duncan's bashed up face. It saved paperwork and he'd had a gutful of Irishmen with his burly house guest in the other cell.

Murphy remained a thorn in Nando's side as the Irish brawler refused to be helpful. Duncan said he knew Murphy from years ago in Ireland. Nando assumed they must be friends and asked Duncan to try talking to the other Irishman. It would save Nando so much energy if that proved successful.

Before going in to see the prisoner, Duncan supplied what he knew of Murphy's personal information. A kid on work experience got busy checking records on the police computer - probably not a conventional task for a schoolboy, but Nando didn't take to online research.

Both Duncan and I were allowed to sit in the next cell and talk to Murphy.

"Good to see you Murphy. Behind bars that is." Duncan prodded.

Murphy didn't bite at Duncan's prodding, at first. Duncan went on:

"I'll be going back home to Ireland soon just to prove you wrong."

"I'm not wrong." Murphy took the bait.

"Surprised you had the wits to find me. Took you long enough." Duncan goaded.

"I knew your ugly dial right off," Murphy growled in a low voice, "I watched you and this tart through a crack in the shed."

Duncan and I made no response. We didn't know what Murphy was talking about, but we didn't let on. *Tart* indeed. I'd have loved to swipe that ugly sneer off Murphy's smirking face.

"That stumped yas didn't it." Murphy sniggered maliciously.

"Have a nice day." Duncan replied.

We smiled and waved goodbye leaving Duncan's old adversary stewing in his cell. Murphy uttered an obscene suggestion in reply, although what he wished upon us would be physically impossible.

The four of us headed for home after truthfully telling Nando we had urgent horse work to catch up on and we would check back with him later.

The menfolk limped about the farm with varying degrees of injury. Murphy sure put his mark on them all. I volunteered to make something to eat while they painfully got on with chores.

"Can't chew." Sid said feeling his sore jaw.

"Me neither." Nobby concurred.

"Scrambled eggs all round." Duncan suggested.

The warriors couldn't even handle toast. I buttered soft white bread instead. Sid had a jelly in the fridge which I served up with ice cream. We sat about the table puzzling over Murphy cropping up after so many years. Together, we summarised what we knew so far:

"He somehow landed in Clemency. Found out Duncan lived in the area. Realised Duncan would very likely be at the picnic races. Then he's put it over the loudspeakers asking for a farrier to lure Duncan in."

"That's about it."

"The main mystery is how did he find you, Duncan."

"That's the mystery. Out of the whole of Australia, how on earth did he land in Clemency."

"And why did he claim to have watched us, Duncan?"

"He said it was through a crack in the shed."

"He couldn't have been anywhere here, or the dogs would have let us know."

Enzo and Shamus followed me everywhere. Murphy couldn't have spied on me at my place or Duncan's farm without the dogs being alerted. Neither dog was likely to attack a person without good reason, but both were very vocal when it came to intrusions.

"Only other shed is the old boathouse."

"Hey, you know what? I remember trying to squint through a crack in the wall when I was locked in there. What if Murphy was in the boathouse one time when we picnicked there? What if he is connected to the drug haul."

"Feasible. Knowing Murphy from years ago he was into all sorts of substance abuse."

"That's it then. Has to be."

Duncan and I drove back to the Clemency police station after lunch, still discussing the situation between ourselves. The lads opted to stay home for siestas. The fistfight with Murphy followed by an uncomfortable night in the watch-house had caught up with the feisty old fellows.

"Remember we're under strict instructions not to discuss the drug sting with anyone."

"Obviously from that ridiculous report in the local newspaper, Nando was left out of the loop. Headquarters must deem it to be a need-to-know basis and Nando is perhaps flagged as a weak link."

"It's been a short acquaintance with Nando, but that seems feasible."

"We don't know how much Nando let on to Murphy."

"Maybe Murphy hasn't seen the ridiculous newspaper story. He might be unaware the boathouse has been busted if he's been hanging about in town stalking you, Duncan."

"True. He could have been sleeping rough somewhere. My guess would be at the showground stables. He might not even know his mate at the stone house has been nabbed."

"Murphy seems confident, but it was a stupid move for him to mention the shed."

"He's never been the sharpest knife in the drawer."

"OK. Guess we play it by ear."

The computer whiz kid found that our friend Murphy was not an Australian citizen. He had once held a tourist visa, but it expired months ago. The efficient little computer nerd read out a finding:

"If you are in Australia without a valid visa, you could face serious consequences including immigration detention and removal. If your visa has expired, you need to apply for a bridging visa immediately in order to become lawful."

Nando said he would run it by police headquarters. Maybe they'd take the prisoner off his hands. He didn't see why he had to help Murphy apply for a bridging visa. Not in his job description, he said.

Duncan and I conferred privately. We decided not to talk further with Murphy in case we let slip anything to clue him in, supposing he belonged to the gang, and imagined himself safe.

"Let's keep him in the dark".
"I vote we tell the city police that we suspect Murphy of involvement with the canola oil stash and why."

Duncan phoned in our suspicions immediately after we left the station, in case Nando let Murphy go free before he could be properly assessed.

Bun Fight

AT THE OK MARQUEE

The following week, Clemency enjoyed a special mega edition of the local newspaper with a comprehensive blurb and lots of photos of the festive picnic race weekend.

Sharing the front page was a star off shoot – *Bakery Lady in Bun Fight*. Bet the local news editor was proud of that catchy headline. He probably had it pinned to a cork board in his office.

Enough people had noticed me walking about with my handsome companion that I had been easily recognised and dobbed in. Gladly I did not appear in any photos and the story line missed the gist:

'A source reported that a drunken man had caused a ruckus in the dining tent and several women including the bakery lass were forced to defend themselves with items from a food cart. The marquee had to be evacuated after becoming unstable during an ensuing free-for-all.

The instigator was thought to be of Scottish descent as his ribald turn of phrase was likened to Billy Connolly's. Unfortunately despite best efforts of the policeman on duty, the offender escaped in the confusion.

End note: Please be aware that unruly visitors to public events in Clemency may be ousted from the venue with no refund of admission.'

Nando chose to ignore my role in the fracas. I got off lightly. Maybe he couldn't be bothered with the extra burden of writing an extra report.

Drug Squad officers arrived at Duncan's farm during the week. Fortunately, not by helicopter, which would have frightened the horses.

Duncan and I explained in detail all that led to our suspicions about Murphy. We were relieved to hear Murphy had already been moved to more secure incarceration in the city. The officers noted the bruised and beaten faces of our trio of men.

"Looks like you've all been in a bun fight." one commented. I'm not sure if that was coincidental or if he'd read the local paper.

Sid made egg and lettuce sandwiches plus a big pot of tea and a batch of fresh scones as it looked like being a lengthy interrogation. Eventually we all had our statements recorded, witnessed and signed. Duncan asked if he was at liberty to leave for Ireland in the near future. My heart sank.

Advice was he probably could go overseas temporarily. To be officially confirmed. As the investigation was ongoing and inconclusive, we were unlikely to be needed as witnesses in any court hearing for several months. The officer suggested Duncan should take his short break sooner rather than later.

The officers seemed to really enjoy the morning tea. Sid had set the table with plates and cutlery, real butter, homemade fig jam and honey. Between munching scones, an officer mentioned rewards, saying any person who contributed greatly to the successful completion of a case might be eligible. That hope was pruned as he added rewards were rarely paid out so not to hold our breath.

All I could think of was Duncan going away to Ireland. I didn't want him to go. It had been wonderful having the company of my big Irishman friend. We didn't always agree but could argue with impunity, knowing any differences would be forgiven or laughed off, eventually.

Day by day I had denied a budding physical attraction for Duncan. If he got too close, I deliberately evaded him or started a silly argument to thwart his advances. At times I pushed him too far, sending him into a sulky mood. Sounds fickle, but I liked how we meshed as platonic friends. I didn't want to spoil it by acting on impulsive physical desires.

Duncan had never seriously propositioned me since that clumsy bear hug incident back at the seaside stables. Now, I wouldn't mind being kissed again by the hunky Irishman. I wanted him. His plans to leave for Ireland hurt so much I had to subdue my emotions.

While Fabio's urbanity and masterly control enthralled me to worship him, Duncan's rougher approach tantalised in an earthier way. Both men were special to me. Variety is the spice of life, after all.

My resolve to keep the relationship non-sexual with Duncan began to cave at the picnic races when he demanded holding onto my hand. That simple gesture had been a turn-on. It made me feel desirable. I'd felt proud to be his companion, noticing wishful glances from other women.

Duncan's handsomeness and impressive build stood out in a crowd. I began to wonder why I was holding back. Surely, we could remain friends even if the relationship developed into sexual intimacy. Desire was blossoming for my Irish best friend. I couldn't ignore it and had verged on doing something about it.

Duncan's plan to leave for faraway shores, across the sea to Ireland, frustrated my new romantic intentions and his prior hopes at the same time.

My Men

ACROSS THE SEA

Bad man Murphy had been moved to the prison infirmary. He was very ill with symptoms of drug withdrawal. Tests proved he had traces of crystal meth in his system, addicted to the drug commonly known as ice.

The crystal meth addiction somewhat explained Murphy's powerful aggression. The man had always bent towards violence according to Duncan, and the drug would only bolster his natural inclinations.

As Murphy's failing condition made the date of any court hearing even later, Duncan was advised he could take a longer trip to Ireland in the interim, if he so desired. There had been a lot to organise before he left. Irrationally I avoided Duncan, in a blue funk because he was leaving.

When the time came, I drove Duncan out to the main highway where he would meet a bus connection going to the international airport.

"Come back to me Duncan. I don't want to come looking for you."

"Would you do that?"

"Probably not. I get air sick." I lied.

The lump in my throat felt as big as Uluru. As the Greyhound Coach pulled up.

"Take care Dimity."
"You too Duncan."

Duncan travelled light. His one kit bag was stowed in the luggage compartment. The automatic coach doors whooshed shut. Then he was gone. There would soon be vast oceans and over 10,500 miles separating us. The distance sounded even longer in kilometers, being almost 16,900 kms.

I kept in touch with Sophia on Sundays at the bakery. My old friend said life was different and more interesting since I'd come to Clemency. The bakery owners said they'd never known such a surge in custom since employing me.

Surprisingly, many customers congratulated me on taking a stance against the hooligan Murphy at the picnic races. Several enthused that the food fight was the most fun they'd had in years.

The caterers had their losses covered by insurance and promised to be back bigger and better next year. Plans were to advertise their luncheon pavilion as: *Home of the Great Bun Fight.*

Unwittingly, within five minutes of residency, in the greater scheme of things, I attained the dubious honour of becoming part of local lore. So much for the quiet life.

Emails back and forth kept me up to date with how Fabio and his family fared in Germany. Fabio was able to rent a two-bedroom apartment for himself and Wolfgang.

"It is our bachelor pad." Fabio told me with no degree of shame over its advantages.

Wolfgang's mental journey from childhood had zoomed through the adolescent period. His therapist counted among those amazed at the swift progression. Fabio put it down to Wolfgang losing his virginity at long last.

Agneta stayed on with her ageing parents who wanted to spend time with their long-absent daughter and get to know Bean, their little granddaughter.

I guessed Fabio did not maintain any ongoing de facto relationship with Agneta, but it was not a topic I would ever broach with him.

Wolfgang's miracle recovery surprised everyone. Fabio continued telling the story:

"Wolfy takes great care over his appearance and hygiene now. His power of speech has fully returned. He is still fluent in three languages, but he doesn't talk much. I didn't expect to take a back seat to my little brother to be honest. However, we find ladies are very attracted to the tall silent types."

Fabio went on to say he had engaged in some private therapy sessions for himself, to talk about his personal hang ups.

"My doctor concludes my philandering nature is an escape from reality. She says I engage in promiscuous behaviour to evade responsibilities and unpleasant facts. So, at great expense I am told what I already know. Ha ha. At least my good doctor is a very attractive lady."

I held no expectations that Fabio would ever change his ways. I dealt with it philosophically.

"Fabio! You are a rogue."
"Perhaps I am not the only rogue. I hear from Aunt Sophie that you have been tossing buns at people Dimity. I find it hard to imagine. Could this bun tossing behaviour be true?"
"Totally untrue. It was actually traditional pudding made of sponge cake soaked in sherry with jelly, custard and whipped cream. There may have also been a few Marello cherries."

Fabio laughed saying if only he knew the real me during all those years we worked together. He said it wasn't until I ventured out for my escape to the country that he realised what he had missed out on.

"You granted all my wishes, Fabio, in that first wonderful night of passion we shared."
"Wishes? I think it had been just one. You wished for the lemon tree property."

"I more so wished for you Fabio. I'm glad you turned to me for comfort after the loss of Giorgio too. You can always come to me if you have the need. I love being with you and being fulfilled by you."

I enjoyed hearing Fabio groan with instant want. His emotion fuelled my imagination. Especially since Duncan chose to distance himself away to Ireland, when I really wanted him.

If we weren't on different continents, repeat performances would be organised with Fabio. I have needs. Fabio reverted to our office etiquette:

"We have unfinished business Miss Minto. I miss your caring nature. My good lady doctor is no match for you *il mio bellissimo amore*."

He had no compunction in confirming the involvement he enjoyed with his unethical lady doctor. He did not expect any jealousy from me, as he had none himself.

Interestingly, a diagnosis of mild autism was firmly rejected by Fabio. He told me of it, as an aside to be shared as an amusing outcome to his therapy. Yet the condition fitted the man.

"If you were here in Germany, I fear Wolfy would also be chasing you. Hmm. Who would you now prefer I wonder, me or my tall silent younger brother."

Fabio himself would always be my choice if it came to that contest. I am certain he knew it. Lock up your daughters came to mind with Fabio and Wolfgang at large and on the prowl.

Conversations with Fabio were diverting flirtations. I could never resist beautiful Fabio if he wanted me again, however fleeting that might be. I cherished his friendship, and his lovemaking transported me to seventh heaven. Secrecy added spice.

Yet, strangely, I no longer felt totally obsessed with Fabio. I blamed that on Duncan.

Fabio would never be satisfied with just one woman. Any expectation of winning his total fidelity paved a sure path to heartbreak. Nevertheless, he could always arouse my physical desire and my heartfelt compassion for his past.

Duncan represented my trusty constant. Fabio my rare exotic treat.

Duncan's possessive nature provided more security insofar as loyalty to one woman. I relished being openly displayed as his date at the picnic races, with no need to hide or pretend.

Once upon a time I never would have imagined wanting Duncan more than Fabio, but to my own surprise, my best friend, Duncan, had taken first place as the man I most yearned for now.

Somehow the planets had reshuffled in my universe.

Without a doubt the Irishman's absence made my heart grow fonder.

Home

IS WHERE THE HEART IS

Duncan stayed abroad for three whole months. Keeping a positive attitude despite missing the Irishman, became my next big challenge.

In the meantime, police exposed and shut down the drug trafficking operations on the river. Once the haul had been found in Gallo's boathouse, other disused boathouses were searched and found to hold similar stashes. Murphy's partner the lads had drubbed, eventually caved under questioning and informed on several others. All were wanted in other countries and faced years in prison. Various overseas authorities joined a queue to have a crack at them.

Missing Duncan, I turned to Fabio for more flirtatious chats online as a distraction. But no amount of kidding around with Fabio dispelled the empty desolation of missing Duncan. Just my luck. Vast oceans separated me from the two men I adored. I abhor self-pity but sank to feeling sorry for myself.

I couldn't let the animals suffer or let the lads down, so had to persist, hour by hour, day by day. Putting one foot in front of the other going about daily tasks seemed an uphill climb.

Nights were long and lonely. Pillows dampened by tears brought on by anguished dreams. At least I didn't resort to alcohol. Perhaps that would make a worthy addition to my virtue list, if I could bother to update it. Keeping that list seemed frivolous in my dispirited state.

Duncan's emails from Ireland were brief and never very newsy. He dutifully checked in now and then to ask if all was well with the horses and his spelling establishment.

Unfortunately, Duncan didn't ask personally after any of us except saying to let him know of any problems. His emails could have been in form letter style, with appropriate boxes ticked.

The lads and I supposed he must be having such a busy good time; we were obviously out of sight and out of mind. Sid, Nobby and I managed to keep everything operating efficiently. Perhaps Duncan might have returned earlier if there had been problems.

I resisted emailing questions to Duncan to extract information or touch on his private feelings. If he didn't want to relate personally, I must allow him that space.

The thought crossed my mind that Duncan might meet another girl like Lexie and never return. I lay awake at night trying not to go there, but it is where my thoughts inevitably fell into deep despair.

Mornings I dragged my weary body out of bed and forced myself to meet the demands of another busy day.

We didn't know when Duncan would return.

Sid, Nobby and I were grabbing a quick lunch on the farmhouse verandah when a rattling farm truck paused at the roadside stall.

A hitchhiker got out and stood rooted to the spot as the truck drove off in a cloud of dust and a lusty fart of exhaust fumes.

At first, we didn't recognise the gaunt bearded figure who alighted there, but Enzo and Shamus knew. It was Duncan. He dropped his kit bag in the dirt and knelt to greet the dogs.

"At last. The wayward traveller returns. About bloody time." Nobby remarked conversationally.

"I'da baked a cake if I'da knowed he was coming." Sid drawled.

The good old lads remained seated possibly so I could meet Duncan alone. I approached Duncan at the roadside. He hadn't taken a step. We stood facing off, neither of us sure how to play it. Finally I broke the impasse:

"Didn't they feed you over there?"

Duncan made no reply, but in the next moment, tears flowed unchecked to mingle in his rough beard. I said:

"You're crying."
"So are you."
"I am not." I sobbed.

We embraced at last. The dogs jumped around us in joyful exuberance.

"Kettles boiled." Sid yelled from the verandah.

We made our way together back to the farmhouse where Sid and Nobby greeted the weary traveller, slapping his back and telling him, truthfully, he looked fecking awful.

Duncan was exhausted for days after arriving home. Visiting his old stomping grounds in Ireland had not been a magic resolution to his concerns.

He'd visited places where he and his friends used to hang out but saw no one he knew. Seemed during the past twenty years, unsurprisingly, everyone had moved on, gotten married, settled down or just grew out of that era.

The cosy pub he'd spent many a Saturday night at with Lexie had been updated out of recognition. It was now a thumping loud teen disco joint with blinding strobe lights.

There were older vaguely familiar faces at the racecourses. He'd touched base with a few who were naturally friendly though he wasn't sure if they could actually place him after so many years. He supposed they would discuss him later and might recall events.

No one accosted him as Murphy had in Australia. Murphy had lied just to make Duncan think people saw his absence as cowardice and that they talked about him still.

The family plot where Lexie lay had her parents' graves added during Duncan's absence. They had passed away separately within the past ten years. At least he didn't have to face them, as he had intended, but dreaded.

Duncan had gone from one place to another. The fatal accident that killed his girlfriend was scarcely remembered if at all. Only Duncan's parents remembered it well. He was sorely reminded of how his past bad behaviour had disappointed his mother and father. As their only child, Duncan had broken their hearts and it could not be undone.

"They made me welcome, but I felt like the proverbial bad penny turning up on their doorstep. Neighbours' curtains twitched when I got out of the taxi so nothing ever changes in that street."

All the sad story of Duncan's journey back home to the Emerald Isle came out over several days as the four of us shared meals at the farmhouse. There was nothing to do but listen and hear him out. The lads and I recognised his need to purge what he'd been through.

"Did you stay with your Ma and Pa?" Sid asked.

"No Sid. I did not. I'd taken a room at a boarding house so I didn't impose too much on their hospitality. Not that they offered me a bed or even asked where I was staying. I felt like a stranger when Mam got out the best china tea set. If only they'd just given me a chipped mug and said, 'oh well shite happens boyo'. But the visit was so stiff and cold, and I couldn't break the ice. I just wanted to get out of there."

I understood how the formal visit must have felt for Duncan.

"That sounds harsh." Nobby commiserated.

"Yeah. Harsh is the word. So I soon left the boarding house as well. It was too depressing. I had no direction or plan I just wanted to get away. I went hiking anywhere I could think of with wide open spaces. I had grown used to a wide sky and missed Australia. I stayed in backpacker joints mostly. A few times in isolated barns. Once I got caught out in bad weather and shared a tent with some friendly Asians on a camping holiday. I guess they took pity on me."

"When we heard so little from you, we all imagined you must be having a whale of a time."

"Well I emailed when I could but places to charge my phone were few and far between."

"We're all just happy to have you home safe and sound."

"This is my real home. I couldn't relate to anything or anyone in Ireland anymore."

That gladdened my heart, ever thankful Duncan wanted to stay in Australia and hadn't met another Lexie in Ireland.

My planets aligned. The moon was in the seventh house. All was well in my universe.

Cruising

THE HIGH COUNTRY

Sid and Nobby were off on a sailing cruise.

Duncan recovered back to his normal cheery self and addressed his obligations. He shouted Sid and Nobby on a three weeks island cruise as thanks for all the extra work they'd done while he was in Ireland.

The lads went to town buying colourful Hawaiian shirts and board shorts to wear on deck.

"I love horses." Nobby said "But I don't mind a break from them."

"Same." Sid admitted. "I could use a breath of sea air myself."

"Just look out for all those ardent ladies after a shipboard romance." Duncan warned.

"Guess you would know all about that Duncan." I said.

Duncan just grinned his old cheeky grin. Glad he seemed over his unhappy home trip. Between the two of us, Duncan and I, we could manage the spelling facility in the absence of the lads. Only a few racehorse boarders were being stabled and only at night. Most had been let down from racing condition gradually. They could be allowed liberty in the broad grassy paddocks with just two-sided shelters and windbreaks for shade and weather protection.

Duncan and I breezed through our work most days so we could spend quality time together. Just the two of us as best friends working out our shifting relationship. Sometimes we rode trails on Nero and Piper but avoided the boathouse area. Instead, we'd pack lunch and head out through the bush, climbing to open highland plateaus.

In that high country, great eagles soared aloft looking for unwary hares and other food animals. The magnificent birds of prey with wingspans over 2.5 metres (over 8 feet) could easily pick up a lamb in their strong talons. A Wedge-tailed Eagle once took a full-grown whippet from a paddock. True story. She miraculously escaped and limped home within a few days. Covered in lacerations, she may have been dropped from a great height or from a lofty nest. No one knew what horrors that tough little whippet endured, only that she must have fought hard for her life in order to survive.

Eagles wouldn't bother us in a group as we were. Enzo and Shamus ran beside us. The dogs were obedient to the point they could be called to heel if necessary. The whippet and border collie ran full pelt, bright eyed with ears flat back and shiny coats rippling, the sight of them a precious memory.

Returning from the high-country rides just before sundown, we'd all be happily tired out. With our respective evening duties to be completed before retiring, Duncan would return to his stables, and I to my lemon tree house.

Wet Dogs

WE LIED

While the old lads were away cruising, Duncan and I worked our properties either singly or together. Some tasks were easier done with both of us.

One morning, we decided to run out new electric fence cable, each on our land, working either side of the dividing fence.

Duncan had something on his mind and had begun behaving quite out of character, sulky and taciturn.

Peeved, I let the big dummy-spitter simmer. His change of attitude upset me. Since returning from Ireland and up until lately, he'd been so nice and amiable.

Duncan struggled with cutting the cable and skinned his knuckles when the pliers slipped.

"Dammit. I wish I could find my good penknife." he cursed.

"Is that all?"

"All? It was my grandfather's. I can't believe I could have lost it."

I knew he valued that pearl handled scout knife, but I wouldn't dignify his churlishness by catering to his bad temper.

"Well, I haven't got the bloody thing." I retorted.

"Did I say you did?"

"Maybe you left it in Ireland."

"No. I didn't take it to Ireland. Airport security would confiscate knives."

I knew I'd made a daft suggestion but said it anyway. On top of that, rain seemed imminent. A few heavy splatters announced a torrential downpour. Frustrated, Duncan abruptly downed tools. The job wouldn't be finished this day.

"I've been thinking." he said at last.

"Yeah, thought I smelt something burning."

I tried to kid him out of his mood. He didn't laugh.

"OK. Spit it out Duncan. What's eating you?"

"That thing you said you did."

"What thing?" I played dumb but knew where this was going.

"With the Italian guy. The one who looks like Kevin Costner."

"Paul Newman."

"So you do know what I'm getting at Dimity."

"I have an inkling."

"So. Did you really do what you said?"

Geez...this again? Duncan's jealous streak became too tiresome. I didn't owe him my life story. He could just like it or lump it. In anger, I stuck it to him well and truly:

"Did I really have a one-night-stand with that delectable Italian stallion and we fucked our brains out all night? Yep. Furthermore, it was truly the best night of my life. I still dream about it. Mmm Mmm. He was absolutely delicious. Totally unforgettable. What a lover. A true maestro."

I stuck my finger in my mouth, sucked it in and out, and licked my lips. I couldn't spell it out better than that. Not that Duncan deserved any explanation, but I hoped he got some kicks out of my hotter more descriptive version. Of course, I wouldn't mention the years I'd craved having Fabio, nor that the lemon tree house indelibly linked me to him.

Duncan's expression teetered between green eyed envy and total scepticism. I don't know why he even asked. I stared him down.

"Yeah right. I'm calling bull. You'd never do that."
"Whatever gives you that idea? Don't you think I'm capable of it?"
"You're too proper. Too prissy. Proper and prissy that's you Miss Minto."

I hoped my cunning smile looked suitably enigmatic just to irritate and further confuse him. I'd given him food for thought that's for sure. He tried to read me. Our emotions were high for different reasons.

Rain teemed down harder than ever. The dogs scarpered back to the house. Duncan and I faced off regardless, becoming sodden to the skin. I felt the chill of water trickling down my back and into my pants. This was too stupid. I put a stop to it.

"Race you back to my place." I challenged.

I do love a race. It appeals to my competitive streak. Plus, I was confident of winning because Duncan was on the wrong side of the fence. Thing is, his legs are longer than mine.

"That's cheating." I yelled as he easily vaulted a gate into my place.

We arrived laughing at our own ridiculous irresponsible childishness, lobbing up cold soaking wet at the same time into my cosy kitchen.

The room was warmed by the wood burning stove, its ashes still hot from the night before as the dogs slept on shared bedding in front of the warmth.

Duncan opened the flue and added more wood while I refilled the big kettle.

"Brrr. I love rain. It's so good to get out of."

Duncan shucked off his sopping wet shirt. He basked bare-chested in front of the glowing flames rising in the stove.

Despite having known Duncan for a few years, I had never seen him without a shirt.

Half naked, the Irishman's fit and toned body was stunning. His wet blue jeans clung like a second skin. Catching me looking, he broke into his confident trademark grin.

"You're admiring my god-like form aren't you."

"Get over yourself Duncan. I was only thinking you'll catch your death standing about in those cold clammy jeans."

"Point taken."

He began to unbuckle his belt, a move intended to bother me. I dead panned the bland face I had practised for years in the office, hiding my true feelings for Fabio. Duncan ogled my body trying to chink my icy composure.

"The wet t-shirt look suits you." he leered suggestively.

To my great annoyance I felt a hot blush rise and my nipples harden. Duncan laughed triumphantly. He had called me too proper and too prissy. How judgemental. How wrong. I'd show him.

My competitive streak emboldened me to prove a point, plus I might dazzle him at the same time. Duncan could eat his heart out once he got an eyeful of what my Italian one-night-stand might have enjoyed, if my story were true. Serves Duncan right for making it an ongoing issue and prodding me about my private life.

My wet cotton shirt and thin lacy bra had become so transparent I might as well be naked anyway. Slowly and deliberately, I peeled it all off. I watched with satisfaction as his eyes adored me.

Coolly I ignored his avid interest. I prepared to bask half naked in front of the stove, as he had done. Just to warm my goose bumps, mind, but I really wanted his admiration.

I waited to hear him utter some amazed or romantic adjective in awe of my naked breasts. I suspected Fabio counted them as my best feature.

Perhaps Duncan might say words like magnificent, beautiful, awesome, creamy or luscious. But NO. He said:

"You smell like a wet dog."

The mongrel.

"That will be Shamus and Enzo under the table."

I replied matter-of-factly. Duncan stepped closer to look over my shoulder.

"So it is. There they are. The little devils."

A wet dog indeed! His unflattering comments were purposely designed to rattle me. He just loved to get my goat.

"You're always going to tease me aren't you, Duncan."

"Just till you're ready." he winked.

Two can play at that game. I strove to shock him. I touched myself lewdly and licked my lips suggestively with a few humping motions thrown in for good measure. His open-mouthed expression was priceless. He hadn't expected that rude and improper response.

"I'm ready now Duncan. Ooh. Ah. More than ready in fact." I crooned.

My overacting was so hammy and such an obvious put on, I expected him to laugh out loud. But he took it another way:

"Babe. Oh wow. I love a good neighbour."

Duncan gasped in a voice gone all husky and sexy. My teasing ploy backfired. I became inflamed by Duncan's keen reaction. We were about to move our neighbourly status up a notch.

He gathered me in, so our bare chests met skin on skin. This was the turning point I'd both feared and longed for. Wide smiles on both our faces made our kisses awkward.

Duncan tried another tack by tracking his kisses lower. This was moving as fast as that raging river. I needed to qualify it:

"Wait. There has to be some ground rules. Ok?"
"Sure. Ground rules. Bed rules. Kitchen table rules. I'm easy."
"You forgot futon."
"No. I didn't."

Fielding Duncan's speedy reaction and our mutual intentions was like trying to slow an avalanche. But I did try to be sensible:

"Wait. Slow down. No false pretences Duncan. I am so very in lust with you. Doesn't mean this has to change our friendship. It's just sex. I'm not in love."
"I beg to differ Dim-ity. You're just slow on the uptake."

My denial faded as he took control. He cupped my breasts, lifting them and kissing my nipples. He sucked hungrily on one side then the other. His warm mouth was the most delicious sensation in the world. My knees buckled. He was ready with a supporting arm about my back anticipating the effect he fully expected.

"Does that hurt?"

He asked but didn't stop, knowing his rhetorical question was unnecessary.

Duncan had honed his skills over the years, and very likely practised with many partners. No innocent amateur, he proved adept and confident in his seduction technique.

I felt certain he hadn't had another woman since he'd moved in next door, which probably accounted for his mood swings. I was curious to learn more of his expertise and didn't have to wait for long.

Duncan worked my damp jeans down. I kicked them off, caring not where they landed. We made it to my bedroom, quickly shedding our remaining clothes in a fever of mutual arousal.

When it comes to afternoon delight, there's a lot to be said for a sturdy old-fashioned bed and a hulking great sex-starved Irishman.

Admittedly by then, I was beyond caring if Duncan was my best friend or just some random pick up. I was so lost in our present delirium.

As evening drew in, animals had to be fed and attended. I cursed that the lads were away on their cruise so no one else could do the work. Duncan rolled off my bed loathe to leave, but duty called. No rest for the wicked.

Running late with much to get done without the lads to help, he cursed not being able to find his boxer shorts. He looked under the covers, under the bed and under the pillows.

"Bugger blast and damn it all."
"Please don't go all romantic on me now Duncan."

It was fun watching him search stark naked yet so completely uninhibited. I stretched luxuriously unbothered with his missing boxer shorts for I knew where they were. He blamed Shamus though he really loved the little whippet.

"I bet that spoilt rotten hound dog of yours has taken my under daks."
"Bet he hasn't."

I could see the truant pair of underwear hanging from a curtain rod where Duncan had pitched them in lustful desperation earlier.

"If Shamus hasn't taken them...I'll...I'll bloody well kiss him on the freckle."

Hearing his name, my dear little whippet wandered in from the kitchen.

"Well here he is, all ready for your promised kiss. Pucker up big boy."

I pointed to the curtain rod and laughed till tears came to my eyes. Duncan retrieved and donned his underwear. His face red. He didn't share my mirth.

"Anyway, I lied." he said.
"That's ok. So did I."

I would let him wonder what I lied about but I vowed to keep my secrets. Duncan dressed quickly and left in a bit of a huff. Talk about an anti-climax. His swift and bad-tempered departure left me feeling disposable, crushed and wrinkled like the bed sheets.

Bedding Duncan at long last had been absolute bliss and amply satisfying. Our inevitable connection should have been superbly liberating. A shame, in the circumstances, Duncan had promptly gone home, without a sweet word or kiss goodbye for me. The spoilsport.

I lay on my lonely bed reminded of Fabio's lightning departure to feed his cat after our first night of passion in the city. I don't know what I expected but had not foreseen a repeat of that let down with Duncan.

Seeking a cool drink, I went to the fridge only to find it was on the blink. That was all I needed to dissolve into tears. It seemed a sign of reprisal for enjoying the sexy afternoon. I couldn't win a trick at a kids' party.

Cursing my luck with men I stepped under a hot shower and soaped away all traces of Duncan's lovemaking. Damn him.

It would be difficult to rewind our rocky relationship back to pre-sex status, but I resolved to try.

Fridge Row

RAIL ROADED

After dark, Duncan returned to my house, offering a ridiculous little posy of flowers of mostly flowering weeds and possibly some nettles.

His dark hair glistened wet from his shower and a spicy aroma of aftershave added to his appeal. The Irishman's emerald-green eyes were full of apology and pleading. He asked ruefully:

"Babe. I'm sorry. Do you still love me?"
"Don't recall ever saying I did." I grumped.

He digested that for a moment before saying:

"Come for dinner at my place and I'll give you another chance."

I went. Free dinner after all. Don't knock it. He had heated up a freezer meal. Sid probably precooked it before going on holidays. It was rather burnt but might have once been cheesy macaroni.

Duncan sliced ripe red tomatoes and tossed them with leafy green lettuce and vinaigrette. There were candles and wine glasses set out on a clean tablecloth and paper towels folded into triangles under the cutlery. He filled the wine glasses with cold beer. The man was really pushing out the boat for me. The meal wasn't too bad. I don't mind the brown burned crusty bits.

Duncan grinned confidently at the end of the meal.

"Your place or mine?"

"That's subtle and rather presumptuous Duncan."

My prissy Miss Minto side came to the fore, just when I thought I'd lost it forever.

"Hey. You're the one who stipulated no false pretences Dimity. Just say if you don't want more of my neighbourly friendliness."

"I wouldn't want to take you for granted." I parried.

"Please take me for granted Dimity. Or any other way."

That was him being romantic. He looked so earnest and hopeful, I melted like butter in the hot sun. Bet he rehearses that facial expression in front of a mirror. So much for my earlier resolve. It lasted maybe two hours tops.

Duncan gathered me into his strong embrace. The dish washing could wait until morning.

Funny how I never knew what I really wanted until I got it. Despite our energetic afternoon of first-time sex with each other, I fervently wanted to be with Duncan again. We spent all night together in his king-sized bed, exploring each other, making leisurely love, sleeping off and on.

I woke to the ornate wallpaper of cherubs blowing trumpets amongst fluffy clouds. Duncan liked the décor and had no plans to change it. He brought me a nice hot cup of tea, to drink propped up on pillows in bed. I could stand this. What a man.

"Any plans for today?" he asked.

"Nothing great. My fridge is on the blink. I'll have to see about getting a repairman."

"No worries. It's still under warranty. I have the receipt in a box somewhere. The electrical store in Clemency will replace it."

"What? What the hell?"

That was news to me.

"Wait just a cotton-picking minute my friend. You didn't buy my 'fridge. Or did you?"

"Who did you think? The fairy godmother?"

No. There was nothing remotely fairy-like about Fabio. I didn't say that of course.

The revelation that Duncan bought my 'fridge marked the moment our initial honeymoon period ended.

"Geez Duncan. I thought you said you didn't do charity."

He clocked my discontent and gave an ill-advised reply:

"I don't do charity Dimity. I bought the 'fridge, you bought the bed."

"Oh! I see! Is that how it works? You make it sound as if it were a done deal that you'd get into my bed. Like you planned it that way."

He had the grace to look sheepish and tried to cover up with his usual malarkey:

"Well since you chased me hard enough, I thought I'd make it easy for you."

"Get over yourself Duncan. I mean it."

Cripes. Since Duncan was responsible for buying the sparkling new fridge in the lemon tree house, maybe he also fixed the front staircase and cleaned everything else up before I moved in.

I'm sure the old people would have helped but it had entailed an enormous amount of work.

Bugger. I probably owed Duncan big time. I had to reassess my loyalties. Duncan not Fabio had been my main benefactor. The thing is, I had so wanted it to be darling Fabio.

Don't get me wrong, I loved that the house had been so welcoming to move into. The new refrigerator, icing on the cake. Not to mention the lovely lemon tree Duncan delivered and helped plant. He did all the hard work. And then there was the whippet puppy of course.

Duncan even picked out and installed the great big bed we recently exploited in our fury of lust. He must have seen his plans falling nicely into place.

I didn't like feeling like an ingrate after my best friend Irishman had gone to so much trouble.

Sadly, the truth was: I did feel rail-roaded. It felt smutty like being a bought woman. Accustomed to steering my own outcomes, I resented having someone else assuming control.

Rather than fall fully smitten into his strong welcoming arms, I revised the situation. I swung my feet off the bed and assessed Duncan anew. I tried to read his thoughts. He soon came up with one.

"One thing bothers me." Duncan began.

"Just one thing? Talk about luck of the Irish."

"OK. I gave you that one. But I've just wondered, when you said you lied. What exactly was that about?"

Got to him. Knew it would.

"What do you think?"

"Could be you lied about that Italian guy?"

Holy Mother, he just couldn't let it go. The irksome persistent cuss.

"Do you still see him?"

"He will always be a dear friend." True.

I wasn't going to assuage Duncan's jealousy by letting him know Fabio was now living in Germany.

"You had the best night of your life with this Kevin Costner guy and that's it?"

I gave him a flippant reply:

"My personal love life is none of your business Duncan. But I can frankly assure you in all truth, cross my heart, I have never had a one-night-stand with Kevin Costner." *(Mores the pity)*.

My frivolous answer didn't satisfy Duncan the nosy parker.

"Thinking you're avoiding the question Dimity."

Grrrr. Did he have no idea? He tread dangerously on thin ice. Primed by new resentment that Duncan assumed too much control, I saw red.

"Avoiding the question? Do you actually consider that I owe you an answer? Just because you bloody well bought the fridge, cleaned the house, got the bed, delivered Nero, gave me a dog that I love by the way, and everything else?"

Duncan was taken aback. He reacted with his own angry retort.

"Oh. I get it." he shouted. "You just can't stand being so damn loved can you Dimity. It would cut into your independence. You might have to bend your strict rules."

"Oh! How dare you judge me! Go to hell Duncan."

I dressed in haste shoving my underwear in pockets and left without even putting my teacup in the sink. It was our first big row. I gathered what shreds of self-respect I could muster and flounced off home.

Stamping into my kitchen, I noticed my damp jeans poking out from behind the refrigerator. They seemed to mock me from where I'd hurled them with lewd abandon yesterday. Only yesterday. How time flies when I'm having fun.

The far-flung pair of jeans had knocked the electric plug out. So at least the fridge wasn't buggered. It began to hum nicely again once plugged back in. I raged around the house doing housework, cleaning, changing sheets, washing laundry, all the while fuming over the row with Duncan.

By nightfall my temper began to cool. Yes, I am a silly fickle woman at times. I blame Duncan.

The Bill

THE ACCOUNT

During the night, I hate to say it but I began to see Duncan's side of the argument and feel bad about my churlish reaction. He had done so much for me. His big Irish heart was in the right place, and I had hurt him. No wonder Duncan became so upset.

My failing was I wanted some of the good things at the lemon tree house to have been given to me by Fabio. Not that he owed me either. But I had credited Fabio with buying the new fridge and had held the idea fondly to my heart.

Duncan had only met my Latin lover once. He observed me with Fabio at Giorgio's wake and sussed there might be some history between us.

I fell for Fabio long before I met Duncan, so the Irishman had no right to jealousy. I valued my shared secrets with Fabio and saw no reason to justify myself to Duncan or anyone else. Nor did I feel unfaithful to Fabio by having Duncan. Fabio and I did not have that kind of relationship. Admittedly, my love life was complicated.

Since I told Duncan my one-night-stand story in anger, he initially suspected I invented it to tease him. Now that he had experienced just how shamelessly wanton I could be, he must view the story as plausible. Seeing I was not the wilting wallflower waiting to be picked off must be sticking in his craw. Not my fault. I hadn't asked for so much help from Duncan and apart from the gift puppy, had always offered to pay.

Still, I recognised that Duncan had always been more than generous towards me. To be fair, I could see it from his perspective.

Selfishly, I knew the situation with Duncan as my neighbour had ideal benefits and I did not want to burn any bridges. I never claimed to be an angel.

With the lads away cruising, I couldn't shirk helping Duncan with the morning horse work. I endeavoured to be nice to him. I would be really, really nice. I would. Sadly, my kinder second thoughts didn't last long.

Despite my diligent early arrival, Duncan was already hard at work, toiling away. He didn't acknowledge my presence, so I didn't say hello good morning how's your temper today you great big frigging sulking oaf. Duncan just brought out the worst in me.

For some reason Duncan decided it was a good day to clean out the stables and replace all the bedding. It was a huge undertaking, shovelling it all out and barrowing the waste to a steaming compost heap behind the vegetable gardens then hauling the new stuff in. It was totally unnecessary to do it all on his own. The job could wait for the lads to return in less than a week. I went about doing light daily tasks without paying his huffiness any attention.

Half an hour in, I noticed Duncan had shed his shirt and was naked from the waist up. His muscles rippled as he strained to cart the heavy loads. Duncan's body looked awesome, though his exhibitionism seemed too obvious. The sun was out, but a cool breeze streamed in and around the stables.

If Duncan thought I'd be mesmerised by his fabulous physique and fall begging at his feet, he had another 'think' coming. Ha ha.

I deliberately turned my back on him, sat on the lawn and played with the dogs in the lukewarm sunshine, letting Duncan know his ruse didn't affect me. My disinterest paid off when he responded in a fit of pique.

"Well if you're not going to help you might as well go home." Duncan growled.

I had gotten to him, but he had gotten to me at the same time. I riled up.

"Not help? Can I remind you I am not in your employ Duncan. Oh, that's right, you bought me with all your favours and gifts. How could I forget."

"OK. If it makes you feel any better, I'll send you a bill. In triplicate." he shouted.

"How will you price that then Duncan? By the number of orgasms?"

"You are bloody fucking impossible Dimity."

"Enjoy your day, Duncan."

Destined to forever stalk off in a dark mood after words with the Irishman, it confirmed my initial gut feeling that sex with Duncan would spoil our relationship. It was a bad idea from the start. I knew it, but I did it anyway. Idiot! Slave to my own desires.

Intimacy removed self-censorship escalating our emotions and giving free rein to run off at the mouth and say too much that could never be unsaid.   I blamed giving in to him when we had been cruising along famously just as friends. Knowing my major part in the seduction didn't make it any better. He drove me mad.

I had nowhere to go but decided to drive out as if I did. Duncan would see my car go past. Let him stew. I hoped he thought I was meeting with my Italian guy since he was unaware Fabio had gone to Germany. I bet Duncan couldn't even recall Fabio's name, he thought of him as Kevin Costner. *If only.*

Anyway, I drove into Clemency and walked around a park. I wasn't dressed for town so avoided seeing people. This was boring and a stupid waste of time. I drove back home without speaking to anyone or buying anything. Halfway home I kicked myself for not getting myself an ice-cream cone in town or even some chocolate for later. It was going to be a night for comfort food.

Duncan's ute was parked in the usual spot, so he hadn't come looking for me. As if he would.

Another lonely night was faced wondering how this thing with Duncan had gone so wrong. No amount of pillow thumping, tossing and turning enabled sleep.

Around eleven o'clock that restless night, I decided to go next door and continue discussions with Duncan. At least I could show him I wouldn't back down or that I didn't hold grudges for long, depending on the outcome.

The dogs were cosily curled in front of the warm stove in my kitchen. I told them to stay. No problems they seemed to say. They just grunted and closed their sleepy eyes again.

The night had grown cold. I strode through a foggy shroud of icy mist along the lane to Duncan's farmhouse. A weatherproof parka worn over my yellow polka dotted purple ski pyjamas kept me from freezing.

My boots echoed hollowly on Duncan's timber floored verandah. I didn't knock. Surely, he would have heard me thudding around, but he didn't come out to meet me. The bloody big sour puss.

I tried the kitchen door and found it unlocked. Huh. Maybe he expected me. Maybe he even hoped I would turn up. Bet he did too. Unless he always left it unlocked. I wouldn't be surprised if he did.

Regardless, I left my boots outside, silently pushed the door open and entered the house like a cat burglar. Thankfully it was much warmer inside but my hands were chilled. I hung my dewy damp parka over a kitchen chair and crept barefoot towards Duncan's bedroom. Creaking floorboards announced my progress through the old farmhouse. Only a very deep sleeper would not be alerted.

A fire glowed in Duncan's bedroom fireplace emitting a golden light. I could see he lay on his side, faced away from the doorway. He couldn't possibly be asleep. Reckon he was playing possum. How childish. My hands still felt blue with cold. Good. I slid into his bed under the doona and put my freezing hands on his lovely warm naked back. He rolled over in record time.

"Aaarghle!" he yodelled like a cowboy. "Feck! Did you have to do that Dimity? Your hands are like ice."

"How did you know it was me?"

"I'm psychic."

"Oh dear. Sorry. I thought my cool hands would feel nice and bracing."

"No you did not Dimity. And that's a horrible way to wake someone from a deep sleep."

I had to smile. He was so transparent.

"Deep sleep was it? Geez. You might have been ravished by some complete stranger sneaking into your bed since you are such a deep sleeper."

"I can only wish." he sulked lamely.

Ignoring his disgruntled attitude, I snuggled against his warmth, kindly placing my cold hands between my fleecy pyjama clad thighs to warm up. He didn't make any move of encouragement. The big sook. I felt absolutely sure he was stringing it out. No doubt he felt warranted in having me chase after him for a change.

"By the way I got the fridge going." I said.

"Bet it was unplugged. You just plugged it back in didn't you."

Perhaps he was psychic.

"Maybe."

"What are you really doing here." he demanded.

"Paying a neighbourly visit."

"Why?"

"I want to have sex with you."

That stymied him for a moment.

"Don't beat about the bush Dimity. Say what you mean."

"I believe that's my line. And I mean what I say."

"What if I don't want to have sex with you." he growled.

"You do."

"How would you know."

"That tent pole you've got propping up the doona is a clue Duncan. That sucker could hold up the lunch marquee at the picnic races."

He coughed a bit. Maybe he had something caught in his throat.

"Are you just along for the ride Dimity?"

"Now there's an idea."

"Seems I've been knocking myself out like a mug and everything I've done to woo you has only made you resent me."

"No. Well yes."

"Make up your mind."

"OK. I did resent you for a split second. But I'm over it. Duncan, I'm flattered and very grateful for all you've done for me. I know I've reacted badly. I've thought about it for hours. I get that you've done so much for me because you actually really love me. Sorry I have been so insensitive."

I considered that an excellent apology for my rude behaviour. He didn't. I had to spoon feed the cry-baby a bit more.

"Insensitive. That's one way to describe it." he brooded.

"You must think me an utter bitch."

"Must I? OK if you insist. And by the way I never said I loved you Dimity."

"Oho. Yes you did. Quote: "you can't stand being so damn loved.""

"That was hypothetical."

"Was not."

I crept a warmed hand over his taut naked belly. The room was feeling toasty warm with the fire glowing in the grate and two of us in the bed. Duncan's breathing quickened but he wasn't quite finished with his grump fest.

"Anyway, you're the one who doesn't want love to come into it. You said you're only in lust with me. You made damn sure to tell me you're not in love. I know you get off on the one-night-stand-lets-still-be-friends thing. I assumed you just wanted a go for the good fun..."

"And it was great fun Duncan."

"... then you get all uppity about it. Even though it was your own fecking rules. You blow hot and cold Dimity. I just don't know from one minute to the next where I stand."

He was right about my attempt at ground rules. I could only think of one answer.

"Changed my mind. Woman's prerogative you know."
"Geez Dimity you drive me crazy. Why are you so cruel? Did you even have to mention your one-night-stand?"
"You goaded me. You know you did. You think a woman can't enjoy a romp in the hay occasionally? Betting you've had quite a few short term adventures in your time Duncan."

He veered off answering that one. Of course. One rule for men another for women.

"Do you get a kick out of making me feel jealous?" he asked.
"It's mildly amusing. You're so easy."
"And that's my line. So what's your alleged one only lie?"
"I do love you. You great flaming hulking bloody idiot of a stupid man."
"Now you're just trying to sweet-talk me." he said.

It wasn't exactly a lie as such, since I was sort of in love with him. At least I'd love to remain friends and have sex with him. Sooner the better.

"Can't it be possible to be in love and in lust at the same time as being best friends? I'd like to have it all with you Duncan."

His sigh sounded more exasperated than pleased. A moment ticked by before he growled a few four-letter words under his breath and mentioned my name in vain with them.

"Aren't you hot in those lurid pyjamas?"
"I am hotting up now that you mention it."

I shed the hot PJs, straddled his waist before he changed his mind, and tentatively pressed my mouth to his lips. He didn't object too strongly. I ran my hands through his hair, kissed his ears, nibbled his earlobes and gently stroked his nipples.

"Ahh Jesus fecking Christ Dimity. I hate you."
"How much. Show me."

I ran my fingers up the rigid length of the part that had a mind of its own.

"Mmm. This much hey? Can this beauty be for me since you hate me so?"
"I think you're toying with me."
"I am. Do you want to play or not?"
"Well. Suppose I might as well. Since you're here now anyway disturbing my sleep."

I settled slowly onto his inviting erection. His hands seemed to go unbidden to my breasts. Writhing to accommodate Duncan's engorged size sped his undoing. He couldn't wait.

Duncan placed his big strong hands on my hips, holding me down hard, as he orchestrated how he wanted it. Duncan yodelled again, this time in ecstasy as he nailed it home.

He really was getting that cowboy thing down pat, but I must take care not to voice every single thought that comes into my head. Be a shame to suppress his spontaneity.

Triumph felt vaguely predatory as Duncan's release shuddered in wave after thrilling wave. All too soon my throbbing response sucked the life out of that whopper.

I wasn't done and he knew it. Duncan flung me onto my back, and none too gently forced my legs apart. His tongue flickered over my most sensitive swollen parts. My fingers clutched his hair. I didn't rip any out by the roots, but it must have been a near thing. Transported to exquisite pleasure my body bucked involuntarily. That brought out the latent soprano in me. Perhaps we could form a duet.

Afterwards, cooling off, Duncan gently nestled my face against his shoulder, rubbed my back and kissed the top of my head. I had tamed the beast in him to my own satisfaction.

"Babe. Are you OK?" he asked. "Sorry if I got a bit rough."
"Turns out I adore a bit of rough."
"I love a woman who knows what she wants."
"I love a man who can deliver."

We fell into a deep sleep, spooned together. This shared time in the afterglow of sex was a rare luxury for me and preferable to having the man bolt for home half dressed in a hurry.

Waking at dawn to the glorious notes of magpies chorusing, Duncan and I were at peace with each other, for the time being. It would be naive to imagine we would never have another argument or falling out. Duncan made a robust sparring partner on many levels.

My big Irishman Duncan brought a nice cup of tea to me again as I contemplated the musical cupids on the bedroom wallpaper. Or cherubs. Whatever.

"So, what's the deal?" he dared to ask. What a brave man.

"Play it by ear?" I suggested. No pun intended regarding my hair clutching performance.

"I don't want this to be another root and run." he said seriously.

"That's a crude way of putting it."

Not sure if he meant another root and run by me, or if he alluded to my questionable one-night-stand with Fabio. It would be hypocritical to pretend I cared either way. I am truly no angel believe it or not.

Duncan could never be certain if that one-night-stand really happened, or had it been just a taunt. He seemed to construe his own version as an educated guess based on probability.

I would never tell of my obsessive love for Fabio and could not expect Duncan's sympathy: That first night of passion at my city unit, just another dalliance for Fabio, had been my private heartache, however sweetened with winning *Albero di Limone*.

After Giorgio died, when Fabio came to me for comfort, my longing changed to tender empathy. I no longer felt subordinate to him. It was a type of closure on the prior enslavement I endured under his charisma.

Later, before Fabio left for Germany, apart from being wildly pleasurable for us both, the sex had been confirmation of our close and secret bond. We became equals. Fabio and I always had that as our own.

Playing my cards close to my chest, I wouldn't be volunteering any secrets to either man.

Never could I explain my complex relationship with Fabio to Duncan, who tended to see everything in black and white and allow jealousy to goad his moods.

On the other hand, I wouldn't have to explain my relationship with Duncan to Fabio. Fabio would understand that I entertained the Irishman as another lover.

I accepted the situation would always be transient with Fabio. We had separate lives. Despite having Duncan, I looked forward to being with Fabio again some day, however temporarily.

Fabio's influence limited my complete commitment to anyone else. Yet I keenly embraced being entertained with the available, delightfully playful Irishman, however pesky, contrary and green-eyed that good neighbour proved to be.

Awkwardly, Duncan wanted to know what the deal was, and I had to come up with a tactful answer. I hedged:

"What do you want this to be Duncan?"

"I know what I don't want it to be. As I said, I'm not a root and run man. I've bided my time waiting for you Dimity. This isn't a passing phase for me."

"I don't want to spend too many lonely nights either. We can be fun together Duncan. When the mood takes us."

He thought about this for a while, holding my gaze, but I couldn't read his expression.

"You seem to really enjoy sex Dimity. I thought you'd never come round."

"You don't know me."

"I'm learning." he said with a shrug.

"It doesn't have to be complicated, does it?" I asked.

"Truthfully, I'd like it to be easy between us. Whatever it takes. I don't want to squash your independence Dimity. But I want to be with you. You like no strings sex with me hey?"

"You know it. I love feeling wanted and sharing my pleasure with a trusted lover."

"I can do that for you. And you trust me?"

"You can Duncan. And I do. Also, I don't like going without for too long."

"I can definitely oblige with that." his green eyes twinkled above that cheeky grin I loved.

"Good. I love that you're so obliging."

"I am obliging, aren't I? You are a very lucky woman to have me as a neighbour Dimity." he kidded himself out of his serious mood.

"Get over yourself Duncan."

Bless him. Big ego. Big heart. I felt lucky.

Sophia

VAI CON DIO

Sunday at the bakery came around without the usual visit from Sophia. Instead, her group of friends drifted in late, to break some terribly sad news: Giorgio's widow had passed away. At least she went peacefully in her sleep.

The shock hit me hard and could not have been more unexpected. Sophia had seemed to be going so well and enjoying her easy retirement in the good village atmosphere.

"Sophia was usually the one to get us up and going on Sundays. When she didn't appear, we knocked on her door and became alarmed to get no answer."

"A woman from management opened the door with spare keys. Sophia lay in her bed as if she was sound asleep. But she had gone. The ambulance has already taken her away."

"Oh no. I can't believe it. This is so sudden when she was doing so well." I gasped.

"She missed Giorgio too much. We hope they are now together again."

I left the bakery early and drove around to the retirement village to ask more of management. I was told:

"Mrs. Gallo had next of kin listed as a Mr. Fabio Ricci. Her nephew."
"Has he been informed?"
"He has. Unfortunately, he had to be told over the phone because he is overseas."

Although it would be late at night in Germany, I phoned Fabio.

"Fabio. I am so sorry."
"Dimity, thank you for calling. It is hard to take in."
"For me too. Your Aunt Sophie seemed to be doing so well and enjoying her retirement."
"She thought a lot of you Dimity, always bringing fruits and eggs from the farm every Sunday. And I thank you for being so kind and for staying in touch with her."

I could tell he wept from the sound of his choked words. He said Wolfgang was asleep, but he would have to tell him in the morning and then phone Agneta as well. They were all part of the extended family.

"I thought a lot of Sophia too Fabio. Can I help with anything? The arrangements?"
"Thanks but I know what has to be done. It has not been that long since Uncle Gio passed. I will follow the same procedure, and I will be back in a few of days."
"Do you want to stay with me at the lemon tree house?"

"Thank you Dimity. But no. I will stay in town to organise it all. I hope to see you soon."

Sadness for Sophia mixed with my rising anticipation for seeing Fabio again. I drove home in a turmoil of emotions. Remembering Duncan also counted Sophia as a friend, I stopped by the spelling farm to break the sad news. He was busy working in the stables but took one look at my face and knew something bad had happened.

"What is it? What's wrong? Dimity my darling, tell me."

I think it was the first time Duncan used the darling endearment on me. He lay down his hay rake and opened his strong arms. I ran to him and lay my head on his broad chest. Duncan's comfort and care brought my tears to the fore. Sobbing I told him about poor old Sophia.

Duncan told Sid and Nobby we had lost an old friend this day. The lads tipped their caps off in respect and said not to worry they'd get on with the chores.

"You get that girl a strong cup of tea with a dash of whisky." Sid advised. "Thanks fellas. I will. Come on Dimity."

Duncan led me to the verandah. Memories flooded back of times I'd sat there with Sophia and Giorgio enjoying their hospitality and the time I ran down there in the night afraid of Wolfgang's intrusion. Then of watching them laugh together at Enzo playing with the new whippet pup. Coming full circle back to Shamus reminded me of how much I owed to Duncan. Maybe I should have held my tongue but in my emotional state I declared it:

"Duncan, I love you."

"I know." he replied briefly.

In the week preceding Sophia's funeral, I had my hair done again at Roberto's. Wanting something pretty and feminine to wear after the funeral I bought a couple of strappy floral sundresses with Fabio in mind, knowing he would have to stay for a while to wind up Sophia's estate.

Sophia's funeral and wake followed the same procedures as Giorgio's. Duncan acted as a pall bearer again, as did Fabio. The same Catholic priest presided. Fabio had come back to Australia alone. I was glad he did not bring the rest of his family. The church filled with many of Sophia's friends and distant family members, but Fabio was her only close relative in attendance.

Fabio looked for me in the church and asked if I might sit beside him during the service, so he would not be alone in the front pew. I held his hand as we sat together, and he openly wept his grief. My poor boy. My Fabio.

Giorgio's grave lay between Sophia's and Fiorella's. There was another space in the family plot. I didn't like to think of when that might be occupied or by whom.

Fabio did his solemn duty of greeting and thanking people at the wake.

Duncan stayed in the background but looked across to catch my eye as the background music segued into Beyond the Sea. I dropped my gaze, waiting keenly for Fabio to complete his obligations and get around to me.

Ultimately, Fabio searched for me and found where I sat at the bar with a glass of wine.

"Dimity. How good to see you again. Thank you for sitting with me in church." Fabio said.

"I am happy to do something for you. Will you be staying in Australia for long?"

"Perhaps I will stay for some weeks this time. I hope we can be together some more."

"I want that."

My knees already felt weak at the implication in his sultry Italian voice. We smiled together in quiet anticipation of the comfort we would share.

A few days later, I met with Fabio at Sophia's little retirement cottage. The place would be bequeathed to him as her next of kin.

"The management are allowing me to stay here for the time being." Fabio said. "It is easier at this time to do so."

Sherman Knickerbacker from the old firm had been putting a lot of work Fabio's way. Able to work remotely anywhere with internet access,

Fabio had his laptop on the table. He had already been working from the retirement cottage.

"I cannot drop everything unfortunately. With all the expenses you understand."

Fabio obviously juggled many balls in the air with his family management in Germany and his commitment to duty in Australia. I didn't want to talk business. My every breath awaited his invitation and willed Fabio to get to the main event. I felt a blush spread over my face. He saw and understood. Fabio smiled at last opening his arms in the welcome I craved.

"Vieni qui, mia cara."

I melted into his embrace. We went to the second bedroom. We did not want to sully or use Sophia's recently vacated main bedroom. The single bed proved adequate for our needs. And our needs were great. We joined eagerly reliving our past passionate encounters.

"Ah. Dimity. *Il mio angelo.*"

Fabio spoke softly and earnestly. How I loved when he spoke Italian to me.

Fabio said he was glad to take some extra time out from his family in Germany. Wolfgang's girlfriend had all but moved into their bachelor pad, making Fabio feel he was playing the gooseberry.

Sherman and Fabio were working on having the firm invest in the Clemency Retirement Village and hoped the complex business might be purchased outright. Fabio said if that happened, he would keep Sophia's apartment cottage as his own headquarters in Australia. He still owned the stone house but internet connection was inadequate out there.

"So Fabio, you will stay for a while?"

"A few weeks. I must return for Christmas and Bean's 4th birthday which is soon after that."

"I hope to visit you here some more in the few weeks ahead then."

"That is also my wish. *La mia bella* Dimity."

Fabio kissed my hand, and I remained hopelessly besotted.

I made the most of the glorious few weeks Fabio was available to me. I visited daily, rushing morning chores to get to him. I spent as much of the day as possible making love with Fabio before returning home to the lemon tree house for evening tasks.

On Fabio's last day before returning to Europe, he asked if we might meet at the stone house which was still boarded up after the drug bust.

He had no interest in going down to the riverside boat shed or anywhere near the river but wanted to check the old cottage. I parked close to the cottage behind Fabio's hire car.

The gardens had become very overgrown during the time of no occupancy at the old place. Other than that, everything else seemed completely isolated and untouched.

Fabio prised some boards from the door and we entered the stone house together. The interior badly needed airing. Fans were out of action since the power was turned off. I had never before seen inside the stone house.

Inside, the house seemed far more spacious than it appeared from the outside. Fabio showed me around:

"This used to be Wolfy's room. And this was Bean's. Agneta slept in here..."

He showed me a room with a queen-sized bed that had been Agneta's. I wondered if he had carried on his affair with Agneta on that bed. Of course he must have. I didn't ask. It was not my place to be jealous or question Fabio's actions. He would never question mine.

Duncan came unbidden to my mind as I thought about that. Of a sudden, I realised Duncan had been avoiding me since the funeral and wake although I'd been home every day before dark to tend the animals in my care. After the love-filled days spent with Fabio, I hadn't missed Duncan at all. I shouldn't feel guilty but somehow it crept in, at least until I fell under Fabio's spell once more.

"Have you ever made love outdoors?" Fabio's eyes were full of come-hither mischief.

"No. Never. Not yet."

I felt my face flush at the exciting variation and all thoughts of Duncan evaporated.

Fabio carried a thick patchwork quilt from the stuffy house and spread it out on a wide grassy area surrounded by flowering shrubs and lightly shaded by eucalyptus trees. Shedding his clothes without shame or hesitancy, he commanded I do the same. He watched as I undressed, then kissed me tenderly, as we knelt down slowly, relishing our anticipation.

Naked with Fabio, I experienced the most wonderful feeling of abandonment there. Sunlight dappled my Italian lover's smooth bronzed skin. Eagerly we joined together beneath fragrant silvery-green foliage of gum trees that laced the blue sky above.

Greedy for more, Fabio urged me to straddle him. It was the first time he ever invited more than a submissive sexual role from me. Fabio usually wanted and needed to feel in complete control of every situation, so being allowed the top position felt like a gift from him.

A blazing sun burnt my whiteness as surely as Fabio's mesmerised gaze steamed my response. Avidly he watched my breasts sway heavily in rhythm as I rode him to fever pitch. As my pleasure built, Fabio fingered my warm nipples expertly triggering a rhapsody of repeat orgasms.

It had never been so good for me. I sang my ecstasy to the treetops. Fabio shouted his triumph at the same time. This was another first. Fabio had always groaned his pleasure softly and had never before been loudly vocal during sex with me.

Finally, we collapsed, sated, panting and laughing to lay smiling together in shared harmony. A light breeze whispered through the treetops, cooling and drying our hot moist bodies.

"This day will be my fondest memory when I am without you in Germany." Fabio promised.

Making love outdoors with Fabio was already my fondest memory. For a few days after Fabio returned to Germany, I went about in a daze, hugging Fabio's loving words to my heart and already yearning for when I might next be with him.

When it fleetingly crossed my mind that I hadn't seen or spoken to Duncan for a while, I wasn't bothered. He must understand I felt obliged to spend time with my good friend in the aftermath of losing his beloved Aunt Sophia. I had a duty of care after all.

Rodeo

A ROUGH RIDE

Life went on. I had to come down to earth and put daydreams of Fabio on the back burner.

My good neighbour with benefits had been neglected lately so I should pay Duncan some belated attention. To be realistic, it might be a long time before I could be with Fabio again and I had needs.

After work the following Sunday, I dropped off a delectable Apple Charlotte to the farm on my way up the lane to my house. I knew the apple sponge creamy treat was Duncan's favourite. Since the cake had fresh cream it needed to go in the fridge. Sid was in the kitchen and was delighted with the dessert cake.

"You've been a stranger lately Dimity. You must come for the barbeque this evening and we can have the cake with coffee after." Sid said.
"I will for sure. I've missed you guys too."

I fibbed the last bit.

"I should warn you; the boss has been like a bear with a sore head lately."

Sigh. Of course, Duncan would have to be difficult.

"Where is Duncan now?"
"He'll be doling out hay nets in the stables." Sid said.

I passed Nobby on the way to the stables.

"Thank God you've turned up. Good luck with that surly bloke in there." the old guy said.
"Duncan needs to get over himself." I replied and meant it.

Duncan would have seen or heard my car drive in, but he didn't show his face. I went looking for him and found him cutting strings of baling twine with his pearl handled knife. He teased out biscuits of fragrant green lucerne for the horses in stables.

"So you found your good penknife. Where was it?"
"Where I last used it."
"Sid asked me to come over for a barbeque this evening."
"The lads have missed you." he said shortly.

It seemed pointed that he hadn't missed me.

"Am I welcome to come or not?"
"No skin off my nose."

Right. Duncan was hard work, but I'd make a special effort to look my best to tease a reaction from him.

Recent outdoor activities had given my fair skin a nice light tan with no sleeve marks. I'd wear one of my pretty new sun frocks to advantage. I chose a summery one with spaghetti straps that tied in thin bows over my shoulders.

With the aid of a torturous strapless underwire bra, I made sure of showing a cheeky amount of cleavage. A gold chain pendant centred in the sweetheart neckline should help to lead his eye.

I admired my image in the mirror. The yellow and pale green floral print dress set off my tan nicely. I changed earrings for the bigger gold gypsy hoops. Lastly, a peach gloss on my lips, a spritz of perfume on my hair and I was ready to beguile Duncan. I hoped.

I took a couple of meaty lamb shanks from the fridge to be lightly browned on the barbeque plate for the dogs' dinners. Since I was walking to the farm with the dogs, I wore short cowboy boots that looked chic with the girly dress.

"Well, well, you do look real pretty tonight. And smell good too." Nobby said.

"Doesn't the lass look lovely Duncan?" Sid prompted.

"Hmmph."

Duncan hardly spared me a glance. He remained coolly disposed towards me. No doubt sulking because I'd spent so much time with Fabio. The old guys weren't blind to the atmosphere and seemed to chat more than usual to cover Duncan's sour mood.

Bugger Duncan he could just get over himself. I chatted along happily with Sid and Nobby and laughed a great deal at their jokes. Even those I had heard before.

We fondly watched Enzo and Shamus gnaw on their lamb shanks down on the lawn. Bending over the railings to see the dogs, I knew my dress hitched up shorter as I did so.

From the corner of my peripheral vision I caught Duncan looking. He quickly averted his gaze as I turned his way. I judged his sitting position gave him a good view of my thighs. Maybe he could see the colour of my knickers if he tried hard enough. He dropped a fork on the floor and stooped to pick it up. Ha ha. So predictable. Finally, towards the end of the meal, Duncan deigned to comment on my tan:

"You've been getting some sun lately."
"I have."

I smiled to myself remembering how that tan was acquired.

Night was falling and my bare shoulders felt cool in the fresh breeze of evening. Nobby gave instructions to his boss:

"We'll clear this lot away. You'd better walk the lass back."

Duncan's laboured sigh suggested walking me home was over the top of his endurance and a bloody lot to ask.

"No need to put yourself out Duncan. I know the way."

I called the dogs to heel and stomped off up the lane. Duncan followed. Climbing my back stairs, I became aware that the rude Irishman was suddenly very close behind me.

Before I opened the door, Duncan spun me around and mashed his mouth on mine. It was not a pleasant kiss. At the same time, his hands ran up under my skirt groping for my panties. I squirmed away. He managed to pull the shoulder bows of my sundress undone.

The dress fell down, and softly pooled around my boots, leaving me shivering in my brief lacy bra and white knickers.

Duncan caught my raised hand as I hastened to slap his face. Somehow his other hand unclipped my bra. My fury was only tempered by the relief of being freed from the torturous under garment.

"Don't." I growled.

"Why not? You dressed to tease me." he growled back.

"I tried looking nice to please you. That doesn't give you the right to force yourself onto me."

He released his tight hold on my wrist and gently ran his hand up my arm

"I said NO Duncan. I've put up with your rudeness all evening and you've blown it."

"I wanted to see your all over tan." he said breathing heavily.

"You've way overstepped the mark Duncan. Big time. Go away. I don't want you now or ever."

I wondered how he knew my tan was all over. He dropped his hands abruptly and took a step back, suddenly contrite and crestfallen.

"Geez. I'm sorry Dimity. You look so beautiful tonight. You're driving me insane."
"I'm cold. I want to go in. You better not have ruined my dress."
"I'll buy you a new dress." he said.
"Go home Duncan."

I picked up the dress and bra and went inside, shutting the door behind me. I kicked off the cowboy boots in the hallway and I went straight to the bathroom for a hot shower. Emerging in my towelling bath robe, I heard a soft tapping on the door. The dogs took no notice, so it was no mystery who was knocking.

"What now Duncan." I sighed.
"Can I come in?"
"Probably. The door isn't locked. But don't expect a warm welcome after the treatment you've given me."

Duncan entered humbly and faced me in the kitchen.

"I'm a complete bastard." he admitted.
"No argument."
"I've been going crazy these past few weeks. I missed seeing you and missed riding the horses out together. It's eaten my guts out knowing you're with your Italian pal."

I said nothing, waiting for him to wheedle his way back into my good graces. Betting to myself he hoped to spend the night with me. Duncan met my silence with more talk:

"I know you're entitled to spend time with your friends, and I have no right to jealousy."
"Fine. Glad you get that Duncan."
"Please give me a break Dimity."

I was in no mood for his attempt at an apology, but I threw him a bone.

"We can take the horses out tomorrow if you want."
"I gave Piper a good long run recently. I remembered the last time I used my penknife. It was when I cut the netting away from Nero's legs."

Clearly Duncan had ridden back to the stone house and found his knife there. Oh. I got it. His behaviour became suddenly clear as day.

"I must have dropped it when I ran to help Sid and Nobby nab that crook. Anyway, I saw the pearl handle gleaming in the sun..."

I felt a calm detachment waiting for him to spit it out, slightly interested in how he would go about it.

"...then I noticed your car parked up at the stone cottage. I started to walk away. But I heard voices coming from outside so walked up further. And I saw you. With him. I hated you both."

I wondered just how much he saw. My mixed feelings did not include guilt, shame or any pity for Duncan. He shouldn't have invaded our privacy. I stared him down.

"I know it was wrong to watch but I couldn't look away. I watched you for nearly an hour."

He must have witnessed pretty much everything and found it highly entertaining, since he couldn't look away. I brazened it out:

"And? How was it for you Duncan?"

"Painful. Erotic."

"And you got off on that." I accused.

"I've been wanking myself silly ever since just remembering seeing you like that."

"Yeah? What was your favourite part?"

"The rodeo. Definitely the rodeo."

"Glad to be of service then. Are you going home now?"

"I want to be with you."

"You think it's your turn now, is that it?"

"I can't think beyond wanting to be with you Dimity. But yes I would love to have a turn."

"Subtle as ever."

"You said you loved me."

"I do Duncan. But I loved Fabio first. Years before I even met you."

He had to suck that up.

"Alright. I see you go back a long way. Why aren't you together? Doesn't he care enough?"

"He's not free to be with me."

"Aha. A married man I take it."

"No he is not married. But he has an illegitimate daughter to care for. He also supports the child's mother and his younger brother who has mental problems. He works hard to keep them all."

"Obviously he's a saint. And I certainly am not." Duncan said.

"It's never been a competition, Duncan."

"Is he better than me?"

"No."

"Then I'm better than him?"

"No. You are complete opposites. I couldn't choose between you."

And I did not want to. Duncan thought about it for a while trying to make sense of it all.

"I thought you didn't know Giorgio and Sophia before I brought you out here."

"I didn't know them or any of Fabio's Italian connections out here. I only knew him as a single man in the city. We lived in the same area."

"What's his connection to that stone house?"

"It was Giorgio's. A family property. Fabio inherited it."

"So he will be living there now?"

"No Duncan. Fabio and his nearest kin all live in Europe now. He has gone back to them."

That was enough information. I would never share all the secrets. Duncan paced the kitchen floor, stopped at intervals and put hands to his hips, changed his mind, ran fingers through his hair, sighed heavily. I watched his emotions seesaw and knew he was hurting badly. I spent enough of my own life in yearning to know and feel empathy. Duncan choked up, near to tears:

"Are you sending me away when I need you so badly Dimity."
"We could have spent tonight together but you turned me off wanting you."
"Dimity. Please. I love you. I hate you."

The make-up sex would be great. I couldn't resist him.

"Alright. Come here you big lug and I'll try to help you make up your mind."
"I think I love you more than I hate you." he said.
"Same." I said.

I led him to my bed. He recovered quickly.

"Can we do the rodeo thing?"
"You won't last the distance cowboy."
"Try me."

I did. He didn't. But he made up for it in other ways.

Dilemma

ANOTHER SECRET

All went smoothly until an unforeseen consequence cropped up. I'd experienced some nausea and dizzy spells. My lunar orbit had gone askew. Panic!

A doctor confirmed I was about seven weeks pregnant. I worried my age of thirty-five could be a problem, but the GP was unconcerned. All was well. I booked another appointment for a later check-up.

I had to phone Fabio. He was my first port of call after the medical clinic.

Fabio had asked me to drop in to the retirement cottage now and then to air the rooms, saying to use that landline if I needed to call him in Germany. I really did need to speak to him urgently. I had my own key and went to the village very early, catching Fabio just as he was about to retire for the night as the time difference made it later than 10pm in Europe.

"Fabio. I have a dilemma."

"What is it? Are you unwell?"

"Not unwell. But pregnant."

Fabio was silent for a moment taking it in. I felt sick with worry.

"So. This will be a big event in your life. May I presume the father is that Irishman?"

"Or you Fabio."

"Not possible. I should have told you perhaps, but I underwent a vasectomy after Bean. You will understand that she was not planned, and I did not want another little mistake."

That was good news.

"That is actually a great relief Fabio. I can be sure the father is Duncan."

"These things happen."

He would know. Fabio had replied rather sadly. I caught the disappointment in his tone. But it was not all about him for once.

"I will soon have to tell Duncan."

"He should be told of course. He will want to marry you."

He might but I didn't want that.

"But Fabio, I never wanted marriage. It would change our special relationship. Yours and mine."

"I am selfish enough to have already thought of myself in this." Fabio admitted.

My ideal set up with two exciting lovers seemed about to be forfeited for this pregnancy. It felt like a great sacrifice. I had never given a thought to motherhood. Yet I knew my biological clock was ticking and this might be a wake-up call to have a child. Maybe it was meant to be.

"I fear you won't want me anymore after I have born a child. Regardless of that, Fabio, I still do not want to commit my life to one man."

"I will always want you Dimity. For my sins, I care not for the circumstances. And you forgave me for siring little Bean, did you not?"

"Of course. But it's not the same thing. My child will tie me down."

"Do not worry *la mio bella* Dimity. We will find a way. And keep our secret."

Surprisingly, Fabio hoped to continue our off and on affair into the future. At least Giorgio and Sophia had never known of it and now never would. Agneta in Germany was too far removed even if Fabio cared about her feelings. I doubted he would care if she found out.

The silhouetted exposure at the office with Cynthia had humiliated Fabio because it played to a much larger audience, invaded his privacy, and undermined his control.

What if Fabio learnt Duncan witnessed our passionate outdoor display at the stone house? Who knows what that might lead to. Fabio must never know.

Another secret of mine to keep, if only the Irishman did not give it away. Duncan represented a loose cannon who might confront my Italian lover someday out of jealousy.

Bloody men and their egos. Let them fight it out. Admittedly, being no angel, I preened a bit and enjoyed the rare circumstance.

My prissy Miss Minto persona wore her slipped halo at a jaunty angle.

The next time I went to an evening barbeque at the farm, Duncan walked me home again. Since I had forgiven his rough behaviour and taken him to my bed again, it became tacitly understood he would stay the night at my house on these after dinner occasions.

My condition wasn't yet noticeable, and I took care to wear clothing that would keep it unknown for as long as possible. However, I knew I must tell Duncan before any gossip leaked from the medical clinic. Nothing was sacred in a small town like Clemency.

Somehow, telling Duncan I carried his child bothered me more than anything, even more than knowing he watched me have wild sex with Fabio. The child changed everything.

Duncan got into my bed and waited for me to return from my shower. Wearing only his boxer shorts and reading glasses, he sat back in comfort propped up with pillows, perusing a magazine. It struck me that this would be my life every night if we were married. It seemed so bland.

"Why are you staring at me?" he smiled. "Admiring my manly form?"
"I have news." I gulped.
"What?" he was suddenly on full alert.
"You'd better sit down."
"I am sitting down Dimity. What has gotten into you?"
"You. Actually."

He had no idea. If he noticed any physical changes in me, he hadn't said.

"Spell it out Dimity. What's the matter with you?"

"I'm pregnant."

"With a baby?"

"Of course, with a baby. What else would it be."

His jaw dropped. His eyes widened. The news alarmed him. He tripped over his words.

"Feck. Holy crap! You can't be. Can you?"

"I am. About two or so months along."

"But... So... How... I mean... Weren't you on the pill?"

"The pill isn't 100% foolproof Duncan. I had a stomach bug for a couple of days. The doctor said that probably caused the failure."

"You've been to a doctor and had it confirmed? No mistake?"

"No mistake."

Duncan's face took on many different changes in a matter of seconds. I could almost hear the cogs grinding as he jumped to possible conclusions. I saved him some brain cells and gave him the verdict:

"You are its father."

"I am?"

"Yes."

"How do I know that?" he dared to question it, though he asked gently.

"You don't know. But I do."

"You can be certain of that can you Dimity?"

I couldn't blame Duncan for being hesitant. It was a shock. He didn't know how to handle the possibilities without insulting me, but I must try to keep Fabio's personal life out of it.

"There are paternity tests these days Duncan. If you need proof."

"It's not that I don't trust you Dimity...but I know for sure you've been well and truly with another man within the time frame."

"And I know for sure you are the father. I'm not trying to trap you. I plan to be a single mother and raise it myself anyway. I'm not asking you for anything. Just letting you know. But for your peace of mind, I'm ok with doing the paternity test thing. If you want."

He looked aghast.

"Geez. I don't want you to raise it alone. Especially if it is mine."

"It is definitely yours Duncan."

"You said the Italian stallion already has a kid so nothing wrong with his equipment."

"Is there something wrong with yours?"

"Of course not." he huffed.

"I know that better than you do Duncan. Because you made me pregnant."

"OK Dimity. You know more about it than I do. What happens now?"

"Nothing. I can still do my work and ride until I get too big and do Sundays at the bakery."

"No way. You're not horse riding or working."

"I have to make a living. And I need to turn the spare bedroom into a nursery."

"I can help with money and fixing up the room." he said.

"Thanks. I'll ask for help if I need it. But I appreciate your offer." I added.

He began to check out my body, feeling that my breasts were becoming a bit tender and larger. He listened to my stomach laying his ear against my belly button. He seemed in awe.

"We made a baby. It's just waiting to grow and get born. And it's in here."

"Yes. That's where it's kept." I confirmed.

"I don't want my kid to be a bastard." he said.

"Then you must try to set a better example." I countered.

"I mean I will marry you."

"Gee thanks but no thanks. I don't want to marry."

Also, it wasn't a dream marriage proposal. Not that I deserved any romantic gesture.

"Why are you always so difficult Dimity. Why do you have to go your own way with everything. This is my baby too. I want to bring him up with you."

"Him? Fifty-fifty chance it might be a girl you know."

"Even so. More so if anything. I have to protect her. Or him."

"Early days Duncan. Time will tell."

It didn't take him long to think of another aspect.

"Can you still have sex? So far?"

"Of course I can. Trust you to think of that."

"I think of it all the time. With you I mean. I only think of it with you Babe. All the time."

"You almost convinced me of that Duncan. Let's sleep on it then."

I yawned, relieved to have shared my little problem with him, I could relax at last. He began to rub my back gently. It would be nice to have his ongoing support. But I didn't want the whole marriage thing. I liked having my own home and personal options. A child would curtail my freedom let alone a permanent live-in man. How hard could it be being a single mother? So many women manage it successfully.

"I can be really gentle. If you're sure I won't hurt anything." Duncan worked at his quest.

"Duncan. The little person is only about as big as a jelly-baby right now. Sex won't affect it."

"Can we have celebration sex then?"

"You might talk me into it. At your best." I stretched languidly.

"Good. Wow. I can really appreciate your blooming titties. When will they be ripe? When do you get milk? Can I have a suck?"

"Hope I get milk when it's born but it has to go for feeding the baby Duncan."

"I meant now. Promise I won't do it too hard."

He knew I loved that. He was gentle. For him. I enjoyed sex with Duncan. He was enthusiastic and fun. I felt content for the moment.

The Fun Part

VS RESPONSIBILITY

Within another couple of months the baby made itself known with flutters of movements. He/she became very real to me, more than an abstract idea or little problem. It was a life.

Duncan drove in unexpectedly with a ute load of baby furniture and other goods.

"I saw this in passing." he claimed, unloading a bassinet, cot and chest of drawers.

"You just happened to be passing the baby shop in town? Isn't it down a side street?"

"I had other business down there." he fibbed.

"What's all this other stuff?"

"The saleslady said we'd need all these things."

"Hmm. You must have made her day Duncan."

"She didn't rip me off. I was going to get a changing table as well but she said no, just use the cot. It's a lot safer because the baby can't roll off. There are so many different baby baths I thought we'd go together and decide on that."

Actually, I had been just passing the drapery store and saw an attractive curtain material. It wasn't exactly babyish but had a pattern of red, blue and yellow beach balls on a white background. I used Sophia's sewing machine at the village to run up some curtains and cushion covers for a single lounge chair Duncan brought over from the farmhouse.

"The baby shop sheila said you'll need a nursing chair."

I still had paint colour cards in a kitchen drawer and picked out pastel colours to complicate the growing scheme. Duncan washed down the walls and ceiling with sugar soap. He brought a ladder from the farm and painted the ceiling white. We decided to paint one wall light blue and three in pale lemon. The room was really pretty with the new curtains. We stood together, his arms about me, admiring our combined efforts.

"I want our kid to have everything." Duncan said. "But not be a spoilt brat. I mean just have the good necessities of life and a decent upbringing."

He hadn't mentioned marriage again. I wondered if he'd had second thoughts on that. Duncan had already passed his 40th year. He had been single a long time and had his own household.

We both realised these nursery room preparations were the easy fun part.

There would be dirty nappies, sleepless nights, tantrums if the child took after either of us. At our ages, we could expect a baby to be a difficult intrusion on our relatively carefree lives.

Nevertheless, we cautiously looked forward to being parents. Most nights, I sat up in bed knitting little garments. Duncan often lay beside me with his reading glasses on, studying a heap of baby magazines, occasionally reading out paragraphs to me. He was so into it all.

"Duncan, I have the ultrasound appointment coming up soon."

"I'll come with you. I want to see it too."

"Do you want to know if it's a boy or girl before the birth?"

"Can they tell?"

"I believe so. But they don't let on unless the parents want to know."

"Why would anyone not want to know? I want to know."

"Do you? Some people think it spoils the surprise at the birth."

"The birth will be a miracle event anyway. And I want to be there for it Dimity."

It was one thing to have him witness me screaming in pleasure with Fabio. I wasn't sure about having him there for all the ungainly panting sweating and shrieking of childbirth I'd heard all about from the two Gerdas at the bakery.

"I don't know..."

"I want to be there! Come on Dimity. You can't deny us everything."

"Us?"

"Me and the baby. My baby."

"What? What are you on about now? Ha ha. You do know the baby will be there anyway."

"I mean you are already denying my baby's legitimacy." he said quietly.

There it was. He meant marriage.

"Duncan, traditional marriage is just a piece of paper."

"Right. If you think that, and I don't by the way, why not do it Dimity?"

Exploring my reasons privately, I knew Fabio featured largely in my reluctance to marry. Fabio said he would still want me no matter what. So far, we had enjoyed our love trysts without harming or forsaking anyone else. But cheating on a marriage was a step too far for me. Duncan had done everything right and very little wrong. I loved both men.

I was forced to admit there was much more to marriage than a certified document. There were vows and a spouse to be honoured. Children to consider. Duncan had been watching my reaction closely. He knew me quite well by now and identified my hesitancy.

"Dimity, I know you value your independence and don't like giving up your sexual freedoms, but I aim to be the best husband and father I can be."

So he definitely realised Fabio figured in this for me. I couldn't deny it.

"You make it sound like a done deal, but I haven't agreed to marriage."

Duncan completely overrode my reply and ventured where angels feared to tread by laying down his ground rules:

"I want and expect a proper marriage. No seeing the Italian on the side."

"If I married anyone, I would respect the vows Duncan."

"I'm damn sure if the Italian stallion offered you marriage you'd jump at it."

"No. Never. I would not marry Fabio is he was the last man on earth."

Furthermore, I was absolutely certain Fabio would never ask.

"You're enslaved to that man Dimity. Can't you see it for what it is? Surely our child is the most important person in this. Not you. Not me. Certainly not your fucking lover boy."

Duncan shouted and slammed his fist on the wall. Bet that hurt. Hope it did. But I knew he was right. Once I began to cry I couldn't stop.

Duncan didn't offer his shoulder to cry on for once. He went home, shutting my door quietly behind himself. The younger O'Day delivered another kick to my guts. From the inside.

Alone during the night, I dreamt of my grandfather and woke remembering a little box of his personal effects I hadn't opened since moving to the lemon tree house.

In the first light of morning, I retrieved the small cardboard box from the back of my wardrobe. Setting it on the bed, I cut open the taped outer casing and carefully lifted out the old wooden music box that had sat on Grandpa's bedside table for as long as I could recall.

The music box had belonged to my grandmother who had been lost in the same car accident that claimed both my parents. I knew by heart what was inside that box. Amongst various trinkets and keepsakes, I found the pair of gold wedding rings, tied together with a scrap of white satin ribbon.

As a small child, I'd sat on Grandpa's knee as he showed me those gold rings always with the reminder that they were a symbol of how much my parents loved me. I slipped the smaller ring on my wedding ring finger. It fit perfectly. The baby kicked me again. I admonished my unborn child:

"Go to sleep you little imp. I know what to do."

I retied the two rings together and placed them back in the music box.

Slam Dunk

GOT HIM

After finishing my horse work that afternoon, I wandered down to Duncan's place with the dogs in tow.

Sid yelled a cheery hello from the verandah where he was grilling steaks. Duncan and Nobby wandered over from the stables.

"You alright?" Duncan asked gruffly.

"Why wouldn't I be?" I snapped.

"Geez. Only asked." he replied.

"You want your steak well done as usual Dimity? With a bit of salad?" Sid called out.

"Yes well done thanks Sid. No salad. Just half a grilled tomato sprinkled with parmesan."

"Her Majesty has spoken." Duncan rolled his eyes.

Throughout dinner, Duncan spoke in sarcastic asides about me to the lads. I ignored him. Sid and Nobby knew the drill off pat by now with the mood swings between me and Duncan. When they'd finished eating, they rose from the table to leave us alone.

"Hey guys. Please don't go. Can you stay for a while? I've got something to say to Duncan. And I want witnesses in case there is ever any dispute over who said what, when or how."

The three men froze. They all looked very afraid of a sudden. Ha. ha. Yes. Be afraid. I was back in control of my own destiny. As I liked. No one was going to lecture me on what I should do. The baby kicked hard in reply to my thoughts. Was it psychic?

"Why do you all look so scared?" I asked.
"You're a scary woman." Duncan replied.
"Really. Am I a scary woman Sid? Nobby?"

The old guys wisely only shrugged and murmured non-committal sounds while not meeting my eye.

"See? You're bloody terrifying." Duncan said.
"Then you'd better think long and hard about your future from here on in Irishman."
"If you've got something to say get on with it." he growled in reply.

I waited a heartbeat for dramatic effect:

"Duncan O'Day. Will you marry me and make our baby legitimate?"

Duncan startled and stared, totally confused at my unexpected U-turn. Sid and Nobby broke out in raucous laughter.

"She's roped you in." Sid guffawed.

"Just as we said she would. Didn't we say that all along Sid? Well done lass." Nobby added.

Duncan almost choked on his indignant exclamation:

"SHE did not rope ME in. It was MY idea all along. I roped HER in."

I smiled in smug triumph. Slam Dunk. Got him. Big time. I'm entering it into my diary as Miss Minto's Slam Dunk.

"Yes or no Duncan. I'm waiting." I looked at my wristwatch.
"Holy crap. Suppose I'm up for buying a ring now." Duncan mourned.
"Nope. I've already got the rings. Had them for ages." I said smoothly.

That set Sid and Nobby off again in peals of mirth.

"One for your finger, one for his nose." Nobby laughed.
"This calls for a celebration." Sid said. "Will we break out the whisky?"
"You guys go ahead. But I would really rather a nice cup of tea." I said primly. It might be my last chance to air Miss Minto's lapsed persona.
"You are one scheming and devious female Dimity Minto." Duncan conceded.
"Thank you." I replied demurely.

In the interim before our quiet validation at the town hall registry office, Duncan accompanied me for the 16-week baby scan. For the first time we beheld the tiny fascinating creature squirming about, viewed on a small black and white screen. We were told the baby would weigh only about 100 grams at this stage but would be fully formed. The eyes would still be closed though sensitive to bright light.

"Baby can begin to recognise voices now. Some people tell them stories, sing and play music to them." The clinic nurse told us.
"Wow." Duncan said.
"This is the heartbeat, obviously." The nurse said, pointing it out.

We were both spellbound seeing the little alien face, hands and feet coming into focus in turn. I knew for certain the baby was the most important person for me now, and any sacrifices were worth making. I liked feeling virtuous for having made the honourable decision.

"Can you tell yet if it's a boy or girl?"
"I think so. But sometimes the first impressions are wrong." The nurse admitted.
"I think I'd rather wait for a definite answer." I said.

Duncan agreed it made more sense to wait. Another appointment was booked for a fortnights time when the baby's gender should be really apparent. In the meantime, we had to be wed to legitimise its birth.

Neither of us had ever hankered after a big church wedding. Or any wedding it must be said. I used to pity girls mooning over traditional white meringue style wedding dresses and a host of attendants. Thankfully, Duncan and I could agree on the registry office.

Sid and Nobby, dressed in their best, witnessed our wedding vows, on a sunny morning at the town hall. They lads were in charge of the gold rings. Duncan had already tried the larger ring on for size. It fitted well. My parents wedding rings seemed made for us.

My barely noticeable baby bump meant I could wear another of my new country sundresses that Duncan hadn't seen me in yet. The pale blue dress had small sprigs of white flowers woven into the fabric. It draped softly in an empire line to just below the knee.

In a nod to tradition, I carried a posy of miniature pink and white roses and wore my grandmother's antique pearl stud earrings and necklace. Duncan looked absolutely gorgeous in his suit. I took a pink rose from the little bouquet for his lapel.

Duncan and I presented ourselves before the officiating Commonwealth registered marriage celebrant in the town hall registry office. Sid and Nobby stood close by.

"You scrubbed up reasonably anyway." Duncan allowed in his idea of a grand compliment.

"You don't look as butt ugly as usual either." I shot back.

The celebrant raised eyebrows but went ahead and asked if we wanted to use the traditional wedding vows that included having the wife obey the husband. Sid and Nobby broke into spontaneous laughter. The official tossed the vows aside without waiting for our answers.

We cut to the chase to declare our promises in a foreshortened ceremony as: Duncan O'Day do you take this woman to be your lawful wedded wife? Suppose so. Alright. Yeah. I do.

Dimity Minto do you take this man to be your lawful wedded husband. Sigh. OK. I do.

Blah blah...I now pronounce you man and wife. You may now k...oh never mind. No confetti on the steps please. As if.

Once outside on the footpath, Duncan seized me in a bear hug and kissed me soundly to the applause of many shoppers and onlookers. Some gave us their congratulations.

Lunch was booked at a posh restaurant but Sid and Nobby planned a gift for us beforehand. They'd hired a professional studio session for photos. We all went to the photographer's place to record our momentous wedding day in both colour and sepia. I thanked the old guys and exclaimed:

"What a lovely surprise! We'll have some forever photos to show for our sins."

I didn't know how well illustrated that sentiment would become. The photo session deal included props and backgrounds. The men wore borrowed cowboy hats, and the old lads held shotguns. It was perfect. We also had a collection of standard wedding poses taken, but the shotgun wedding photos became our forever favourites.

A Rose

BY ANY OTHER NAME

Our supposed honeymoon period was spent at home, and it wasn't long before we had another disagreement. It blew up a week before the baby scan that would reveal it's gender.

"If it's a girl, can we call her Lexie?" Duncan asked.
"What? You must be kidding! No way!" I exclaimed.

I couldn't believe Duncan would even dare to ask such an insensitive question. It was akin to me asking if we could call a boy Fabio or Paul, Newman, Kevin or Costner.

"You really imagine I would name my daughter after your old flame? Get real. Geez Duncan. I can't believe you'd even ask me that."
"Why not? I just think it's a nice name for a girl. Not about naming her after anyone."
"I would name her anything but that."
"That's a bit long." he joked.

I didn't reply. I felt unsettled. We were in my bed which had become our bed. Duncan also kept the trumpeting cherub room at the farm as his own spare bedroom. I turned my back on my husband and mumbled more complaint:

"And you can bloody well forget suggesting Darlene as a name as well."

He tried to kid me out of my mood with another lame joke.

"Hey, I can't believe it. That was my second choice. You must be piss chick."
"Believe this Duncan: I am beyond piss chick at the moment."

I suggested he attempt something anatomically impossible with his name choices.

"Yeah alright. I see you're going to be hormonal about it."
"Just keep digging yourself deeper Duncan."
"Babe. I know what you need."

He began to rub my back in soothing circles. I began to forgive him. We were good together. Part of my unsettled mood was that I hadn't yet told Fabio of my marriage. This was not a problem I could share with Duncan. But I'd made my bed now. I planned to phone Fabio after work on Sunday.

The two Gerda's at the bakery noticed my wedding ring immediately. I told them I'd had a shotgun wedding because I was pregnant. That gave them something juicy to go on with.

After my bakery shift, I went to the retirement village to phone Fabio from the landline.

"Fabio. I have done what I said I wouldn't." I began.

"You have married?"

"How did you know?"

"I foresaw that you would. With the child in mind."

"Yes, my Fabio. I am also tied to family as you are. You will understand how it is now."

"*Cara Dimity, sarò sempre qui per te.*"

He translated for me: "I will always be here for you."

How often had I spoken those words to him. Fabio's blessing meant everything to me.

"*La famiglia è la cosa più importante...*family is the most important thing."

"Yes. I know that now Fabio and this has given me a deeper understanding of your commitments too."

"Duncan will be a good husband and father. I will not come between you and your duties. Unless you ever decide differently *mia cara*."

Fabio added the temptation to continue our affair. The choice would be mine should we find the opportunity to be together again. Fabio's intimate seductive tones caressed me so, I had to force discipline upon myself. It was not easy to do the right thing, but I made the responsible and mature decision not to speak over the phone to Fabio anymore.

I saw no reason to axe our long-standing friendship completely and would stay in touch with Fabio by email from time to time.

He held me as his best friend. We shared so much together. I would always love my Fabio from afar.

Danny Boy

WE CRIED

On the next baby scan, Duncan and I were inexplicably amazed to learn our baby was a boy. Out of only two alternatives, we'd have been just as amazed had he been a girl. Go figure.

"It's a boy!" Duncan shouted to the lads as we drove back into the farmyard.

"What? She can't have had it already…!?"

"No, we saw him on the scan. It was incredible." Duncan enthused.

Duncan came around to help me from the ute. A growth spurt had expanded my figure and now made my condition unmistakable. Sid had the kettle on, and lunch prepared on the farmhouse verandah. The lads listened dotingly as Duncan raved about seeing our unborn son, saying he looked just like a proper bought one. The subject of baby names cropped up again.

"I'm saying nothing. My darling wife has already told me sweetly where to stick my ideas and it would be a difficult feat to do her bidding." Duncan said.

"They must've been pretty bad ideas then." Nobby ventured.

"They were really bad ideas." I confirmed.

"Just because they happened to be names of a couple of my old girlfriends?"

Duncan spoke artlessly assured of sympathy for being hard-done-by.

Sid and Nobby exchanged looks of disbelief between themselves.

"You're still learning then, aren't you son." Sid rolled his eyes.

"What? I just said I liked those names. I can like the names. Can't I?"

"Jesus wept." Nobby remarked mildly while shaking his head.

That night all Duncan and I could talk about was the little unborn boy seen on the screen that day. We surveyed the nursery room again in eager anticipation. Patting the cushions I imagined sitting there nursing the baby. Duncan wiped specks of dust from the windowsill.

"If you agree Duncan, I would like to name him after my grandpa who brought me up."

"Now you want my blessing for your name choice?"

"If possible. But I might do it anyway."

"Now there's a backhander. What name then."

"Daniel."

"Danny." he compromised.

"Fair enough."

"Danny Boy. Now that has a wholesome Irish ring to it."

On our next clinic visit, a starchy matron advised having a bag packed for the hospital and alternative preparations in place early. As we lived out of town, we were put in touch with the nearest midwife who happened to be Maria Russo, the boy Baldwin's mother from the dairy.

"That is opportune. We've already met Maria Russo." I said.

The matron replied: "Oh that's right. I remember now. You work at the bakery and live out near Gallo's roadside stall. Young Baldwin made a big drug bust and saved you from the river didn't he Mrs. O'Day? You know you shouldn't have been swimming there. But all's well that ends well. I'm sure you'll be more careful with a little one to consider. I suppose with your man coming from the coast you are used to swimming almost anywhere. Even in the sea."

The matron received no reply until adding more of her knowledge: "Good for you doing the right thing Mr. O'Day. A pity it took a shotgun. But as I said. All's well that ends well."

"Just wait a blasted minute. It took me a bloody long time to convince Dimity to marry me. Not that it's any of your bloody business." Duncan retorted red faced.

"A baby's welfare is everyone's business Mr. O'Day, and I certainly hope you won't use such coarse language in front of your child."

"I only said bloody."

"I heard blasted as well. And for your information, toddlers that are brought up with frequent swearing in the home usually learn and use those words first."

Duncan fumed all the way home muttering curses under his breath.

"That's put you in your place Mr. O'Day." I laughed.

"Bloody cow. I'm going to teach our Danny Boy to curse in Gaelic just to spite her."

"You will not!"

"Well, my dear, unless you're familiar with the language you will never know, will you."

Ten days before the baby's due date of birth, I took a stroll down to the creek after lunch as light exercise. Duncan had been busy down at the spelling farm all day. The baby took up so much room inside me now, a few minor twinges I put down to indigestion.

Feeling hot, I bent to scoop a handful of cool creek water when a severe cramp wracked my body. I was unable to straighten up for several excruciating seconds.

Feeling alarmed that my time had started early, I managed to move well away from the waterside and get back up the creek bank. I was not into having an underwater birth.

I didn't get far before having to double over again. It was easier to kneel down on the grass. I laboured in increasing agony all afternoon in the pasture before I felt my waters break.

Now I had horribly soggy knickers and couldn't rid myself of them. I tried to rise and continue up the incline to the house only to be gripped in vice-like cramps again and again.

The three horses in the paddock, Nero, Piper and an old racehorse mare snuffled around me for a while. The dogs snapped at the horses' heels warning them away. I rolled onto my back trying to ease the pain. Perhaps I'd never have been discovered before dark but for Enzo and Shamus.

At last, I heard Duncan calling my name. The dogs barked and raced away to bring him back to me. I screamed as the seizures clamped down again.

"No. No." Duncan shouted as he ran down the slope in panic.

"He's coming early." I panted in a lull between contractions.

"He isn't due yet."

"You tell him then."

"Can you get up to the house if I help you?"

"It hurts so much. I can try. I don't know if...."

I screamed again. The urge to push was strong. I just had to get this baby out. Duncan had a quick assessing look, took out his pearl handled knife and slit each side of my soggy knickers, tossing them aside.

"Go. Get the midwife Duncan." I gasped.

"I can't leave you."

"You must..."

"Too late. I can see his head appearing. He's got black hair. Don't push until you get another contraction Dimity."

Duncan had delivered foals and studied so much about the human birthing process he was as good a midwife as any in the circumstances, and no other choice could be had. Duncan removed his cotton work shirt. I felt the baby coming...

"Wait! Wait! Stop pushing. Dimity hold on. Don't push."

In a delirium I saw Duncan take his pearl handled knife out again. He toiled urgently without telling me what was happening. Suddenly the baby came out in a rush. I saw and felt Duncan zip a long rope of umbilical cord from my body.

I wished he would say something. He looked worried. Duncan silently held the newborn to his chest. The baby looked blue. Duncan tried rubbing the life into him with his shirt, to no avail. In desperation, Duncan held the baby up by his ankles and smacked his bottom.

The baby took a breath and emitted his first cry. Duncan and I cried with our son.

"Thank God. Are you alright Dimity?"
"I think so. Let me have him."

Placing the baby gently along the front of my body, Duncan covered us as best he could with the mucky shirt. There was nothing else. A chill breeze sprung up.

The horses crept closer out of curiosity, sniffing and snorting. Duncan pulled the cotton paddock sheet from the old mare and used it to cover us. I badly needed a drink of water but would not put more demands on Duncan. He had done well.

"What did you do with the knife?" I croaked.

"The umbilical cord was wrapped around his neck strangling him. The more you pushed the more he choked. I couldn't get a hold to pull it over his head. I had to cut it. He's OK. I didn't nick him at all."

In the fading light of day, Duncan had cut the noose of umbilical cord but much of it remained attached leading from the baby's navel.

"Shouldn't it be clamped off?"

"Nothing is sterile. I don't know. Yes, maybe I should tie it off. It has gone flat now so he must have received what blood was in it. What can I use to tie it off?"

"Cut the ribbons from my dress."

Duncan made the crude tying off. We hoped for the best, praying for no infection.

Evening settled in. The glowing rim of a full moon nudged above the horizon in the east like a bright orange peel of brightness. It visibly rose as we watched and cast its silvery light over the land.

"I have to get you both up to the house. We can't stay out here all night. Even if I have to leave you here with the dogs and take the baby up first before he gets too cold."

I tried to get up again but almost blacked out with the effort.

Guess What

LACY

As we worried over how best to get up to the house, we heard Sid and Nobby calling us. Light from their torches waved about the paddock. The dogs barked and ran to meet the old guys.

"We heard screams earlier. Probably a bird, we thought."

"Then we noticed there were no lights on in the house. Is all ok Duncan?"

"Mother and child seem to be recovering. It might take me forever to get over it."

"Jesus. You've done it." Sid exclaimed.

"We need a stretcher to carry them up." Nobby took charge.

"Get the futon mattress." Duncan suggested.

"What the hell's the futon?"

"It's the fecking most uncomfortable day bed ever invented. But the hard mattress will do to carry them. It's in the living room."

They left us one of the torches and hurried back up to the house. Duncan inspected what else came out as I groaned with aftershocks of more cramps.

"It's the afterbirth. Best it all comes out sooner than later. All good Dimity. Just relax. Let it happen."

Sid was smart enough to bring down some big bath towels and Duncan helped me roll onto the stiff futon mattress, while the lads held and cooed over little Danny.

Sid and Nobby took two corners of the mattress and Duncan the other two. The baby travelled laying on my chest with my arms around him. Baby Danny had already began smacking his little lips and feeling for a teat. He was a big lad just like his dad, black hair and all.

Safely upstairs, Sid and Nobby went for the midwife, while Duncan gently wiped bits of grass and dirt from Danny's back with a warm washcloth. I felt stronger after a sweet drink so made a supreme effort to get into the bathtub and rinse myself down. Feeling faint again, I knelt in the tub until Duncan came to help me out. While this happened, he left the baby wrapped in a clean towel on the floor.

"He can't fall any further than that." Duncan reckoned.

By the time midwife Maria Russo arrived, I was tucked up in my own bed, suitably padded and between clean sheets, holding a sleeping Danny Boy to my breast.

"My word. You've done well for first timers." The midwife said.

Maria efficiently inspected the baby, sprayed the navel cord with alcohol and clamped it off in a better way, closer to his body. Maria said by rights we should go to hospital. I wasn't keen on leaving my bed and said so. Duncan said:

"It was hard on Dimity. I only found her near to the last minute. I am afraid it wasn't the most hygienic of conditions. The birth happened down the back paddock and I had to cut the cord with my old penknife to get it loose from around his neck."

Maria seemed to envy him.

"It's called Nuchal cord. Very common. But I've never had one so tight it needed cutting. I wish I'd been there for that experience."

"Believe me it was too tight. And with my big ham fists and the light fading...."

Duncan gulped fighting back exhausted tears. I loved him more than ever before.

"You both did very well. A robust healthy boy and mother doing well. I'll leave a digital thermometer with you. Try to monitor their temps frequently. Get them straight to hospital if either of their temperatures look like going beyond normal either way."

"Thanks Maria. Actually we have our own digital thermometer." Duncan said.

"Oh no. Not the rectal horse one Duncan." I hoped.

"Of course not. I bought a new one with all the other stuff from the baby shop."

The midwife prepared to leave with the promise to return early. She wheeled the bassinet on its stand to sit beside the bed with strict instructions on how the baby should be and not to sleep with him in our bed. Duncan had spent months going on and on about all this but we thanked Maria for her help and advice.

Sid and Nobby returned, put the kettle on, made tea and warmed chicken soup and buttered toast for us. We were so grateful for their caring help. The old lads spoke in stage whispers:

"We fed the dogs. Get some sleep. Hang a big sheet or something out the kitchen window if you need help. We'll keep a lookout." Nobby promised.

Maria returned early next morning, pleased to see the baby was latching on well at this early stage. Danny would have received the important colostrum, she said, but it might be another couple of days before my milk came down in full. She warned it could be painful. Was there no end to it?

"I'll leave you to it. You're all doing well. I must rush now to get home and cook Baldwin's tenth birthday dinner. He wants a roast with gravy and home made apple pie with cream."

"These boys are keeping you very busy Maria."

"Always. You'll find all this will be easier next time."

"Next time!"

Duncan and I chorused a denial of there ever being a next time.

"Everyone says that." she laughed.

"So how many children have you?" I asked the jolly midwife.

"Just Baldwin." Maria admitted with a crooked smile.

I continued my part-time Sunday work at the bakery and expressed milk for Danny to be bottle fed in the interim while Duncan got to spend some quality alone time with his baby boy.

The two Gerdas were full of advice that had a long-lasting effect our lives. I should never have given credit to their expertise on reproduction. Here's the crunch: You can get pregnant while breastfeeding. As soon as my second pregnancy was suspected I went to Maria Russo to ask advice.

"Oh dear Dimity. Fancy listening to those Gerdas." she chided mildly.

"I don't know how Duncan will react. I'll have a test to be sure before I say anything."

"Well, don't be surprised if you have fallen again."

"It's so soon after Danny and I didn't want to wean him yet."

"See how you go Dimity. It can be done. Keep up a healthy diet with plenty of calories."

"I really believed those Gerdas. They were so full of advice." I cried.

"A temporary reprieve from ovulation only works if the baby is exclusively breastfed and suckled. Expressing milk doesn't work. The pump action doesn't send the same message to the mother's brain." Maria explained.

"Wish I'd asked you first Maria."

"Now now Dimity. Count your blessings. It will be great having the two as playmates together. I wanted more but it was not to be. Still we're lucky to have Baldwin. He's a good kid."

A test confirmed my second pregnancy. I returned home to find Duncan sitting in my nursing chair and reading a highly inappropriate story to little Danny. Fortunately, our son was yet too young to understand a word of

Duncan's book choice of murder and mayhem: *The Bruiser - Bad to the Core.*

"Hey Danny Boy, here's your Mummy with her lovely titties."
"Hi guys. Guess what Duncan. You can get pregnant while breastfeeding."
"Well that always seemed too good to be true...wait...you're not?"
"Yep."

I waited ready to burst into tears while my surprised husband digested the news.

"This just proves it. I'm one hell of a virile man. Haha. Nailed you again!"
"It's not that funny to me Duncan."

I changed places with Duncan and put our son to my breast for a feed before his afternoon nap. My tears began to flow as I lay Danny in his cot, fast asleep.

"Babe. Come here. I know what you need."
"That's what got me into this mess."
"But now we're safe until after the next one and we've got an hour before Danny wakes up."

Had to give Duncan full marks for logic.

"I'd rather have a nice cup of tea. First."
What the hell.

Our daughter was born safely in hospital, arriving just one year after Danny, their birthdays only a week apart. We named her Lacy. Duncan swore he never had any girlfriend with that name.

"Are you sure?"
"Not that I remember."
Hmmm.

Danny grew and thrived. Despite being born down in the horse paddock with the horses and dogs as witnesses, our boy suffered no setbacks. Lacy however, contracted a slight infection in hospital and could not come home for a fortnight. I am not advocating horse paddock births. Just saying.

The Kids

BIRDS & BEES

Danny and Lacy shared the second bedroom while they were small. The pair were very close as brother and sister but not always in a good way. They frequently fought like cats and dogs, hitting, kicking and hair pulling.

They got their combative streaks from Duncan obviously.

Neither Duncan nor I had siblings. We thought our kids must be particularly terrible brats. People laughed at us saying it would be unusual if they didn't fight.

Duncan was not a great disciplinarian. He was good cop to my bad cop. Once when little Danny smart mouthed me, I took Duncan to account to back me up.

"Duncan!" I demanded his input.

"Danny Boy it's not nice to backchat your mother. Can you tell us why?"

"Because Mummy is a big scary woman?" Danny asked in innocence.

"Oh Duncan! What have you been saying?"

"Daddy says we have to behave because you are a big scary woman." Lacy dobbed.

"You reap what you sow Duncan." I frowned.

Eventually after a particularly big row between our darling children, our son announced he was leaving home. Lacy had never been one for dolls but loved her action figures. She had knocked down part of Danny's Lego building while playing rough with her superheroes. Danny had spent hours on that project, so he pulled the heads off Spider Man and Wonder Woman. When Lacy kicked down the rest of the Lego building in rage, Danny packed his school bag and walked out growling a parting threat:

"I'll be back for my other stuff later and you better not touch anything Lacy."

Danny commandeered a spare bedroom at the farm and apparently told Sid and Nobby he was up for adoption, to their great amusement.

"Don't worry, we'll look out for him." the old guys promised.

"Duncan. Do something. Danny is too young to leave home. He's not even eleven yet."

"Mind of his own. He gets that from you my love."

Duncan said it was high time we split the pair up anyway. I felt like we failed as parents. Lacy came to me in tears.

"I didn't want Danny to go." she bawled heartbroken.

"Never mind my darling. He's only two minutes walk away."

"But what if he stays at the farm forever and ever?"

"Then you can redecorate your room. Make it girly and pink if you want to, or we could look for some action figure material for new curtains."

Lacy's tears dried up as if by magic. She began making plans for her own space. That's my girl. Time flew by. Danny followed Duncan everywhere around the farm but came back to see me everyday before and after school.

"I miss you Mum, but I don't miss Lacy." he declared.
"Not even a little bit?" I prompted.
"Well. Not very much."
Just saying that much told me Danny missed his sister a great deal.
"I hope you look out for her at school. Lacy is still your little sister, and nothing will change that." I reminded him.
"I know. She's a right royal pain in the butt. Anyway, I biffed some wanker who pulled her hair."
"Right royal? Some what? Where exactly did you pick up those words?"
"Around." he replied.

Interrogation never worked on my son. I blamed the all-male environment at the farm.

"And you shouldn't be fighting at school." I offered lamely.
"But you said..."
"Danny!"
"Yes Mam." he grinned charmingly like his Daddy could.

Danny would break some hearts when he came of age; of that I felt certain.

By the time Danny finished high school he knew everything about running the spelling farm business. All he wanted was to work alongside his father and the old lads. Duncan encouraged him, so I had to concede my son was never going to make any other career choice. The business was bound to become O'Day & Son. Could be worse.

Lacy liked to write, so we gave her a computer for her 15th birthday. She had work experience at the local newspaper and said that was the type of work she most wanted to do. Eventually, she began full time work at the newspaper office with opportunities to contribute article material.

As our son and daughter advanced into later teens, Duncan gave them cars so they could socialise with their wide group of friends in the town. I worried they might come to harm.

"You can't keep them tied to the apron strings." he had said.
"I know. But have you had a birds and bees talk with Danny yet?"
"Good God no! I wouldn't embarrass the boy. Kids know everything anyway these days."

Lacy had already asked me all about it and corrected me on a point or two. She was the forward one.

Empty Nest

NOT FOR LONG

This period, as the children matured into young adults, became the loneliest time ever in my life.

Both my dogs, Shamus and Enzo had passed on. They had lived long happy lives. Each were tearfully laid to rest in the front yard, not far from the lemon tree.

That namesake of *Albero di Limone* had thrived and filled out bushy and tall. Its fruits were abundant and prized. Sid often made a tangy marmalade that sold well on the roadside stall.

Nero and Piper, after serving well as the kids' first mounts, also succumbed to old age, and went the way of all living things. One by one I felt my family drift away, every loss a knife in my heart.

Good old Sid and Nobby had become slow and doddery though they limped about achieving what they could. Danny gradually took over their jobs unasked.

The spelling farm expanded over the years to provide a good living. Duncan and I were what could be described as comfortably off. We strove to take care of Sid and Nobby in their dotage as the old lads were dearly loved and valued family to us.

Duncan and I discussed investing in the retirement village, asking the agents to let us know when another cottage became available. We snapped up a three bedroom place overlooking the lake and set Sid and Nobby up in easy retirement. They soon made other friends at the village and were in popular demand to ply their old yarns onto new ears.

The times I'd contacted Fabio had grown few and far between over the years. He had long since sold Sophia's retirement cottage to supplement buying a villa in Italy, which he shared with Wolfgang. Fabio's daughter, Bean, also went to live in Italy with them, after Agneta met and married a German man.

Asked what I would like for my 56th birthday, I told my little family I'd like nothing more than a quiet meal together. Just the four of us at home in the lemon tree kitchen. It seemed such a small and simple wish. Between them, Duncan and Lacy produced a roast dinner and a crème caramel dessert. Danny arrived with a six pack of lager. At twenty years old, he wasn't a big drinker but enjoyed a beer with Duncan on occasions. All went well until Danny made a short startling announcement:

"Mum, Dad. I might be getting hitched."

Danny said it with such studied nonchalance we took him dead seriously.

"What? Getting married?" I wasn't ready for this.

"You're only young son. Sow some wild oats before you settle down."
Duncan advised.

I could have strangled Duncan for that sage advice. Surely Danny did
not have to follow his father in every respect.

"Ahem. I think Danny Boy has already sown a wild oat." Lacy butted
in.

"Shut up Lacy. No one asked you." Danny retorted.

"Are we the last to know what you've been up to?" I cried.

Danny blushed. Something he rarely did.

"Look. I'm sorry. I got a girl pregnant. This probably comes as a shock
to you both with your staid old-fashioned backgrounds. But people often
do have physical relationships before marriage."

"Do tell. Is that so."

"He means he's been bonking her silly. She's really old too."

Lacy had to put in her two-bobs-worth.

"Lacy! That's crude." I reprimanded.

"Well, he has, and she is."

Danny retaliated:

"What about that old bloke you're seeing Lacy. He must be thirty if he's
a day."

Duncan jumped up from the table upsetting a glass.

"What! Who have you been seeing Lacy?" he roared.

"Why don't I know any of this?" I exclaimed.

Lacy looked daggers at her brother but stood her ground:

"Baldwin Russo. And he could teach you a thing or two about good
manners Danny Boy."

Little Baldwin from the dairy farm. Maria Russo's boy. I remembered him well.

"Oh Lacy! Baldwin is so much older than you."

"Only about twelve years older Mum. But he is young and naïve for his age."

"Where did we go wrong!" Duncan yelled.

"Calm down Duncan. One thing at a time." I said.

"Lacy. You better bring Baldwin home for a meal one day soon."

"Sweet. Thanks Mum."

Lacy poked her tongue at her brother.

"Danny. Is this true. You've got some older woman in the family way?"

"Seems so. I want you to meet her of course. Her name is Benita."

I dissolved into tears. This was the worst birthday ever. Baldwin was one thing. I liked him but not for my young daughter given the age difference. Danny getting trapped by some conniving old slag was the worst.

I'd never felt more nervous about meeting someone than waiting for Danny to bring that damn older woman home.

Lacy decided to stay away during this meeting. Thank heaven for small mercies.

It was only for an afternoon tea. I set the big coffee table in the living room with my best china, made fancy little sandwiches and cakes and ironed linen napkins. The futon had gone long ago, replaced by a nice three-piece lounge suite.

I went to some trouble to show *that woman* that my boy Danny came from a respectable family and could not be the one to blame. Obviously the old tart had led him astray. I heard Danny's car arrive. They had arrived. I took deep breaths.

"Mum. Dad. This is Benita. My fiancé."

Danny introduced a petite blushing dark haired girl. She actually looked quite young. A frisson of deju vu made my hair stand on end. I felt I knew her somehow.

"I am sorry to bring disgrace on your family Mrs. O'Day. I do not know where to turn. My father would never understand. So I hoped Danny and I could be wed before he finds out."

I looked into the girl's brimming eyes and instantly forgave her. I well knew how it was with men. The poor little thing. In fear of her father.

"Are your parents a local family? Italian?" Duncan asked her.

"We lived in the area long ago when I was small. Now we live in Italy. I don't remember much about Australia and my father doesn't speak of it."

"What of your mother?" I asked.

"My mother does not live with us. She is married to someone else."

"What brings you back here?" I asked.

"My father took me to Parco Zoo in Poppi where there are kangaroos that reminded me of my early childhood. I kept nagging Papa – finally he agreed to let me travel to Australia with two of my girlfriends as chaperones."

Hmm. A lot of good those chaperones did. After we'd finished with morning tea, I asked Duncan and Danny to clear the tea things away. I wanted some private time alone with the young woman. I figured her age to be around mid twenties, perhaps only five or six years older than Danny.

"Where are your girlfriends now?"

"They went back. They were disgusted with me. But you see, they both were after Danny as well. They were jealous when he chose me."

"He didn't?"

"Oh no Mrs. O'Day. Danny has only been with me, in that way."

Thank goodness for that. The more I looked at the girl, the more an idea grew.

"Do you know what *Albero di Limone* means?"

"Yes. In Italian it is lemon tree."

"Does it have any special meaning for you personally?"

"Should it?"

"Ok Bean. Come and look at this."

She automatically rose to follow me but paused in confusion.

"You called me Bean? That is actually my name."

"I thought so. You are the image of your grandmother. Your father's mother."

"You knew my grandmother?"

"Only in spirit my dear. This was her house. She named it *Albero di Limone*."

I showed Bean the brass front door plate. The young woman was confused and amazed.

"How can this be? I don't understand."
"Did your father never tell you of it?"
"No never. I only know my grandmother was named Fiorella and she died when Papa was very young. He mourns his mother still and lights candles in church for her. But he does not like to talk about it."
"It's a long story my dear. Some day your father might tell you more. It is not for me to say. But for now, your close connection to this house must be kept strictly secret. Can you keep the secret?"
"If it is what you want I will keep the secret Mrs. O'Day. Cross my heart."
"Call me Dimity. Why do you go by the name Benita now?"
"Because Bean is such a stupid name."

I had to agree. I had always thought so too.

"So, Mrs...um Dimity. Will you tell Danny of my real name?"
"That is your business not mine. And I can keep a secret."

I smiled at Benita.

"So, we have your blessing to be wed?"
"Absolutely. I feel it is meant to be."

I hugged her.

"I am so happy and relieved. Thank you. Now I only fear to tell my father."

"Don't worry Benita. I believe he will accept it as preordained."

Benita gave me a puzzled look but did not question my belief.

In the meantime, while Danny and Benita made wedding plans, Lacy brought Baldwin home for afternoon tea. I'd asked Lacy how she came to know Baldwin since she claimed he was a homebody who did not socialise in the town. She explained:

"I came across an old news article at work mentioning him finding a drug stash. I was curious knowing he lived not far away from us on that dairy farm that is split by the river. Anyway, one day I decided to drive over to the Russo place to question Baldwin about it. I thought of writing a follow up story."

I declined enlightening Lacy about the old dramas. My connections with the boat house and the stone house might bring up details of my long association with Fabio. Now I had Benita to think of as well. The last thing I needed was Lacy getting wind of all that.

"You questioned Baldwin? What did he say?"

"He said it wasn't strictly factual, and the local rag rarely was."

"That's a fact." I agreed.

"I'm working on changing that. But Mum, Baldwin mentioned you getting into some brawl at the picnic races years ago. Was that factual?"

"Ask your father." I hedged.

Deftly changing the subject, I began a saga of how Baldwin's mother had been midwife to Danny and asked if Lacy had met Maria Russo yet.

"No. Baldwin's parents moved into town, his mother is on call at the hospital and his father is pensioned off with rheumatism."

"So Baldwin runs the dairy alone now?"

"A couple of school kids help in the afternoons. But pretty much alone. He is always busy."

"He would be busy with running the dairy seven days a week. Lucky he took the time out to talk to you Lacy."

"I guess so. He was just finishing up after morning milking when I got there. He told me to go in the kitchen and put the kettle on and he'd be in soon. Imagine that. He didn't even know me, and he tells me to put the kettle on. I thought that was really funny. He is so different to the vain and cocky young guys I know in town. Baldwin is solid. What you see is what you get with him."

"So you like Baldwin a lot?"

"Yes Mum, I really like Baldwin. A lot."

"How much is a lot? Does he like you a lot as well?"

"I'm working on it Mummy."

I knew there must be much more to that story. Lacy's Mona Lisa smile was a clue.

"Hmm. What do you want me to do for Baldwin's visit here?"

"Can we have a verandah barbecue at the farm? Dad might not sound as loud outdoors."

"I'm sure we can manage your father between us." I smiled.

Baldwin duly arrived on time for the planned barbecue lunch. Circling his truck in the broad driveway space, Baldwin parked it facing out to the road.

"Ready for the quick getaway." Duncan observed.

"Don't you come over all Irish and surly on him Daddy." Lacy hissed.

Baldwin turned up in clean jeans, an ironed plaid shirt, work boots and a gift of a big jar of fresh jersey cream. He had always been a tall boy and had grown into a tall and handsome young man. I admired his long and easy athletic stride as he walked over to the verandah. Lacy went downstairs to meet Baldwin and pecked him on the cheek. He blushed charmingly.

Polite greetings were exchanged. I thanked him for the cream and Duncan offered Baldwin a beer. Lacy had already told me Baldwin didn't drink alcohol, but he nevertheless accepted the ale.

Lacy took a seat at the table and Baldwin chose to sit opposite her. A few shy adoring glances Baldwin bestowed on our lovely daughter made me wonder if she'd already seduced him. What was I thinking. Of course she had. It was plain on her face and in her manner. It was written all over him as well. I felt confident Lacy would have been the instigator in that conquest. Don't ask me why.

Chatting throughout the meal the subject came around to Baldwin living alone at his family farm. He said he managed ok with his dog and a few farm cats for company.

"That's right. You had kelpies." I recalled.

"Gone now. Dad got me a border collie bitch pup a few years ago. Flick."

"We used to have one named Enzo.. He was a lovely dog."

"Flick's got her first litter due soon." Baldwin mentioned.

"I'd love to help with the pups when they arrive. I could stay with you for a few weeks." Lacy declared.

"No Lacy. That would not be proper. Not being wed." Baldwin replied in gentle reproof.

Lacy did not argue but I saw in her gaze Baldwin might pay for that refusal later. Now we were getting to the crux since Baldwin had brought up 'not being wed'. Duncan got himself another beer. Baldwin said no thanks he was driving. I made a pot of tea and brought out a plate of cakes and sweets.

Baldwin spoke up bravely:

"Mr. O'Day, sir, if I was ever to pose the question would you have too many objections?"

"Well now Baldwin Russo. If that ever came about. I would let you know my thoughts in no uncertain terms."

I cast a stern glance at Duncan's grim face. He read it well. Lacy defied her father's mood quietly during the uncomfortable silence that followed:

"I love him Daddy."

That was her ace. Baldwin's whole face softened in misty reaction to Lacy's words. He loved her for sure. Duncan met Lacy's eye. He had never denied our daughter anything in all her nineteen years. Duncan gave a gruff warning:

"There'd be me to answer to if you ever hurt her."

"Mr. O'Day, I would never cross her. That's a promise. For one thing, and this might surprise you sir, but your beautiful daughter can be a very scary woman."

Duncan's expression lightened and brightened. He'd missed having Sid and Nobby around as back up and suddenly saw an ally in Baldwin.

"Call me Duncan son. Have you seen the latest mulcher slasher? I just got this..."

Our two men sauntered over to the sheds to look at boring farm machinery.

"Mum. What just happened?"

"Baldwin asked for your hand in marriage and your father gave his blessing."

"But Baldwin hasn't even asked me yet!"

"He will. Let him think it was his own idea my darling."

Lacy thought about this.

"Do you know everything Mummy?"

"Enough."

Lacy reverted to calling me Mummy whenever trying for an innocent approach. She didn't fool me for one moment. My daughter was too much like myself to be a mystery.

"Are you happy for me?" Lacy asked.
"Yes. I am very happy for you Lacy. I think you and Baldwin will be good together."
"We already are."
"I know that too."

We smiled together as women. Having met Baldwin as an adult I could see he was right for Lacy. Despite his 31 years she was probably his first serious encounter with a girl, and clearly, he adored her. Lacy felt empowered by his natural artlessness, and he possessed the maturity to let her be herself. Within reason.

Parents

THE THREE OF US

For my next trick, I had to phone Fabio in Italy.

"Dimity! *Tesoro mio, quanto è bello sentire la tua voce.*"
"Fabio. My friend. It is good to hear your voice as well."
"It has been too long." he said remembering to switch to English.

A little small talk ensued before I got to the point:

"Fabio. I have news."
"Uh oh. Good or bad?"
"Different. Our children have met. My son and your daughter."

Fabio needed a moment to consider the possible ramifications.

"Ah. Bean wanted to holiday in Australia. I thought there was little chance of contact with the past. She even goes by another name now. How did they meet?"

"By chance. Socialising in the town. Fabio, I have to tell you, they have formed an... that is, they have an... actually they wish to marry."

This revelation was met with a stunned silence.

"Each other?"

"Of course. Each other."

"Is there more to this?"

"We are to share a grandchild Fabio."

"Your son of the Irishman has made my little daughter pregnant?"

"They are in it together Fabio. And your daughter is terrified to tell you."

Fabio of all people would not want to be a frightening father after suffering his own violent upbringing with Lupo. The silence dragged on. Fabio still clung to his fear of having past deeds discovered. I gave him time to work through it.

"It has been so long. Can my daughter learn of the past by this? How has it come about?"

"Danny brought her, as Benita, to the lemon tree house to meet us. I recognised your daughter because she looks exactly like Fiorella. The similarity is uncanny Fabio."

"Yes. I agree this is so. Bean is like a reincarnation of my dear mother in appearance. Also, by the sound of her voice and in her gentle loving manner. How did you see this Dimity?"

"Giorgio and Sophia showed me many old family photos. Fabio, they also spoke of the tragedy and heartbreak. I have felt close in spirit to your poor little lost mother."

"How can you feel this closeness Dimity? You never met my mother." Fabio said it not unkindly.

"Because I loved her only child. I live in her lemon tree house; I cried by her graveside. I planted another lemon tree for her. It thrives here still."

"*Capisco come può essere, ma non l'ho mai saputo* - I never knew this."

"But it is so Fabio."

"Do you not love me still Dimity?"

"Yes. But it's different now. I have made a good marriage with Duncan, and I love him dearly."

"*Ti ho sempre amato tesoro mio* - I have always loved you my darling...but so far away."

"And what of you Fabio?"

"Ah, the women come and go. You know how it is."

I could just imagine his Italian open palmed gesture when he admitted how it would always be. Fabio ventured a memory:

"I will never forget our last time together, under the sun. It was the best for me."

"For me too. It may be difficult to revisit that place. But that will be our task." I told him.

"Our task? What do you mean?"

Here was the clanger:

"Danny and Benita choose to have a garden wedding. They said it will be in a grassy area they are renovating behind the stone house."

"Where we..?"

"Yes on the same ground. The exact place."

"I did not imagine this would happen when I agreed to let those girls stay there."

"Of course you could not foresee how it would go Fabio."

Fabio thought about it some more.

"I think it will be alright. We will be aware, but our children and others will not know and could never guess." Fabio said.

Duncan didn't have to guess. But I couldn't tell Fabio that.

"Did you know the other two girlfriends returned to Italy without Bean?"

"They left Bean alone out there? But my daughter has led such a protected life. She would be like a babe in the woods."

"The girls had a falling out. The other two also vied for my son. Danny is a handsome lad."

"Bean would be easy prey for the Irishman's son."

Fabio's words sounded brittle.

"Babes in the woods Fabio. Both of them. Danny is much younger than Bean. That has to be taken into account."

"So now it has come to this."

On top of feeling outrage for Bean, Fabio had the concern that had hounded his life:

"How much does my daughter now know of our family history?"

"Only that *Albero di Limone* was once her grandmother's house. I asked her to keep it secret and she promises to do so. Although her curiosity will need some satisfaction. It is up to you Fabio how much you tell her. It will never come from me."

"I hoped to keep all connections to Lupo buried. I will think of a way to edit the tale."

"You will come for the wedding? It will mean the world to Benita...Bean."

"I know she prefers to be known as Benita...I keep forgetting. Yes of course I must. I will be there."

Fabio's imminent arrival had me run to the mirror for a critical assessment. I had aged and gained a little weight since we lay together, but I might pass muster with some special effort.

My personal vanity was the least of my worries. The wedding venue was the tricky problem. Duncan had seen my erotic behaviour there and was unlikely to have forgotten the wild passion I had shown for my Italian lover.

Fabio surely blamed Danny for getting his daughter pregnant. It might not take much to ignite a fight.

I felt Duncan was the one most likely to break the peace seeing me with Fabio again, but I could hardly ignore my old friend and lover. He would be Danny's father-in-law. It tied us as family.

The three of us as responsible parents must stand composed to witness our children marry in that garden arena, despite strong memories the place would surely evoke.

I prayed the two hot heads would not spoil the wedding day for Danny and Benita.

Danny & Benita

CLOSE KNIT FAMILIES

The day dawned perfectly for the marriage of our son Danny and Fabio's daughter Bean, now always to be known as Benita.

Fabio flew into the nearest international airport and hired a car to drive out to his stone house for the wedding. He would stay there for the few days he had in Australia.

Age had not diminished Fabio's masculine allure. If anything, snowy white hair enhanced his smooth olive complexion.

Duncan, Lacy and I had driven into town early to collect Sid, Nobby and the mature lady wedding celebrant who also lived at the retirement village.

Between us we also picked up several eskys of foodstuffs from a local hotel that catered to Danny's orders. Originally the kids planned to honeymoon in the stone cottage, but Fabio gifted them a fortnights holiday at a plush coastal resort. Lacy and I would stand in doing Danny's chores at the spelling farm in his absence.

Danny and Benita organised their wedding day in the way they wanted with no interference from others. The lady celebrant who presided over the simple ceremony had been suggested by Sid and Nobby.

Duncan and Fabio exchanged stiff formal greetings. As fathers of the wedding pair, they strove to be on best behaviours.

Benita wore a long gown in sprigged muslin. A delicate tiara adorned her shiny dark hair. She carried a fresh posy of flowers and ferns from the garden. Danny was as handsome as ever, a younger replica of Duncan in a suit. They were so alike.

That morning, we had all helped set out chairs on the lawn. The same chairs to be later carried to the patio for a smorgasbord luncheon set along a row of three tables joined together.

The couple did not want any bridal attendants. Smiling, they had walked into the wedding area together, holding hands. No formal arrangements were in place.

Lacy sat with Baldwin among the few other guests. Duncan and I took front row seats behind Danny. Fabio sat beside us behind Benita. Sandwiched in between the two men I loved; I couldn't help but be highly aware of both.

In the rush to be settled I had little time to think of the last time I'd been in this garden. Now the thought came that I sat directly over the area of lawn where Fabio had spread the patchwork quilt for our pleasure, so many years ago.

When the familiar words were spoken: '*who gives this woman to be married to this man*' – Fabio rose, bowed elegantly and made his solemn reply "I do."

Benita looked back adoringly at her father. The young woman had insisted on the tradition of being given away. It confirmed her father's acceptance of the marriage. Smart girl.

Having been announced man and wife, Danny and Benita turned to greet the little congregation to cheerful applause and well wishes. If Benita missed her mother, she showed no sign. I later learned she despised the German man Agneta married and had become sadly estranged from her mother because of him.

Without Agneta and Wolfgang being there, it saved explaining the complexity of Wolfgang being a half-brother both to Fabio and to Benita.

Wolfgang and Benita shared Agneta as their mother. Fabio and Wolfgang shared Lupo as their father.

It brought up the fact that Fabio sired Benita to his own stepmother if anyone cared to work it out.

Uncertain how much Benita realised, it went without saying, the sexual relationship I had with Fabio must never be revealed.

Talk about close knit families.

Benita threw her bouquet posy, fairly obviously in Lacy's direction. Lacy caught it and winked. Despite Lacy's lifetime love-hate feud with Danny, she'd become friendly with Benita. I hoped this marriage would encourage harmony between my two children.

In the interim before the wedding breakfast, we toasted the couple with champagne out on the lawn. I caught Fabio watching me over the rim of his glass. As our eyes met fleetingly, a spark fired between us. We would never forget. A smile flirted about his lips and hovered in the age-old question. My body betrayed my loyalty to Duncan with an electrifying thrill.

I had long ago relinquished the physical side of loving Fabio and would never risk acting on his tantalising invitation now. Our time together as lovers had been beautiful, but it belonged to my wild past.

Duncan had been on high alert, and he did not miss much. My husband came to my side and placed a proprietary arm about my waist. Duncan and Fabio faced off in a silent duel. No one present would notice the tense significance of that moment. I held my breath. Fabio bowed with grace, smiled coolly and walked away. Ah my beautiful Fabio. Such aplomb. Such class.

The fraught moment I feared might spoil the wedding day for Danny and Benita, fizzled out. Handled well by both the men I loved.

A while later, I casually surveyed the surrounding hillsides. I wondered where Duncan had hidden as he watched that long ago frenzy of lust I enjoyed so much with Fabio. Duncan read my mind:

"I was behind that big ghost gum." he told me quietly without being asked.

"Don't bring that up now Duncan." I whispered.

"Babe. It can't be helped. It has a mind of its own." he twinkled.

"Keep a civil tongue in your head Duncan."

"I will for today. But not for tonight."

"Why what happens tonight?"
"I think you can guess." he grinned.

Duncan's flirtatious grin stirred my interest. He still had it, and he knew it. My big brash gorgeous husband was dearly loved. Assuredly I would never betray Duncan nor our marriage vows.

I had always been Miss Minto from the office and a trusted confidante for Fabio. We'd embraced our friendship in every way. However, despite all the ways Fabio coloured my world, the Irishman emerged as my life partner and trusted soul mate.

Back in the Day

WHY GILD THE LILY

Danny and Benita had organised such a fun and easy wedding. Everyone lent a hand at setting out the luncheon with an array of cold meats, salads, mini quiches, finger foods and sweets.

Sid and Nobby directed the conversation unwittingly letting out past events. For a variety of reasons, we had never told much of anything to the younger generation. Fabio raised eyebrows at some of the disclosures as well.

"This is where we trounced that crook hey Sid? Right here. On this patio."

"Yep. We got him good. Those were the days." Sid replied dreamily.

"Huh? What's this?" the kids were stirred to instant curiosity.

"That time your mother escaped the kidnappers and put herself in the river." Nobby said.

"She reckoned if she had to be drowned it would be her own idea." Sid laughed.

Fabio and Benita exchanged shrugs that clearly said what can you do? They are Australians.

"I saved her." Baldwin spoke up conversationally.

"You saved my mother?" Lacy was astounded.

"He sure did." I confirmed. "Such a clever and capable little lad. He pulled the bridle off his pony and used it as a lifeline to help me climb up the muddy bank."

"She was really fat." Baldwin recalled. "The pony! The pony was really fat."

Everyone laughed at Baldwin's embarrassment.

"From what I recall, little barefoot Baldwin gave me a good dressing down about swimming in the river." I laughed. "I've never really thanked you Baldwin. I should have and I do."

"I have thanks enough."

Baldwin replied with his love-struck gaze adoring our Lacy.

Nobby continued his tale:

"Then Dimity, bless her, refuses to go to hospital. She says: Duncan ain't my boss."

"That is so. After riding her horse home for her, I had to spend the night on guard on the damn hard uncomfortable futon in case she had a bad reaction to all her injuries." Duncan mourned.

"What futon?" Lacy asked.

"A futon used to furnish the living room long ago." I supplied.

"Why on the futon?" Danny asked.

"We weren't wed at the time."

Duncan replied in a travesty of prim innocence. I tactfully changed the subject:

"Good old Nero. He wasn't even spooked by the police helicopter."
"Police helicopter?" the kids repeated in wonder.
"Just lucky that I ever found my good pearl handled knife again." Duncan remarked.
"Huh? Here's us thinking you oldies led such staid and boring lives." Danny exclaimed.
"So, Mum and Dad. What exactly was the thing about the brawl at the picnic races?" Lacy asked.
"Even I heard of that in Germany, from my Aunt Sophie." Fabio added.
"The legend of The Great Bun Fight." Baldwin recalled.
"There weren't any buns were there Duncan? I remember trifle pudding."
"I remember getting the worst black eye ever." Duncan added.
"I remember the awful bunks in the lock up. You think that futon was bad." Nobby said.
"I remember my sore jaw and I lost a few teeth. I didn't have that many to lose either." Sid said.
"And people talk about the younger generation!" Danny marvelled again.
"Why weren't we ever told all this?" Lacy wanted to know.
"We aimed to protect you from fearful events. It was all in the past."
"Family is everything." Fabio summarised quietly.

Later Duncan and most of the others went to play cricket on a makeshift pitch below the house. The rest of us watched them from the verandah.

In a quiet aside, Fabio asked if I ever found the truck keys in the hollow tree. His teasing intention was to remind me of the ploy we used to initiate sex in my bedroom. My answer surprised him.

"No Fabio. I never looked for those keys. But I did find the truck."

"The truck? But it sank deep in the river."

"Over the years it washed downstream to lodge against the bridge footings. When I escaped the drug pushers, a log I clung to snagged on the old truck body. That is what saved me from drowning. Apart from young Baldwin of course."

"*Spettrale!* I mean, did this feel sinister to you Dimity? Knowing what I did."

I could put Fabio's mind at rest on that score.

"No. It didn't ever feel sinister Fabio. I saw it as an intervention. You know I used take lemon tree sprigs to throw in the river as a tribute to Fiorella. I imagined all sorts of things."

Fabio seemed surprised that I had never discussed my fanciful rituals with him.

"So, Dimity. You have never told me everything."

"Have you ever told me everything of yourself Fabio?"

"Only one thing I have not told you." Fabio said with a wolfish grin.

"Oh? And what would that be?"

"Your Duncan watched us making love together under the sun, that last time. He hid behind the white tree up there. I think we performed well for him. No?"

Finally, I understood why Fabio had urged me to take a less submissive role and why he had shouted in triumph so unexpectedly that day.

"Fabio! You urged me to ride on top so Duncan could see how much I wanted it with you."

"I orchestrated that victory." Fabio admitted.

"You wanted to taunt Duncan. It was a game to you. I was your pawn."

"Perhaps."

"You could have told me sooner." I stage whispered.

"Why would I do so? Knowing would quash your keen responses to me."

Fabio smiled shamelessly.

"Are all men such bastards Fabio?"

He laughed softly, liking where our verbal duel headed. Fabio replied softly:

"Yet now you limit your pleasure to just one Bastardo."

"You played me that day only to gratify your male ego. Not for my pleasure."

"No. The height of your joy was a bonus. Even I did not expect such a wonderful result."

"And you played me expertly Fabio."

"That exciting time in the sun need not be our last Dimity."
"Why gild the lily, Maestro? Let us enjoy our memories as they are."

Fabio picked up on the Maestro title but perhaps not on my refusal. We laughed in quiet irony together for our different reasons. Still, twenty and more years allowed us to appreciate the comedy element of that past event.
Benita wandered over to ask if we would like coffee.

"This is nice Papa. I am glad you and Dimity are getting acquainted."
"I feel I know your Papa so much better now." I replied.
"This is your day, Benita. Allow your Papa to make the coffee."

Fabio easily adopted the gallant role he did so well.

Holidays

A RARE GIFT

Over coffee, Fabio and I spoke quietly of how the river featured in our past lives. Fiorella's drowning. Lupo's drowning. My close escape from near drowning.

"If you had also drowned in the river, it would be too much to bear." Fabio told me.

"Of course, if I had not survived to produce Danny, Fiorella's beautiful granddaughter would not now be returning to live in the family home. I like to think Giorgio and Sophia would be pleased."

"My daughter will now live in the big house that was once my Uncle Gio's?"

"Yes. Danny runs the business there with Duncan now. It is strange how things work out. The place will become theirs some day of course."

"What of your lovely daughter?" Fabio asked.

"She is keen to marry Baldwin and live on his farm."

"They are engaged to be wed?"

"Close. I wouldn't be surprised if Baldwin pops the question soon after seeing Danny and Benita so happy today."

"Forgive me. But the young man Baldwin seems quite a lot older than your girl Lacy."

"He is about twelve years older, but he is young in experience. I doubt he has had another."

"Ah. The charms of a woman. A lonely man. I can see how it might be. He is sure to be faithful and protective." Fabio smiled.

I agreed that Baldwin possessed those admirable qualities, and Lacy was drawn by that. My heart and mind confirmed that Duncan earned my trust and undying loyalty for those same reasons.

Fabio said his Australian property would go to Benita someday so both our daughters were well set up for their futures. He looked over the rustic stone walls and solid beams of the house that his grandfather built.

"Danny and Benita have the farmhouse as their residence so this place could be let as holiday accommodation."

"That's a good idea. This is a beautiful spot and a shame for this sturdy cottage to sit empty."

"Perhaps you will manage it for me as a country getaway venue Dimity?"

"I would enjoy the challenge. As business partners." I replied.

"Of course. As business partners." Fabio agreed.

Surely Fabio viewed our proposed shared project as another coup to taunt Duncan. Armed with realising that side of Fabio's intentions, I let him have that harmless little ego trip.

"I am happy to have your Danny as my son-in-law and father of my grandchild."

"And I am happy too. Benita is a lovely young woman."

Fabio smoothly suggested future trysts to be enabled with the holiday let as catalyst:

"I will return from Italy to see our grandchild and meet you here from time to time."
"Who can tell what the future holds."

I smiled knowing it would not go precisely as Fabio planned. Any business or family connection would never curb Fabio's enthusiasm for sexual conquest. However, I would not entertain any ongoing affair with my beautiful but flawed Italian ex-lover.

In consolation, I had his flirtatious interest to bolster my ego, a rare gift to be had for a woman of my years. Staying true to Duncan and our marriage empowered my confidence and self-respect.

I liked feeling virtuous. At one time, I kept a personal virtue list. It wasn't very long.

My Man

FLINT & JASPER

Lacy and Baldwin married within three months of Danny and Benita. My family regenerated to form a stronger unit as time marched on.

With the lemon tree house to ourselves, Duncan and I rediscovered some freedoms and privacy denied to us while raising our children. Even venting our frequent numerous disputes openly, instead of in hoarse whispers seemed a luxury. Or just walking naked from the bathroom. Not to mention the worry of making noise in the bedroom. Duncan rediscovered his talent for yodelling.

Before long, Danny and Benita invited us for a barbecue on the farmhouse verandah, with Lacy and Baldwin as well. The young couples got along well together and were fast becoming firm friends. I felt satisfied that we'd done a fair job of raising our pair of brats.

Duncan squeezed my leg under the table and gave me a loving smile and a wink. He always knew my mind.

In the course of conversation, Baldwin said he would like to gift me a puppy from Flick's litter, if that was ok. The pups were ready to leave the mother.

"They are pedigreed." Baldwin said as if to convince me.

I didn't need much convincing. The prospect of having a dog again raised my spirits along with seeing our children happily settled. It was a good day that marked a turning point.

I had so grieved for Enzo and Shamus that I hadn't faced getting another pup. Now with our empty nest at the lemon tree house, the time was right.

The very next day we visited Lacy and Baldwin at their dairy farm to view the puppies. Six healthy active and adorable black and white babies scrambled for attention. One little male had odd-coloured eyes, one brown, one blue, just as Enzo had.

"I said Mum would pick that one."

Lacy and Baldwin shared a smile. I named the pup Flint for his flinty blue eye. To restore the balance of two dogs in front of the fire, we found another red brindle whippet pup and named him Jasper.

At home, Duncan and I enjoyed a quiet cup of tea at our kitchen table and admired Flint and Jasper snuggled together in their basket bed.

"They look cute together." I smiled.
"We might have to deal with a few puppy smells for a while."
"I remember when you told me I smelt like a wet dog."
"I never did!" Duncan said in a shocked voice.

"You did so!"

"Did not!"

"You so did Duncan."

"When?"

"That first time you finally got your wicked way with me in this very kitchen Duncan O'Day."

"What? You were the one! If I remember rightly, you begged me for it. You pleaded."

"Oh! I did not!"

"Babe. You did some raunchy stuff."

"I never begged. And you did say I smelt like a wet dog."

"Yeah. Ok. Maybe I did. But I knew it was just a game to you Dimity."

"Alright. Sometimes it was just a game back then because I was afraid of spoiling our relationship. Anyway, you weren't serious, always covering up with your Irish malarkey."

Duncan rubbed his face and suddenly became deadly serious.

"Because I loved you more than you loved me Dimity. I was your bit of rough on the side and that bloody Italian was always in the way. Now he's invented that damn holiday let scheme to keep you on the hook."

Credit where it's due, Duncan got the gist down pat. But he was wrong about one thing.

"Duncan. Admit I was slow on the uptake, but I always loved you. You're my man. I don't want anyone else, and I'll never betray you. If you want to renew our marriage vows properly in front of everyone, with a priest, in a church, I will do that for you."

Duncan took that to heart. He looked suitable horrified.

"Geez woman. Don't go overboard."
Phew thank Christ for that.

I took his big hand in mine and kissed his palm. His face softened.

"Come here Babe," I said, "I know what you need."
"Suppose I could let you have your wanton way as usual." he grinned.
"You're so kind."
"It's my sweet charity again for sure."
"But you don't do charity remember."
"That's right. I forgot. So just leave the money on the fridge. I take instalments."
"Get over yourself Duncan."
He laughed at his own brilliant wit. I could've let him have the last laugh, instead I said:
"Okay. I should have some loose change somewhere, perhaps a few pennies in the bottom of my bag."
"Get over yourself Dimity." he replied.

I probably won't. I'm working on it.

The End